Gray

A NOVEL

Book One of The Firebrand Trilogy

David Kettlehake

BROTHER MOCKINGBIRD

Cover Design by: Alexios Saskalidis
www.facebook.com/187designz

For information please contact:
Brother Mockingbird, LLC
www.brothermockingbird.org
ISBN: 978-1-7344950-1-0
First Edition

For my daughter, Nikki.
Thanks for believing.

CHAPTER
ONE

I found a new book today.

Sometimes I find books when we're out scrounging, but most of them are ruined beyond salvage, little more than blocks of moldy, spongy pulp. The condition of this one is better, even though the leather cover is black and crusty and I can't make out the title. With patience and care I'm able to tease a few stubborn pages apart with my tweezers, one by one, my hands trembling in anticipation. The pages separate grudgingly, with a soft tearing sound, reluctant to reveal their printed secrets. Their words transport me away from this place, from now, from this thing we call life.

Lord shoots me a stern look, so I take a break and tend to the fire. I'm the Firebrand. Keeping the fire going is my real job, one I've been charged with for more months than I can remember. I'm good at it, too, and better yet it keeps me out of the slop. Most of the time, at least.

I carefully rearrange the logs and expertly add

a few more to the existing pyramid shape. The damp wood hisses and pops, but eventually catches, flaring and lighting up our cramped room at the Motel 6 where we've been living for the past few weeks. We punched a small hole in the ceiling where the smoke escapes. Rain drips down from the rim of the hole and sizzles and spits when it hits the fire.

I look up at him. "We're going to need more before the night is over, you know."

Lord nods and leaves without a word. He doesn't say much, not anymore. I go back to my book, tweezers in hand. In the flickering light, I carefully convince another page to part ways with its neighbor.

Seven months ago while scrounging in the remains of a small town in northwest Ohio, we found a library. I was so excited I thought I was going to pee myself. I was only able to find a dozen books worth saving. They were in the fiction section, which pissed off everyone but me. They only want reference books, ones that tell us how to do things that help us survive, like what wild mushrooms we can eat, and which ones will kill us, how to deal with injuries…stuff like that. But not me. I long for the escape of fiction.

Give or take a few weeks, I'm one hundred and ninety-eight months old. I'll be dead before I hit two hundred and forty months. Guaranteed. In fact, everyone who's still alive on Earth knows when they'll die. I'm not sure it makes you appreciate your time here any more than people did before the Storm, but it makes you more aware, if you know what I mean. At least I hope it does.

Lord is back. In his strong arms he's carrying sticks and branches. It's not much, but it should get us through the night.

"Is that all of it?"

He drops the firewood at my feet. It's wet, but I expected that. It's raining outside, of course, and like so many of the buildings and houses now, the rest of the rooms in the hotel are ruined and open to the nearly constant deluge outside. I'd asked to keep the supplies here, but the fire pit and the eight of us are already occupying every square inch of floor space. I can hear the rustling and restless murmurs of the others in their various stages of sleep. Someone whimpers and cries out. I'm guessing it's little Carly.

"Yeah. Is it enough?" he asks. His voice has changed in the last few months. Now it's a deep rumble so low I'm pretty sure it vibrates my internal organs. This newfound baritone bothers all of us, and it should bother him, too, but if it does he isn't letting on. Maybe that's why he doesn't say much. It means adulthood has arrived, and he's running out of time. He just turned two hundred and twenty months old last week. He could go Gray soon. I try not to let it worry me, but I can't help it. After all, he's my big brother.

I spread the new wood around the outside of the fire to dry. The coals are hot, and glowing a deep, comforting orange, and the fuel I added a few minutes ago is burning nicely. Every night I go to sleep, worrying if I've done enough to keep the fire going. As Firebrand, it's my responsibility, and I protect what's in the pit like it's the last chocolate bar on Earth. I doubt we could survive without fire, and with the constant rain and humidity thicker than a steam room, starting a new one can be a bitch. We need it to cook, and sometimes to boil water to drink, and, of course, to keep away the Grays. They don't like fire.

Lord looks at me, his dark eyes deep in shadow. Unlike me, he hasn't cut his hair in months and it's almost down to his shoulders now. There are a few drops of water suspended from the ends, hanging there and glittering like delicate jewelry in the flickering firelight.

"You good now, Scout?"

I survey the new supply and estimate that it should be enough. "Yeah, we're good."

He settles down next to me, accidentally bumping into me as he sits. I stifle a grunt. Lord's so solid and muscled it feels like he just punched me. He's not the skinny boy he was before the Storm. He looks at the book cradled in my hands and raises an eyebrow in that way he has. Actually, he pretty much has a unibrow now. When did that happen?

"Where'd you find it?"

I cradle it in my hands. It's thick, heavy with age and knowledge. I dredge up a word I've never said out loud, one I read somewhere: gravitas. This book has it.

"It was in a bedroom dresser in that house this afternoon, where we were scrounging. That white frame house up on the hill? You guys were in another room. It was wrapped up in an old towel and shoved in the back of a drawer. I almost missed it."

"What is it?"

"I don't know. I've been able to read a few pages, but the English is weird. Old, I guess. It's hard to figure out what they're talking about."

"Like what?"

I pick out a sentence at random and point to it. "Like this: 'Well, God'ield you! They say the owl was a baker's daughter. Lord, we know what we are, but not what we may be. God be at your table.'" I looked at him. "God'ield? The owl was a baker's daughter? I have no idea what that means. But I like the rest of it, especially the part about knowing what we are, but not what we may be. That's...nice. Profound, you know?"

"Yeah. Now put it down and get some rest. You can work on it tomorrow if there's time."

I'm tempted to argue, but I know I'll lose that battle. If nothing else, Lord is a pragmatist. He's the leader of our little group and what he says goes. I remember when I was young, before the Storm, reading under the covers with a flashlight, long after my parents had ushered me to bed and tucked me in. My warm breath would fill the small, comforting space as I silently turned the pages. But Lord has spoken. And besides, we haven't had a working flashlight in dozens of months, so it's a moot point.

It's warm in the room, comfortable, and even though I don't need to, I pull my thin blanket up to my shoulders. Because of the thick humidity it feels damp and heavier than it should, but I always have to be covered up when I sleep. It helps keep the mosquitoes away, too.

I don't have the luxury of a pillow, so I slip my newest treasure under my head. It's not much, but it's better than resting my head on the floor, and the old leather against my skin gives me an odd, warm sensation.

Despite one or two more whimpers from Carly, I'm asleep before I know it, the fire dancing behind my eyes. Eyes that I can never truly allow to close.

CHAPTER
TWO

I wake up in the morning before everyone else. My first, slightly panicked thought is of the fire, how it might have died after its three o'clock feeding. I jump up to inspect it, exhaling with quiet relief when I see the hot embers shifting and glowing nicely. I blow gently on the coals and a small bluish-yellow flame dances to life. I have a few pieces of wood from last night, and I carefully add those, placing them just so. Within minutes, the fire is crackling along, and I can relax.

The first thing we did when we got to this hotel room weeks ago was rip up the disgusting carpeting. It was thick with bugs and beetles, and so rotten it fell apart in our hands, more like moss than carpeting. We tossed it out over the railing where it splashed into the muddy water below. The floor beneath the carpeting is concrete. We built up a ring of stones to contain the fire, and it's served us well since then.

I stand up and stretch, then pick my way carefully across the still sleeping forms toward the window. The curtains are long gone, victims of rot and decay.

The rod and rings are there, but they hold up nothing but memories.

When I look out the window, I see a vast expanse of toxic sludge covering what used to be the parking lot, a gentle drizzle dappling its surface. No cars are visible, since the rusting hulks are all under ten or more feet of the stuff, but I can make out the tops of a few minivans and SUVs, their once bright colors muted and dulled by rust, time, and brown water. Beyond the parking lot there's a ring of trees; tall, thin ones that tower forty or fifty feet into the air. Their branches are bereft of leaves, even though it's the middle of summer in west-central Ohio. I don't know for sure, but I guess all the trees died, simply drowned, unable to cope with a flood that's lasted over sixty months. I miss the color green.

I jump when I sense someone standing beside me. It's Lord. His long black hair is tousled and he's rubbing the sleep from his red eyes. He's tired, but I get it: the strain of responsibility shows in the wrinkles around his eyes, the tight way he holds his mouth and the stiffness in his shoulders. Honestly, he looks much older than his two hundred twenty months.

"When the others are up we're going out scrounging. But not you."

Inside I smile. Scrounging in the slop is no fun, and I won't miss it. It's killing me that I can't continue my work on the book right now, but I know that's a pipedream at this stage of the day. Too much to do, and too many people to care for. Maybe if I'm lucky I'll have some time later tonight.

"I want you to take the canoe and gather as much firewood as you can. Get the hatchet and move out."

"Okay by me." I can hang around nearby and work the trees around the hotel. Plus, Grays don't swim so they won't be able to get to me. They're unpredictable as hell, and you never know what one will do, but you live a lot longer these days without taking unnecessary chances.

"The rest of us will head out and scrounge. We're getting low on food. We'll find a grocery store or something and grab what we can."

I nod at him, still staring outside at the dead trees and calm, toxic water. There's always so much water. I think back to before the Storm and vaguely recall adults talking about a drought battering parts of the country. Out West, I think. Right now a drought sounds wonderful. I can't remember the last time I was completely dry.

"There's that building we saw a mile or so away, just outside of town. It could be a Wal-Mart or something. You going there?" We spotted it yesterday. All we could make out was a huge flat roof with silent, rusting air conditioning units on top, but it sure looked like a Wal-Mart to me. We've noticed that in small towns like this they're usually built a short distance outside the city limits. This one was on a slight hill, which meant it should be more accessible than most.

Of course, if we can easily get to it then the Grays can, too. I shiver.

"Yeah. We'll be gone a few hours, at least. Back well before dinner."

"Okay. Be careful, please." I try to hide the worry in my words, but I'm not very successful. I'm a lousy actress. When I'm concerned like this my already high voice betrays me by jumping up an embarrassing octave. I clear my throat to try and mask my emotions.

Lord lays his hand on my thin shoulder and squeezes once. I smile up at him. My expression is forced, but my affection for him is not. He's my rock. I don't know what I'll do, what we'll do, without him when the time comes. My smile softens and becomes more natural the longer his hand lingers there. He glances around the room.

"Let's get busy."

People stir as I start making breakfast. Today it's dry oatmeal from packets we found last week, supplemented by chopped up morel mushrooms. The combination tastes just as bad as it sounds, but we eat mushrooms more often than I care to admit, since they're everywhere. I'll mix it all up with clean water that I'm heating over the fire in my favorite cooking pot, a big cast iron one with long legs that sits above the burning logs. There isn't any milk, of course; all the cows are either drowned or eaten by Grays or survivors like us. So the oatmeal will be watery and taste like crap, but it's still better than nothing. I remember it cooked the right way. I long for it, and my mouth waters at the thought.

Next to my feet Dog stretches and groans, yawning. No, he's not an actual dog, he's as human as I am, but that's what we call him. We don't have a clue what his real name is since he's never offered to share it, which is fine. To be honest I think he likes the uniqueness of the nickname. His ability to sniff out food and Grays makes him invaluable to the group. He's scrawny and like the rest of us suffers from that unhealthy, malnourished look you'd associate with starving kids from third world countries. His narrow face is completely overshadowed by his massive nose. A beak that size would've been the source of cruel, adolescent mocking in elementary and junior high school, but not with us, not here. Here it's an asset. Here it makes him extremely valuable. He sits up and spies us at the window.

"Morning, boss. Morning, Scout. What's on the agenda for the day, huh?" He talks fast, rapid fire, like his mind is speeding along at a hundred miles an hour and his mouth can't keep up. Sometimes his words run together to the point where it's hard to understand him, and you have to tell him to slow down. He's such a twitchy little guy.

"Scrounging," Lord tells him. "Get something to eat, and let's go."

"You got it, boss. Gimme a minute and I'll be ready to go, you bet."

I know it bugs Lord when Dog calls him "boss," but he's given up correcting him. The kid doesn't mean anything by it; it's just the way he is.

Dog scurries out the door to the porch that circles the third floor, probably to take a pee. The others continue to stir. Annie sits up, her wavy red hair mashed flat on one side. She's proud of that hair and I have no doubt she'll brush it out later. I look to the back of the room and see Hunter is still out cold, one pale leg hanging outside his blanket. Figures. He's always the last one up, not counting the kids, and it pisses me off for some reason.

Singer's up and moving around, which is normal for him. His ebony skin is such a contrast to the whites of his eyes. He's tied his long black hair into a thick ponytail behind his head, which pulls his hair tight against his scalp. His skin is perfect, smooth and flawless. He kneels down and his shoulder accidentally brushes mine as I stir the pot. At least, I think it was an accident.

"Need any help?"

"Yeah, sure. You could get the bowls and spoons out. They're on the shelf in the closet."

He smiles at me. "You got it."

Singer was some sort of musical prodigy before the Storm. He's been with us for almost twelve months. When we can convince him to sing, his voice is nothing short of fantastic. I've never heard anything like it, at least not in person. Like Dog, we don't know his real name, and to be honest, no one cares. And like Lord, he doesn't talk much.

He picks his way with care and grace, navigating between the stirring bodies, and comes back with the bowls and spoons. He hands them to me.

"Thanks."

He dips his head, then makes his way outside, probably for the same reason Dog did. In the back pocket of his jeans I spot a thin, rectangular shape, a permanent faded outline in the fabric. It's his Suzuki harmonica. We found it a few months back while scrounging through the remains of a music store, tucked away on a back shelf in the office, buried under a stack of crusty, rotting sheet music that was riddled with silverfish. Its black case was covered in the usual dried scum and muck, but the harmonica itself was in pristine shape, silver and shiny and as good as new. Lord presented it to him at dinner that night, and I swear I thought Singer was going to cry. He held it and couldn't even speak, his hands shaking, his mouth opening and closing like a hooked carp. Singer never shows too much emotion one way or the other, so this display caught all of us off guard. It hasn't left his person since then. He plays it almost every night. We all love it.

Annie plops down next to me with a heavy grunt. She's a few months older than I am. Her shocking red hair is so bright in this drab, brown world. As she brushes it out, my eyes are drawn to it, almost as if her head is ablaze and I need to tend to it. Of all of us, she's the only one who doesn't have that constant, hungry, darting look about her. I suspect she's hoarding food, even though I've never been able to catch her. But I cut her some slack because she takes care of the two kids with a gentle hand and passion that are beyond my capacity. It's been a long time since I've met anyone as positive and upbeat as her. She can see colors in a black and white world.

Plus, there's no way I could ever do what she does, not day in and day out. Her patience with the little ones seems infinite. Children are a liability to surviving in this crappy new world, but to her they're as necessary as air.

"Come on, Carly, breakfast is ready," she calls pleasantly over her shoulder, as if she hadn't just spent the night on the hard floor in a smelly, crappy hotel room, while the world outside slowly drowns. "Let's go, sleepyhead."

I start ladling out the oatmeal-mushroom stew into bowls. Carly stumbles up with a blanket draped over her shoulder, and I'm not sure how but she doesn't trip over it. Her black hair is flopped across her face, and she yawns so big I bet she could stick her entire fist in her mouth. We found her six or seven months ago cowering in a small mom and pop grocery store outside of Elyria, to the west of Cleveland. She was filthy and ragged and wouldn't talk, which is such a contrast to the chatty Cathy she's become. She's naturally so bubbly and helpful that she might actually warm my cold heart.

Carly takes her plastic bowl and, at Annie's gentle urging, thanks me in her sleepy, mumbling morning voice. She sits against the wall with the bowl in her lap and spoons the warm oatmeal into her small mouth. She'll never know the meaning of "leftovers." While she's eating Annie goes over and picks up a small bundle, cooing to it softly. Wrapped in the bundle is Tiny, an infant of only seven or eight months. We found him a few weeks ago in the destruction of a house on a hill outside of Lima. He was alone in an upstairs bathroom, tucked underneath a sink and thick with a thousand mosquito bites. Everyone else in the house was dead, slaughtered by Grays or some other nastier version of us. We figure the only reason he survived is because he never makes a peep. And by never, I mean never. Either he can't, or he won't, but in the time he's been with us he hasn't uttered a sound. To me it's creepy as hell, but not to Annie. Like I said, thank God for her. She does what I can't do.

With Carly taken care of, the rest of us take a turn. Dog is first, then Singer, Annie, me, and finally Lord. Around his first mouthful he glances at me.

"Where's Hunter?"

I tilt my head toward the wall. "Over there. Still sacked out."

Lord's face clouds and he walks over to him. He's never said anything to me or anyone else, but I get the feeling Hunter bugs him, too. He looks down at the still form under the blanket and gives it a gentle kick with his boot.

"Wake up. Let's go."

His real name is Scotty, but we've called him Hunter from day one. He was raised by his dad in northern Ohio, where they really did hunt for a lot of their food. Deer season is in the fall, but according to him they went out whenever they got low on meat and took down a buck or doe. They'd skin and gut it in their barn away from curious eyes, and they had a butcher in town process the meat for a wink and a few pounds of venison. His dad never saw anything wrong with it, and by default Hunter never did either.

Can he be a pain in the ass? Hell, yeah. He's moody, grumpy, and strong-willed, but he's also the reason we're not in worse shape than we are. In the last month he's been able to take down a scraggly doe, about a dozen squirrels, and more rabbits than I care to recall. Real honest-to-God protein.

He's also an able fisherman, but we only let him break out the rod and reel when we find an isolated pond or lake, one that hasn't been polluted by the toxic floodwaters. We never eat anything from that nasty stuff, and we never drink it. It's poison.

Hunter grunts and rolls over, angrily shoving away Lord's foot. He sits up and looks around, his face screwed up in doubt and confusion, as if he can't believe we're still here, that the world is still so messed up. He has a round face full of faded freckles: we haven't seen the sun in months, and we're all as pale as vampires. His dark eyes slowly blink away the sleep.

"There'd better be some left for me," he mumbles, a typical, gritty edge to his voice. For some reason he's got a southern accent, even though he grew up near Toledo. I never figured that one out.

I scrape the last of the oatmeal from the pot into a bowl and hold it out in his direction. I'm not taking it to him. No way. He can get his ass up and get it himself. Carly, her dark hair still hanging in her face, scurries over to me, always eager to please.

"I got it! I got it, Hunter. Here."

She takes the bowl and holds it out in front of her, cautiously walking heel to toe over to him with all the care of a drunk driver taking a sobriety test. He takes it from her without a sound and digs in, slurping loudly.

"Hunter, a thank you would be nice," chides Annie.

"Whatever," he mumbles back.

She purses her lips and shakes her head at his lack of social graces, but leaves it and walks around collecting bowls and spoons with one hand, Tiny tucked away in the other and resting on her ample hip. Hunter finishes his breakfast and tosses the bowl down. From under his blanket he withdraws a rifle.

He's told me what it is, but I don't know much about guns. I think it's a 30/30, or something like that. It's his very own from before the Storm, and he's jealously guarded it this whole time. All I know is that it's deafening and can take down a deer from a hundred yards or more. We're always on the lookout for more guns and ammo when we're scrounging, and we've got a pretty decent arsenal stashed in the closet, up high, away from young eyes and hands: some handguns, a few .22 rifles, and a short-barreled shotgun. I've shot each one a few times, but I'm terrible at it. The broad side of a barn fears nothing from me. And the shotgun nearly dislocated my shoulder the one time I tried it, so that's not happening again anytime soon.

My preference? I've got a six-inch hunting knife strapped to my thigh. I've never been forced to use it for anything more vicious than stripping bark from a branch to rejuvenate a flagging fire, or for mundane tasks like cleaning out my nails, cutting my hair, or digging out splinters. The edge is so killer sharp that Lord uses it as a razor to scrape off the burgeoning whiskers adorning his chin. For fun I named it Chuck. Chuck's handle is brown leather, wrapped tight, with a heavy silver knob on the end. It looks menacing as hell. The long blade is so shiny I can see a twisted fun-house version of myself in it, my own thin face, brown hair hacked short, and dark eyes that are too big for my face.

When I was young, my mom would place a

loving hand on my face and call me her little pixie, then plant a dozen kisses on my cheeks. I wonder what she'd think of me now. Would she even recognize me?

While Annie spoons the remainder of the cooled oatmeal into Tiny's mouth, the rest of us clean up. When I step outside into the drizzly morning, the stench slaps me, the same stench that we've endured every day since the Storm. It's the constant stink of warm mud and polluted water, of rotting drywall and a million rusting cars. It's the reek of an entire world's worth of personal possessions decaying a little more each day. And underneath it all is the road-kill stench of hundreds of thousands of decomposing bodies. The putrid soup is so thick and cloying it sticks to the inside of your nose like rubber cement. It's disgusting. I hate it.

One time, long ago, I remember my parents and me driving past a landfill on a hot August after-noon in the family SUV. The wind was not in our fa-vor and the reek that washed over us was an almost physical thing, a punch to the face that nearly had us puking. Laughing, noses pinched closed, we shut the windows and cranked up the air conditioning just to get away from it, dad making fake retching noises the whole time and accusing us kids of farting. That land-fill stench was roses and lilacs compared to what we live with every day now. Even after several hours of exposure it's still there, just under the surface. We nev-er joke about the smell. There's nothing funny about it.

When everyone else is set, I toss on my black plastic poncho, grab the hatchet and head back outside. I wish like every morning that I had toothpaste and a toothbrush. I'd kill to be able to brush my teeth. The guys are talking in low tones and preparing to go, getting their guns and supplies ready, suiting up in ponchos and knee-high rubber boots, required gear for trudging in the slop. Annie will hang back with the two kids, just like usual.

I wave goodbye to Lord, and he throws me a two-fingered salute, his typical parting gesture to me. I trot down the steps at the end of the porch where our boats are tied up. We've got two aluminum row boats, what my dad used to call Jon boats. We've also got a two-man canoe, which is not as stable as the row boats but is so much easier to handle in the water. It's a dirty silver aluminum one with a fading Ohio license sticker on the side. I carefully check for snakes, then step in, untie it, and push away from the steps. With even strokes I aim for the tree line a few hundred yards away, at the far end of what used to be the parking lot. Once in a while my paddle clunks against the roof of a submerged car or truck as I glide along. Trash and debris float on and just below the surface. Rain patters against my plastic poncho.

I coast up to the nearest tree, one where the branches are low enough for me to easily reach, and I tie up. I break off a few dozen smaller branches and stack them in the stern of the canoe, then start hacking away at the larger ones, the thunk of the hatchet against the dead wood loud in the eerie silence. In no time I have to switch arms as my right one begins to tire. I'm sweating under the poncho and figure I'll soon be just as wet as if I hadn't worn it. Now that I'm stationary the mosquitoes start descending on me like vultures on road kill, circling my head in a thick, angry fog. I'm so used to swatting them away that I barely notice I'm doing it. Even so, I'll have a dozen welts on my hands and face before the day is done.

I notice movement off to my left and see the guys starting out in the row boats. Lord and Singer in one, Hunter and Dog in the other. Hunter's rifle is across his lap. They shove off and paddle away from me, toward the front of the hotel and the suspected Wal-Mart outside of town. Under my breath I wish them well, and pray they'll be safe. Annie and the little ones are on the porch, little Carly jumping up and down and waving energetically. I turn back to my work.

I hack at more branches until the stern is full. I cautiously row back to the steps and unload, then go back for round two. This time I have to head deeper into the trees before I find one with low branches. I tie up again and repeat the process, slowly stacking up the precious firewood. I do this three more times, until my hands and arms are so sore and tired I'm not sure I can hold the hatchet any longer, much less swing it. I take a break and lie back in the canoe, my face up to the sky, and let the warm rain splash against my face. The black, somber trees around me tower into the gloomy sky, the unique perspective making their trunks lean in to a single point far above me, a million raindrops silently zeroing in on my face. The sight is hypnotic.

The Storm was born over sixty months ago. It began as dozens of hurricanes and typhoons, pounding almost every corner of the globe at the same time. In fact, there were so many that scientists burned through the standard naming conventions, and had to move on to the Greek alphabet. Then the unimaginable happened—all those dozens of individual systems combined into a single huge one. This storm-pocalypse was initially called Zeta, but it quickly grew so massive and destructive that everyone eventually dropped the Zeta. From that point on, it was simply called the Storm.

The torrential rains were like nothing we'd ever seen before, a waterfall that pounded us for months. It eventually eased up, but never stopped completely. Before our eyes entire cities vanished underwater, each one a new Atlantis. Rivers, once secure in their banks, became lakes. Lakes grew and merged into oceans. Glaciers shrank. Mountains melted faster than ice cream on a blistering Ohio summer day.

There were a thousand explanations, of course. Scientists on talk shows postured, weathermen poured over conflicting and hopelessly overwhelmed computer models, and politicians pointed fingers at everyone but themselves. Environmentalists enjoyed the last laughs, wagging their fingers with a dire "I told you so." Then there was the obligatory gnashing of teeth by holy rollers of all faiths, not to mention the tsunami of overnight religious conversions. In the end, no one could explain why it started, or worse yet, when it might stop.

And then civilization simply…dissolved.

I hear a noise and sit up. For a second I think the guys are back, or that Annie and the little ones are on the porch, playing or talking. But looking around me I don't see anyone or anything, so I dismiss the sound. Maybe it was a squirrel, or one of those big black snakes, or a branch falling into the water? Either way, my break is over and I heft the hatchet again with an aching hand. With the blade back, ready to swing, I look through the trees, and I see a Gray.

It's standing on a ridge, only fifteen or twenty feet away. I hadn't noticed this before, but there's a set of railroad tracks beyond the forest, peeking above the water line. From here I can see brown weeds jutting through rocks, and steel rails thick with rust. The Gray is staring at me, then begins pacing back and forth like an angry dog behind a fence. I yelp and jump back in shock and almost tumble out of the canoe, falling flat on my ass, my back banging against the seat support behind me. The impact hurts like hell but it barely registers. My gaze is locked on the creature. How long has it been watching me? It's shirtless and barefoot. The tattered, sagging remains of pants are held in place by a filthy leather belt. It's so emaciated its ribcage is thrust forward, each rib clearly defined, its chest heaving in and out with every breath. I can clearly discern the sharp outlines of bones in its arms and shoulders. Its cheeks and eye sockets are so sunken that if it didn't have a nose it would be a skull. Every visible inch of it is a sickly, ashen color except its hands and forearms. They're stained brown almost to the elbows with what I'm guessing is dried blood. It's been Gray for a long time. It looks…hollow.

I snatch at the oar and frantically try to paddle away until I realize I'm still tied up to the tree. The last time I was this close to a Gray was just a few weeks ago. That Gray attacked and killed Tommy, a nice, quiet kid who'd only been with us a few days. I can still hear his shrieks and cries for help as I fought through the slop, my eyes cloudy with tears and terror.

"Lord! Hunter! Gray!" I scream instinctively, before it hits me that they're not here, and they can't hear my voice even as it reaches new and shocking octaves.

I fumble at the knot keeping the canoe tied in place, but the rope is slippery and wet and my fingers are shaking. I can't get it undone. I tug Chuck from his sheath at my thigh and slice through the nylon rope with a fierce swipe. Free now, I paddle backwards like a crazy person, with a lot more splashing than actual results. The Gray is still pacing, and stares at me with its head lowered, panting and agitated.

My heart is banging in my chest, but my panic ebbs with every watery foot I put between it and me. Grays don't swim, I keep reminding myself. I concentrate on the oar in my hands and settle down, rowing backwards with more purpose. Ten more strokes and I'm out of the flooded woods and into the parking lot. I catch a glimpse of the Gray between the dying tree trunks. I start to turn around so I can paddle correctly when I hear a tremendous boom from behind me.

I spin around and see that the guys are back from their trip to Wal-Mart. Hunter has his rifle up to his shoulder and a wisp of smoke leaks from the barrel. I spin back toward the railroad tracks and see the Gray with its left arm missing. Hunter's shot blew it off at the shoulder. A wound of that magnitude wouldn't kill a normal person right away, I'm pretty sure, but they'd be dead in a few minutes. However, Grays aren't normal people, not any longer, and this one doesn't seem to notice or care that it's suffered a horrific injury. Grays have an amazing ability to heal from just about anything short of complete decapitation. In fact, I'm so close that I can see that its shoulder has already stopped bleeding. If anything, this injury may have pissed it off even more. It's stalking back and forth faster than ever, its dead eyes locked on me. Its arm is forgotten, twitching on the muddy ground next to it.

I hear a click-click as Hunter chambers a second round, and another boom shatters the stillness. The Gray's head explodes in black blood and bone. It staggers backwards but refuses to fall over. I watch in horror, hissing under my breath, commanding the thing to just die, dammit, when it finally topples backwards onto the tracks. Its legs flop and convulse a few times and then stop.

"Hot damn, what a shot!" I hear Hunter shout with a laugh and a whoop. "Did you see that? I took its head off from almost a hundred yards. And I was in a damn boat!"

I start paddling again and pull up next to my brother and Singer.

"You okay?" Lord asks. His voice doesn't betray his concern, but I can see it in his face and I'm thankful for it. Singer and Dog stare at me. Dog's eyes are bigger than quarters.

After a moment I nod. "Yeah, I'm okay. It just startled me, I guess. It was so close, and I remembered Tommy, you know?" My hands are shaking and I feel a little sick. I'm still sweating, but it's no longer from the heat. The skin on my face is clammy. I'm trying really hard not to throw up.

"Yeah, I figured that. Head back and unload. We're going to look around and make sure there aren't any more."

Hunter hefts his rifle and grins ear to ear. "And if there are, I'll take care of them, too. I'm on fire!" He turns to me, laughing. "Hey, Scout, after I blew its arm off you should've asked that thing what the sound of one hand clapping makes! Ha!"

Fighting to remain calm, I ignore Hunter and paddle to the steps. Once there I tie up with difficulty using the cut rope, then unload the firewood. With the stacks from my prior trips included there's quite a bit, and it takes me at least fifteen minutes to finish up. I keep looking out at the guys in the boats as they paddle cautiously among the trees, searching for more Grays. Thankfully I don't hear any gunshots, but my heart is still heavy. I know what this means and what we'll have to do now. We saw one Gray, which means there are probably more nearby: they almost always travel in small packs. It means we'll have to leave. As skanky and nasty as this place is, it's been our home for weeks. We've grown used to it. With a sigh I trudge toward our room to break the news to Annie and the others. Our time at the Motel 6 is over.

CHAPTER
THREE

We pack and we're ready to go in no time, which is pretty easy to do when all your worldly possessions fit into or strap under a backpack.

Of course I've got my new book. It's tucked into the front pocket of my pack and protected in a plastic bag, as safe as I can make it. I'm terrified something will happen to it, that it'll fall into the water, or I'll lose it, or the bag will rip. It's tearing my heart out that I have to leave the other dozen behind, but I don't have any room for them. They're lined up neatly on the counter by the sink. I run my fingers over their spines one last time, feeling their textures, reliving their adventures, their romances, and mysteries. I rest my hand on them before I force myself to turn away.

Also tucked in my pack is a block of magnesium. I've used it before to start a fire, but it's a tremendous pain and rarely works. My blanket is wrapped tighter than a cigar and secured underneath the pack, and everything else I own is stuffed inside. My main concern – besides the book – is the fire itself. Using tongs, I gathered up the freshest, hottest coals and carefully positioned them in the bottom of the cast iron cooking pot. For the duration of the trip I'll feed in small sticks and bark to keep it going, blowing on it, whispering sweet nothings to it, and praying it stays viable.

Carly whined and fussed when we told her we had to go. She's not keen on change either, and the hotel room was becoming home to her, too. At some point she drew pictures on the walls with some crayons, scenes of sunshine, flowers, and smiling stick people, and was upset at having to desert them. In soft, comforting tones, Annie promised she could draw new ones, at our new home. I'm curious how in the world the little girl even knows what those things look like. I can't remember the last time I saw the sun, much less a flower.

With minimal fuss we're in the boats and under way, the smelly Motel 6 slipping silently away behind us. I'm a little shocked at my reaction, but I think I'll miss it, too. We're not even out of the parking lot when I turn to Lord.

"Did you guys find anything at that Wal-Mart?" I'm really hoping they did. Our food is running low, and we ran out of dried fruit a few days ago. From a cupboard in a bomb shelter up north we scrounged some packs of dried mango well past their expiration dates, but thanks to the miracle of chemical preservatives they were still good. Carly didn't like the yellowish-orange, chewy strips of fruit in the least, but Annie sweet-talked her into eating some of it. Still, the lack of nutritional variety is one of our biggest ongoing problems. Packets of oatmeal and mushrooms mixed with water is okay for the short-term, but not forever.

Lord rows with strong, even strokes, keeping his focus ahead. "No, it wasn't even a Wal-Mart. It was an office complex, or something like that."

"I think it used to be one, but not anymore," Hunter chimes in. He makes a gross, hacking noise and spits into the water. "Didn't figure we'd need any staplers or easels, so we didn't stick around. Good thing, eh?"

"Yeah, good thing. Thanks." I don't want to talk about the dead Gray, but I'm so grateful they came back early. Still, it sucks that they didn't find anything good. We're going to be starving in no time at this rate.

We paddle out of the parking lot and into a vast, open expanse of water. Interstate 75 used to be the main highway that began in Michigan and ended up down in Florida. Now it's a concrete ribbon a dozen or more feet below us, four lanes slowly dissolving to gravel. Around us are the very tops of green highway signs sticking up out of the water, proclaiming that there's an exit for some streets I've never heard of, going to a place that no longer exists. This part of Ohio is flat, and by flat, I mean pancake flat, with barely a hill to break the monotony. We keep going, sliding quietly between the signs, the paddles making small splashing noises. A million raindrops dimple the brown swill around us, tapping on our plastic ponchos in a steady beat that I don't even notice anymore, background white noise that no longer registers. Someone slaps at a hungry mosquito. There's a sniff and a whimper from behind me and I suspect it's Carly, still sad about leaving her artwork behind. I wish I could feel sorry for her, but I can't. Not now.

Singer is behind me in the canoe, and I'm glad of it. He's strong and he'll row until his arms fall off. As soon as that image strikes me, I shudder inside. Seeing that Gray's arm blown off is just one more nightmare I'm afraid I'll never be able to forget.

Ten feet ahead, Dog and Annie are doing their best to row their boat in a straight line. Neither of them is great at handling the awkward things, and they expend a lot of energy without much return. But they get along well together, so we've learned to live with it.

"Boss, hey, boss," Dog says rapidly, inhaling the thick air, his wide nostrils flaring. "I just caught a whiff of something. More Grays, I think. Yeah, more Grays. That way, I think."

He points a thin finger ahead and all of us look. Hunter has a telescope and he pulls it out and snaps it to its full length in a single motion. He puts it to his eye and begins scouring the water ahead of us.

He swears he prefers the telescope to binoculars because of its size and portability, but I'm pretty sure he keeps it because he thinks it's cool. Like he's Captain Jack Sparrow, or something.

Lord calls a halt, and we all drift to a stop. "Where?"

Dog sniffs the air again. He wrinkles his nose before pointing ahead, away from the Motel 6, toward the south, in the direction we're going.

"There, boss, I think they're up there. Near the overpass."

I strain my eyes to see the concrete overpass in the distance. It's got to be almost half a mile away, and even squinting I can't spot anything. I can tell that the overpass is at least partially collapsed, but I can't tell how badly. I guess that sort of thing happens with a flood and sixty or more months with no road maintenance crews. To the right the road travels a hundred feet or so before it vanishes under water. Quite a bit farther in the same direction it breaks the surface, then goes underwater again, undulating like a giant asphalt sea serpent.

"Hunter, what do you see?" Lord asks quietly. When Hunter finally speaks his voice is muffled because his hands are in the way, the telescope still up to his eye.

"I see two, no, three Grays. They're on the right side of the overpass."

Oh crap, more of them. I shiver like I'd just

stepped into a freezer. My mouth has gone dry, which I find only mildly ironic considering the drowning world around us.

"Damn," Lord whispers. Then louder, "How did they get there? The road to the overpass is under water."

Hunter blinks a few times as he thinks about it. "Beats me. Maybe jumping from one car roof to the other? It doesn't look too deep there."

Lord stares straight ahead, his mouth working. "What are they doing?"

Hunter shrugs. "Nothing. Just standing there."

In the beginning, just after the Storm, there were Grays everywhere. Hundreds of thousands of them. Maybe more. Maybe even millions. No one could ever come up with a head count because the world fell apart so fast. Those of us who managed to survive the first few years only did so because we were holed up in places they couldn't reach: the upper floors of buildings surrounded by water, like the Motel 6, or bomb shelters, or way out in the sparsely populated country where there simply weren't very many. Hunter is a survivor. He made it by himself in a tree house fifty feet above the ground and used his rifle to pick off any Grays that got too close. Lord and I lived in a nearly finished apartment complex on the west side of Cleveland where the first three floors and dozens of blocks around us were submerged, living off of whatever we could find in nearby buildings or stores. Those first few years were horrible beyond belief. So many people died, screaming, confused, being torn apart, helpless and unable or unwilling to fight as their own relatives went Gray and turned on them. And my parents...

I snap back to now. As bad as it is, the present is preferable to traveling back to those dark, awful days. We're still drifting a bit so Singer gently paddles up to Lord's boat and grabs hold. No one is saying a thing, they just stare at my big brother and wait for his orders. There's no way we can go back the way we came and avoid them. They almost certainly know we're here, and they'll do anything to get at us. Like I said, Grays are unpredictable as hell, but we can't risk a surprise encounter. If they're in the area they'll eventually find us. We have to do this on our own terms.

Lord looks at us, his mouth a hard line. "Okay. We'll have to take them out."

I knew he'd say that. It's the only way, really. But I hate the thought of getting close to them. He shifts his gaze toward Hunter.

"Think you can do it? If we get closer?"

Hunter's aggrieved sneer tells the story. "Seriously? You saw what I did back at the hotel, right? Get me close enough and I'll clean house."

I've seen my brother like this before. I can tell he isn't completely convinced, but he's smart enough to know that, as our leader, he can't appear wishy-washy or uncertain. Lord sets his face and looks straight ahead at the overpass and the acres of water separating us. His brown eyes squint in concentration. Finally he looks back at Hunter.

"Fine. You and I will go ahead and take them out. Everyone else stays here."

Hunter grins and his face lights up. He lives for this stuff, and as much as that scares the hell out of me, I know we desperately need him and his skills. Out here he's nearly as important as our fire. He claps his hands together loudly, the report echoing across the water. Carly jumps in surprise.

"That's what I'm talking about!" Hunter exclaims with a fist pump.

"We'll ferry the supplies into the other boat. Hunter, you and I will just take what weapons and ammo we need."

I know it's the right thing to do, and I would've made the same call myself. But having both of them exposed and in danger gives me the chills. Especially Lord. I start to say something but hold my tongue. There's nothing I can say that will change his mind.

The row boats come together with a metallic clunk and we offload most of the supplies. The ammo box is heavy. I'm always astounded at how much bullets weigh, so we set it in the middle of the canoe. The trusty aluminum craft handles the added weight easily, just settling lower in the water. The ammo is only a few feet from the cook pot with the simmering coals, which gives me a little pause. Both Singer and Lord see my concern. My brother waves it away.

"Don't worry. It would take a lot more heat than that to light them up," he assures me. While he's talking he gathers up the shotgun and one of the handguns, which he stuffs in his belt. Hunter keeps his trusty 30/30 and straps a holster and pistol onto his hip. The only weapon I've got is Chuck. I glance at Hunter for a moment, and notice that he's staring at me. He holds his eyes on me for a heartbeat longer than I find comfortable before he looks away.

My brother shoots me another two-fingered salute, and the two of them shove off, paddling toward the overpass. They each have an oar and they use them in perfectly timed motions. If synchronized rowing were in the Olympics, those two would be Team USA. Even though they don't look like they're working at it, their powerful strokes move them away from us quickly. The wake behind the boat travels out in even ripples, flattening, eventually dissipating to nothing.

Before long the guys are far enough away that it's hard to distinguish between the two of them. I can't tell how close they are to the overpass, but they have to be getting near. Then I see a small flash, and a second later a deep boom rumbles across the still water. I jerk in my seat a little, startled, even though I was expecting it. Then there are two more flashes and delayed booms, and finally a fourth. We wait, staring ahead, the only sound the rain as it hits our ponchos and the metal of the boats, a sound that for some reason right now reminds me of wind chimes tinkling in a breeze.

Finally we hear a whistle, the kind you get with fingers in your mouth, a whistle that would likely cause hearing loss in someone standing next to you. Hunter. I exhale a breath I didn't know I was holding and we all look at each other and smile, big, goofy grins that seem to extend beyond our faces. We're all so relieved we could laugh out loud, and Carly claps her little hands together in glee, picking up on our mood. Now that the drama is over I take a moment to remember my duty as Firebrand and add some scraps of bark to the coals, blowing gently, my hands shaking. The fire rewards me with a tongue of flickering yellow flame. I feed some twigs into the pot and blow some more. A gentle, attentive touch is imperative.

In no time the guys are back, Hunter smiling so wide his face might split. Lord's grin is more muted, but still there.

"Four shots, three dead Grays!" Hunter whoops with pride, his fists raised above his head in triumph. "See that last one? Damn thing moved so quick I couldn't get a bead on it. But it stopped long enough for a head shot after I put a round in its chest. Nothing to it, boys and girls! Boom!"

Carly laughs at this and imitates him, a pretend gun at her shoulder. "Boom!" she cries out.

"Good job, Hunter! You did it, yes you did!" Dog laughs. The threat is over, but I can hear how his voice trembles, nerves and fear eclipsing his relief.

The rest of us congratulate him warmly as well, which he happily eats up. He's still beaming as the two boats bump together and the youngsters and supplies are handed back. With this latest threat gone I feel tension leak away, replaced by exhaustion. Incidents like this take more of a toll on me than I thought possible, even though I was safely tucked away from the danger. I wish this stuff didn't hit me like this, but it does.

The mood has improved by a magnitude as we begin rowing. Dog and Annie start out, with Dog and his magnificent nose taking the point. I'm a little nervous since I don't even think his amazing talent will be able to discern live Grays from dead ones, but Hunter and Lord follow close behind, their weapons at the ready just in case. Singer and I bring up the rear, which, if pressed, is just where I want to be. We paddle along in single file and before I know it we're easing up to the ruined overpass.

I was right. The center section is completely collapsed, like it was bombed. Long, rusted fingers of rebar jut from ruined concrete on either side of a twenty-foot wide chasm. Chunks of concrete cling to those gnarled lengths of black steel, unwilling or unable to let go. Somewhere below us is the fallen span, completely hidden from view by the dark water.

Above me I see a bloodied, gray arm draped over the side. The twitching fingers could be tapping out its obituary on a phantom keyboard. No one is speaking and the atmosphere has gone hushed and eerily silent. Death of any kind will do that to you, I guess.

Dog and Annie's boat is the first to ease into the collapsed opening, with Lord's tucked close behind. As our canoe gets closer I see tendrils of thick black scum coating the concrete supports below the waterline. The small wakes of our passing disturbs the dark filaments, pushing them into a slow, nearly hypnotic underwater bolero. The only sounds are the small splashes of our paddles as they dip into and out of the water. I'm gripping the paddle so hard I'm afraid it might splinter.

The first boat is nearly through when I catch movement out of the corner of my eye. Before I can shout out a warning a Gray launches itself from behind a column.

CHAPTER
FOUR

The creature crashes into Dog so hard they both fly off the boat and into the sludge, Dog's yelp of shock sliced in half as they go under. Hunter shouts something incoherent and jumps to his feet, rocking their boat dangerously, his rifle up to his shoulder and tracking back and forth in jerks. He's unable to lock onto the submerged Gray. He can't shoot what he can't see.

"Oh, no, Dog!" Annie shouts, her hands to her mouth in terror. She's tumbled into the bottom of the boat and is laboring to get up, Tiny on top of her. I hear high-pitched screaming and realize that it's me. Lord has the shotgun aimed down at the churning water, but he can't pinpoint the Gray either. He's scanning madly back and forth. I've never seen him panic before, but this is close.

"I don't see him!" he shouts. "Does anyone see him?"

The almost black water near the canoe is churning and bubbling, and for just a second I swear I see them, flashes of lighter brown movement at least ten feet down. But I don't know what to do. I'm frozen in place, paralyzed, every muscle and joint seized up. My hands are gripping the sides of the canoe so hard they could be nailed in place.

Dog bursts up out of the depths, spitting muddy water from his mouth and nose. His arms flap like a duck at takeoff, splashing and grasping at nothing. Just for a second, a split second, our eyes lock and I see the panic there: a wild and desperate look that I've never seen in anyone's face before. It's the face of imminent death.

I feel a tug at my thigh and see a flash of silver as Singer rips Chuck out of my sheath. He dives from the canoe with my knife in hand and is immediately swallowed by the disgusting water. Dog's head and arms are sucked under as the Gray yanks him back down into the black abyss. Lord and Hunter both cry out, but they're powerless to do anything. We can do nothing but watch and pray, although prayer hasn't done squat for us in the past. My chest constricts and I can't draw a breath. Like Dog. Like Singer.

I can't tell how much time passes. Thirty seconds? A full minute? Lord slumps down. He runs his hand through his long hair, anguish crushing his face. The shotgun clatters to the bottom of the boat. Annie whimpers and starts to cry. Hunter screams in rage and I swear he's going to start shooting randomly into the water. I've never seen him like this before, not this angry. His normally pale face is bright scarlet, his freckles standing out in a dark red swatch across his nose and cheeks.

Just when I've given up hope, Dog bursts out of the water, spluttering, the skin on his face laid open from his left eye across his cheek. There's no blood yet, but there will be. Lord's hand shoots out and he latches onto Dog's flailing arm. With a powerful yank that almost tosses him over the other side, he pulls Dog up and out of the water and into the boat.

"Singer! Where's Singer?" he screams at him.

Dog is coughing and rolling around. His chest heaves and he vomits out foul water and the remains of breakfast. He tries to talk but collapses face down, his chest shuddering. He's still breathing, but barely.

Lord looks like he's about to grab and shake an answer from the unconscious Dog, but before he can make a move Singer's head breaks the surface. He shakes water from his face then swims over to the canoe in two even strokes. I'm more relieved than I should be when I spot Chuck still in his hand. He tosses the knife into the bottom of the canoe and slowly climbs in, flopping heavily over the side. His breath comes in huge gasps, his chest moving up and down rapidly, and he lies in the bottom of the canoe, exhausted. His head is propped up in the V at the bow and his eyes are squeezed shut.

Hunter is the first to talk. "What the hell happened? Did you kill it?" he demands loudly. He's still aiming his rifle into the water as if the Gray might leap up and go for round two. Now is not the time to remind him that Grays don't swim. They don't seem to feel pain, like the one at the railroad tracks, and a headshot is one of the only surefire ways to kill one. But as fast and strong and tough as they are, they sink like stones and can't breathe under water. It has to be dead by now.

Puddles form in the bottom of the canoe around Singer. His clothes are stuck to him, accentuating his slender frame. His black hair is glistening, water dripping from the end of his ponytail. He isn't answering, but just lying there, regaining his strength. I don't blame him.

Hunter starts to yell again, but Lord holds up a hand for silence. Hunter's lips compress so far they disappear and his eyes flash, but for once he obeys without a fight or snarky retort. He glances at Singer with a hard expression that I don't understand, but I don't have time to think about that now. He's still got his gun locked onto his shoulder.

"It's okay, everyone," Lord says, his hands out to calm the flock. "The worst is over. Singer, you okay?"

For a few seconds Singer doesn't respond, but after a moment he flashes us a shaky wave. Looking him over I figured he was all right, but I couldn't relax until he confirmed it. Like all of us, I've grown to like his soft-spoken nature. I'd hate to see anything happen to anyone, sure, but Singer is so...nice. His manner and bearing take me back to those times I love, back to the days before the Storm. It just wouldn't be fair if he were taken from us.

Now that the danger is over, Lord is his calm and stoic self again. I can see the next steps whirling behind his eyes. He's so good at planning and working things out, and he's even better at getting people to follow those plans. This is where he shines. I'm so very proud of him, and I know mom and dad would be, too. It's too bad they'll never see the person he's become.

"Hunter," he says, his tone leaving nothing open to interpretation, "keep an eye out for others. I'm pretty sure that was the last one, but let's be safe. Annie, you and Hunter switch places so you can tend to Dog. He's got a nasty wound across his face, and who knows what else. Let's go."

Without a word the two get to work. Annie hands Tiny to me. Surprised, I take him awkwardly, not exactly sure what to do with him. Once Annie is in my brother's boat she and Lord manhandle Dog over onto his back so he's propped up in the bow. She wipes the dregs of vomit off his face and inspects the wound, which isn't bleeding nearly as much as I thought it would. As she lightly touches the edges of the gash Dog moans and groggily swats at her.

"It's pretty bad," she states. "He's going to need stitches, for sure."

"Can you do that here?" Lord asks.

She stares at the wound. "Yeah, I think so. But I'll need to clean it up, and then someone's going to have to hold him while I do it. We don't have any anesthetic."

We try to maneuver the boats around so we can all help, but it just doesn't work. In the end we tie up to the overpass about twenty yards away, where the roadway first dips into the water, and Lord carefully drags Dog up onto the concrete. The drizzle has slowed to a light mist that covers us with a shiny glaze, as if we've been working out and have a good sweat going on. Singer is up and about now, too. He looks a little glassy-eyed and groggy, like he just woke from an afternoon nap and isn't quite with it yet.

Annie opens the first aid kit, one of the several we've scrounged and keep handy for emergencies just like this. Inside there's gauze, bandages, tape, and lots of expired medicine like antibiotics, painkillers, and aspirin. There's also tons of other pills and capsules with weird, unpronounceable names that we hold on to just in case, even though we rarely know what they're supposed to do. Better safe than sorry, I guess. The names of people and pharmacies on the bottles are all long gone. These bottles are likely their only legacies.

Lord and Singer hold Dog still while Hunter stands guard. Annie calls me over and tells me to put his head between my knees and squeeze hard. I set Tiny down next to us. He stares at the proceedings with his big blue eyes.

"I don't want him thrashing around when I get going," she explains. "This is going to hurt."

She carefully pours disinfectant on the wound. It bubbles and foams and Dog jerks, but his eyes stay closed. He's still out cold. Next she takes a hooked needle with black plastic thread and goes to work on his face. I look away each time she pierces his skin, and I have to give her even more credit. There is no way I could do that, not to a living person. I'm amazed at how she's so clinical and methodical about it. This isn't the first time she's struck me as being so much more mature than the rest of us.

"Where'd you learn how to do that, anyway?" Hunter asks, peeking around her hands, admiration and awe clear in his voice.

Annie doesn't look away from the task at hand, but does take a second to brush away a dozen mosquitoes that have found a helpless target. "My mom used to watch all kinds of medical shows on TV. Documentaries. We only had one television, so I watched them, too. You learn stuff, you know?"

Dog starts to wake up halfway through, and Annie orders us in no uncertain terms to hold him still. I'm squeezing his head so tight I'm afraid I might crush his skull, but a few minutes later she's all done and wiping up the wound. I chance a look and see that poor Dog must have twenty or more stitches in his cheek, starting above his lip and ending near his left eye. Annie tapes a mass of gauze over the wound. Honestly, he wasn't a good-looking guy before, and this isn't going to help.

"I did the best I could, but I'm sure it'll get infected. He was in the water. Plus who knows what he might've caught from that thing." She picks through the first aid kit and holds up a green bottle, checking out the label. "I think this is an antibiotic. I took one like this for an ear infection I had once. I'm sure it's lost some of its strength, but if he doubles up on the dosage it should help. I hope so, at least."

Dog is starting to wake up, but he's too weak to stand, and way too out of it to paddle. We help him into the front of the canoe and I climb into Lord's boat. Singer quietly insists he's okay, so we let him take the rear of the canoe where he can both paddle and steer. Annie and Hunter are together in the other one.

"Hold on, guys, I want to make sure the fire is fine before we go," I tell everyone. In matters such as this the Firebrand's orders take precedence, even over Lord's. I spend a few minutes clearing out some of the dead ash from the bottom of the cook pot, then carefully add fresh fuel. After a couple of minutes of gently fanning the flames the fire is in good shape, and I give the okay to move out. Once we're back in the middle of the expanse of water, Lord speaks up. His deep voice is confident and strong again, just the way it should be.

"We'll keep going for a few hours," he states. "We need to get as far away from here as possible. We're not going to take any chances."

No one argues, not even Hunter. We're all painfully aware that there may be more Grays around. Our sightings have fallen off dramatically over the last twenty or twenty-five months, but they'll never completely stop. That's just not possible given how Grays come about.

"Let's keep our eyes open for another hotel or office building, one surrounded by water like the Motel 6," he continues, never faltering in his steady paddling. "Something that's basically got a moat. Once we find that we'll hole up there for the night. Questions?"

No one has any. We're all too shaken from the attack and Dog's injuries. We move out with only the sound of our oars methodically dipping into and out of the water. A feeling of dread weighs on us all. Each of us realizes that the Gray could have attacked any of us instead of Dog, and we're unscathed only through the lottery of luck.

CHAPTER
FIVE

I often think back to when the Storm came, probably more than I should. It usually happens when I'm falling asleep, or in the morning twilight of my dreams. I think back to how totally and painfully unprepared we were for such a cataclysmic event. I mean, who plans for a global killer like this?

The rains battered us, floods ravaged the land, and entire sections of the country sank under dozens of feet of rainwater. Coastlines marched inland for hundreds of miles, wiping out hundreds of cities, and maybe even entire states. Even so, we gutted it out and civilization gamely held on. But as the waters rose, bit by bit the world began to sputter and fail: power stations shorted out, wastewater treatment plants flooded and died, the roads washed away, and communications went silent. You should have seen our collective reactions when the last cell phones stopped working. It's like we didn't believe it was real until then, and it might have been funny if it weren't so tragic. Still, people are pretty damn resourceful when their backs are against the wall, and many of us were able to keep moving to higher ground and survive. My dad used to tell me, "Do what you can, with what you have, when you have it," which I thought was a pretty cool saying. And we were doing just that, together, as a family.

But then the Grays happened, and the plug was pulled.

I think I should clear something up right now. Grays aren't zombies, even though at first we thought they were. Zombies were always portrayed as the shuffling, mindless dead brought back to life, or reanimated, or something like that, and their sole purpose was killing and eating the living. That's what pre-storm movies and TV shows taught us, although why zombies have such an appetite for human brains is beyond me. But no, Grays aren't zombies. They're not dead, or the dead brought back to life. Grays are people.

Nobody could ever explain why or how, whether it happened independent of the Storm, or was somehow tied to it. But not long after the rains started, people began to change. It hits not long after you become a young adult, certainly before you hit two hundred and forty months old, usually sooner. You know it's starting when your hair begins to turn gray almost overnight. You go to sleep and you're fine, then you wake up with these gray shocks of hair and it's the beginning of the end. You've only got a few days left, a week tops. This is when most people freak out, and I don't blame them. Once your hair goes, other changes soon follow; your skin turns that horrible ashen color, you lose the ability to speak, but worst of all, your mind, your personality, your essence, I guess, deteriorates and vanishes, replaced by a being with no more intelligence than a two-year old. It's instant senility.

On the plus side, and this may be the only plus, we know that Grays don't live very long. They usually die a few months after they turn. I don't know why, but it's as if they're consumed from the inside out, like no matter how much nourishment they take in, their bodies can't process enough fuel to keep going.

I do have to keep reminding myself that a Gray is still a living being. And like any living, breathing creature, they get hungry and need to eat. But unlike a normal human, a Gray doesn't have the smarts to scrounge for food, recognize an old grocery store, or even open a can of tuna. They'll eat whatever they can easily find or run down, and these days that ends up being people. People like us. Like me.

We have such a short time before we go Gray. I think about it all the time. I can't help it. I doubt it's healthy, but there it is.

This is why I escape into my books. This is why I long for the world the way it was. I can't stand much more of this one.

I don't know how long we paddled this afternoon, but it had to be at least four or five hours. Our arms are a collective ache, and I wouldn't be surprised if we all had blisters across our palms. On the plus side, the worst of the rains held off so I didn't have to call a halt to protect the fire. Even so, by the time we found a place to hole up, I had to work hard to bring the embers back to life. Thankfully I'd kept the kindling dry under my poncho. I was a nervous wreck until it was going again.

We're on the eighth floor of an abandoned office building, one of a complex of three that must have been under construction when all hell broke loose. We chose the one that looked the most finished. The eighth is the top floor, and while we don't have to go up that far, the higher we go the more secure we feel. The first two levels are underwater, and the brown sludge outside extends for miles in every direction. There's no way there are any Grays here. But to be on the safe side Hunter and Lord carefully checked every nook and cranny to be sure before letting the rest of us enter. Nothing is alive here, although desks and chairs are overturned, construction equipment is broken, and there are brown stains all over the walls and floor. It's clear that Grays have been here before, probably in the very beginning. All of us try to ignore the underlying nasty odor we've come to recognize as residual death.

The top floor is the least damaged. Amazingly, blessedly, it's untouched by the elements. This is a real treat. The windows and roof are intact, which we almost never see, and there are no broken pipes, busted water heaters, or signs of fire or smoke damage. The flooring is all marble or granite, and the tan, painted walls are just beginning to show streaks of mold. Most of the fixtures and furniture are plastic or aluminum, which means they can't rot. And since it was buttoned up pretty tight, there aren't any mosquitoes. This is the nicest place we've seen in dozens of months, and certainly the nicest that little Carly has ever seen.

When we're all together in the central room, Lord clears his throat to get our attention. He has to wait for Carly and Annie since they're playing on one of the rolling office chairs. Carly is holding on and Annie is spinning her round and round while the little girl squeals with joy. She finally stops and grins at us, her dark hair almost completely covering her face. She's wobbling and dizzy and looks a little green.

"Okay, listen up. Annie, get the little ones settled and tend to Dog. Scout, let's go down a floor and get the fire going. This floor is dry and bug-free for once, and I'd like to keep it that way. We'll break out a window to exhaust the smoke down there."

I don't argue with him, although that means I'll have to either sleep alone with the fire, or leave it while I come back up here. I've got to admit, I'm not too keen on either option. He looks at me for confirmation, and I give him a two-fingered salute. He grins at that, which I count as a win.

"Singer, you and Hunter row over to the other buildings and see what you can scrounge. There's got to be something of value over there. Some food, hopefully. Okay?"

"What are you going to do?" Singer asks. He looks none the worse for wear after his fight with the Gray, although his clothes reek from the dunking. I have to admit that I'm impressed with him. I don't think I've got the guts to go in after anyone like that. Well, no one except maybe Lord.

My brother tilts his head down to me. "I'm going to help Scout get the fire settled, then I'll poke around. There's bound to be some food or something here I can scrounge."

Hunter grabs his rifle and leaves without a word to Singer, who follows in his wake. Lord and I head down the dark stairwell to the seventh floor. We see right away that it's not as finished as the eighth. There are stacks of building materials, wood scraps, slabs of granite and sawhorses everywhere. Plastic sheeting is hanging up to keep dust away from certain areas. Our shoes make gritty crunching noises as we walk over the concrete floor. But there are no bugs or snakes, so that's a bonus. We've got the heavy cook pot between us. The handle is warm, but we've protected our hands with rags.

We poke our noses into several different rooms, and after about ten tries we're rewarded with a section that contains one of those yellow construction chutes. It's about two feet in diameter, fixed to the windowpane where it descends into the water far below us.

I'm sure there used to be one of those huge garbage dumpsters down there. Construction workers would toss their trash and debris into the tube and, voila, down it tumbles into the dumpster. Easy peasy.

"This could work," Lord muses. He grabs the hard plastic edge and grunts with the strain. Screws pop, duct tape tears, and after a few moments he's ripped it loose from its moorings. He gives it a kick and it twists and flops down fifty feet, splashing in a loose coil into the swill.

"Nicely done," I commend him, looking out the opening at the huge yellow worm still floating just above the surface.

"Thanks," he replies, barely winded from the effort.

For the next ten minutes we shuttle square slabs of white flooring granite into the room and make a new fire pit, one that's surprisingly handsome this time. Hell, it's bordering on ornate. Happily, there are a lot of wood scraps and paper about. Using the hot coals transferred from the cook pot, in no time I've got a nice little blaze going. There's not much of a breeze outside, but it's enough to pull most of the smoke out. And this high up I don't think the flying pests can find us. This is about as good as it's going to get.

Once that's all set, we go back upstairs. Dog is finally awake, but he's just sitting on the floor wrapped up in a blanket, shivering. His color isn't good. He keeps touching his face and wincing. It has to hurt like hell, and I give him mental bonus points for not complaining about it. The kids and Annie have their sleeping area made up and ready for the night. I can tell Carly's hungry by the way she's staring at me, and to be honest, I'm starving, too, but that's the norm. I'm trying to figure out what to do about dinner when we hear some commotion from the stairwell.

Hunter and Singer burst into the room, and such is the nature of our lives that we all jump in shock and fear. My hand flies to Chuck's handle. Thankfully it's a false alarm, since the guys are sporting huge smiles and laughing. They've each got something in their hands.

"Dinner time!" Hunter yells and upends a huge plastic bag onto the floor. I can't immediately tell what it is. Wait a minute, what? I can't believe it.

"Candy bars? Oh my god, where did you find candy?" I shout. Dozens of Snickers, Milky Ways, and more, along with bags of chips and other snacks, tumble out of the bag onto the floor in a colorful heap of cellophane and crinkly paper. I haven't seen a mother lode like this in more months than I can count. My mouth explodes with saliva and I stare like a crazy person at our newfound treasure.

Hunter takes the lead. "There was a candy machine tucked away in a closet one building over. One love tap with the butt of my rifle was all it took to break the glass. But better yet, look what else we got."

Singer steps forward and lowers another bag

to the floor. It's heavy. He unwraps it to reveal two cases of Dasani bottled water, still shrink-wrapped and unopened. Involuntarily, my hand goes to my mouth to cover my shock. Bottled water? Candy?

For ten minutes we do nothing but eat junk food and drink pure water, and it's glorious. We limit ourselves to two candy bars each, along with two bottles of water. At first Carly doesn't want to try her Milky Way because she wrinkles her nose and says it looks like a turd. But after she nibbles on the end I think she'd gladly dive off the roof into the sludge for another one. As far as meals and nutritional value go, it probably doesn't rate too high on the FDA food pyramid, but it sure kicks ass on my awesomeness scale. I opt for a Payday and a Snickers bar, and I do everything but eat the wrapper when they're gone. For "dessert" we launch into bags of potato chips, while doing our best to convince ourselves that they're good for us since potatoes are, after all, vegetables. Singer is laughing around a mouthful of chips, a few crumbs stuck to his lips. I'm laughing too, until I glance over his shoulder and see Hunter staring at me again. I wish he wouldn't do that. It's starting to creep me out.

Carly wants more chocolate, but Annie won't hear of it, saying so much sugar at one time isn't good for her. Instead, she cuts up a Payday into slivers and doles out a few pieces to her, convinced that at least the peanuts are healthy. I've still got a few packets of oatmeal left, so I stir one of those up with some bottled water, and she patiently feeds that to Tiny. He dutifully and silently gobbles up the entire bowl. The cold paste doesn't look the least bit appetizing after my meal, but he doesn't complain. Not that he would.

I'm still licking my fingers and basking in the glow of chocolate nirvana when I realize I'd better check on the fire. Plus, it's getting dark outside, and since we're in a new and foreign place I'd rather get things ready before it gets too dark and I'm forced to fumble around blind. I take one of the waters and my backpack and head down to the seventh floor.

The fire has settled into a comforting blue and yellow glow, lighting up the small, plastic-shrouded room where it's housed. I wander around in the quickening gloom and gather up all the scraps of two by fours and plywood that I can find. The stack grows until I've got enough to last days, not just overnight.

I sit by the fire and relax. For once I'm not hungry, or scared, or swatting at the annoying insect vampires. Okay, I might be a smidge shaky from all the sugar, but that's it. Really, I'm just content, and I marvel at what a weird feeling it is. I take a deep breath of the smoky air and peer out the window. It's getting dark now, and outside the building I can see nothing down below, while the sky above is a shade or two lighter. I also realize that this is the first time in ages that I can't hear rain falling, and that's probably the oddest thing of all, because it's always raining. I crane my neck out the open window and for a fleeting second I see a bright smear of light through the clouds. It's the moon. I swear it is. I can't remember the last time I saw the moon. It's only there for a few seconds, then the clouds drift back, the hole closes up, and it's gone again. But I saw it, and it takes me back to before the Storm, and I'm happier than I can recall in a long time.

I decide that I'll sleep down here by myself after all. It won't be so bad, and a peaceful night away from everyone sounds pretty attractive after such a shitty day. I roll out my blanket and carefully draw my book out of its plastic bag. I lay it on my blanket near the fire where I can see. It doesn't make a sound as it opens, but in my mind I hear ancient, rusted hinges creaking like the doors to an old English castle. I find that I'm smiling, and I didn't even know it.

I've just started teasing some pages apart when I hear footsteps. Annoyed because I think it's Lord checking up on me, I'm about to say something snarky when the plastic sheeting is pulled aside and I see Singer.

"You okay? You didn't come back upstairs." His voice, like always, is soft. There are no hard edges to his pronunciations, no hard stops and starts. Toss in a background melody and I bet whatever he says could be put to song. He must have been something before the Storm.

I smile, kind of surprised that I'm this happy to see him, especially since two minutes ago I was looking forward to being alone. "No, I'm fine, thanks. I just decided to spend the night down here with the fire."

He stands there for a moment, and neither of us says anything. He's quiet by nature, but I'm not. This sudden tongue-tied episode is not like me at all, and I'm very aware of his proximity to me. It takes me a second to realize this is the first time the two of us have been alone together. With so much to do and so many people to care for, it just never happened before. Simply getting through each day is enough of a challenge.

Finally I motion to the floor next to me. "Want to sit down? I'm trying to figure out what this book is."

Singer smiles and smoothly settles down, cross-legged. The room is getting darker by the second and his black skin is becoming one with the night. Except for his eyes. And his smile. He gestures toward the book.

"Can I take a look at it?"

A flash of selfishness hits me and I nearly snatch the book and clutch it to my chest. Then with a blush that I hope he can't see, I force those feelings aside and slide it towards him. With what I judge to be the proper amount of reverence, he picks it up and thumbs through a few of the pages that haven't been fused together. His lips move ever so slightly as he reads in the dim light. After a moment he hands it back to me.

"It's Hamlet. Shakespeare's Hamlet. We did a production of it in school."

I smile again, amazed that I've smiled twice in as many minutes. "Really? Hamlet? We were going to read it in school my next year, but, you know..."

"Yeah, I know. Not my favorite," Singer makes a face.

"Really? Why not?"

"Well, mainly because pretty much everyone dies. It's one of his tragedies. It's not what you'd call a feel-good story."

"Oh, okay. I've tried reading what few pages I've been able to pry apart, but it doesn't make much sense to me. The language is so old, and I can't under-stand what they're talking about."

He nods knowingly. "Yeah, it's tough, I know. We spent a whole semester on it. Thankfully the teacher let us refer to the updated version, the one with modern English. The language is hard enough to understand, sure, but there are so many references to things and places that just don't mean anything to us today."

I suddenly find that I'm inexplicably sad. No, that's not it. Perhaps I'm more let down than sad. I'd hoped this new find would help transport me away like some of my other books, but now it's clear that won't happen. Even if I could magically wish apart each and every page, there's no way I can read and understand what's there. It may as well be written in

German, or Swahili, or even Klingon, for that matter. Singer flips through a few more pages. "I can read it to you, if you like. I don't remember what it all means, but some of it's familiar."

I sit up a little straighter. "Really? Could you?"

"Sure. Tell you what, I'll start from the beginning, in my own words, and tell you the story. I'm sure I'll screw some of it up, but I'll be able to hit the high points. Want me to?"

Want him to? That's like asking if I'd like another Milky Way bar. I vigorously nod yes, and throw some more wood on the fire. The edges of the pale two by fours quickly blacken as they catch, and the room lightens up to the point where I can clearly see him again. I notice for the first time that his face has narrowed recently, and there may be the beginnings of stubble on his chin and down his cheeks.

"Well, oddly enough, it starts off as a ghost story," Singer begins. "King Hamlet is dead, and his brother, Claudius, takes the throne and marries the dead king's wife, Queen Gertrude. But the ghost of King Hamlet appears in the castle, and is spotted by some guards and a scholar named Horatio."

"Ghosts? In a Shakespeare play?"

"Oh, sure. Ghosts in Hamlet, naked witches in Macbeth. Shakespeare loved that kind of stuff. And audiences ate it up."

"Well, it's working. You've got my attention already."

"Good. So Horatio finds the prince, also named Hamlet, and the ghostly king tells his son that he was in fact murdered by his brother Claudius, and that Prince Hamlet is supposed to exact his revenge on Claudius and kill him, too."

Honestly, I'm not sure how much time passed after Singer got going. I'm spellbound as he tells the story of Prince Hamlet, his apparent descent into madness, and all the royal intrigue of this twisted, convoluted story. While Singer talks he flips through crusty pages and finds sections that deal with the story at hand, and when he does he reads the lines in old English, just as Shakespeare intended. They make a little more sense now, but most of it still flies over my head.

Eventually, I feel my eyelids begin to droop, but instead of telling Singer to stop I snuggle on my blanket. My eyes close and I listen to him, listen to his beautiful voice as he transports me away from our drowned, dying world. Somewhere around the time the evil Lord Chamberlain is killed by Prince Hamlet, I drift off completely. My dreams are confusing, filled with images of Lord and Singer in medieval dress, speaking in words and phrases that I don't understand, an unsettling smear of blood spreading across the front of Singer's shirt.

CHAPTER
SIX

I wake up with somber gray light against my face and a person's warm breath on the back of my neck. They're the deep regular breaths of someone still asleep, and there's an arm draped across my shoulder, which isn't too odd considering we're usually bunking together as a group; I've woken up with half a dozen arms and legs sprawled over me before. Now I'm hunkered down on my blanket, and in the background I can hear the ubiquitous, white noise hiss of rain outside. I'm lying there thinking how peaceful this is when a trace of smoke drifts my way. My eyes fly open.

The fire. I didn't wake up and feed the fire!

I leap up, about to freak out, when I spy the faintest glow of embers at the bottom of the pile of ash and blackened wood. Next to me Singer bolts upright at the commotion, his head whipping side to side, searching for an enemy or an attack. He somehow found a long piece of two by four and he's wielding it with both hands like a baseball bat.

"What's the matter?" His expression is full of

panic, his nostrils flaring.

I don't answer because I'm back down on my hands and knees, gently blowing at the base of the fire, my lips pursed like I'm about to kiss the coals. I'm blowing hard enough to remove some of the dead ash, but also to feed oxygen to the embers. I keep this up until I'm slightly dizzy, then I take a quick break, just long enough to grab some kindling and slivers of wood that I've got at the ready. I carefully lean them against the coals and blow some more. I can't believe I slept right through the three o'clock feeding. I know I've got the block of magnesium in my pack, but getting a new fire going with that is nearly impossible. I wish for the millionth time that we still had a working lighter or hand torch, but we haven't had one of those since we found Carly.

In a few seconds I'm rewarded with a gentle poof and a tongue of fire licks upward. With an inward sigh of relief I lean larger pieces of wood around the tiny flame, and eventually they catch and start burning. After another minute or two I've got a strong blaze going, and I can relax. I sit back down and look at my hands; they're black with soot and smears of charcoal.

"Sorry," I eventually say. "I didn't wake up in the night and tend to the fire. I'm the Firebrand. It's my job, and I almost screwed it up."

Singer tilts his head at me. "It's okay. You got it handled just fine."

"I know. But that was close. I don't know if I could get another started. My last lighter died a long time ago. We'd be in big trouble with no fire, you know?"

"Yeah, but we'd figure something out. You'd figure something out. I've got faith in you."

I'm not so sure I'd be able to do anything, but I'm grateful for his trust in me, misplaced or not. I'm struck again how nice he is, how warm. There's too little kindness in this horrible, awful world. I find I'm smiling again, and I'm surprised how easy it is to do that around him.

"Thanks."

He dips his head shyly in what I'm beginning to figure out is his way of saying "you're welcome." We both sit there in silence until he hands me a bottle of water, which I drink greedily, noisily, the thin plastic of the bottle crackling as I squeeze it dry. We never lack for clean water, not really. We've become very adept at putting pans, buckets, kiddie swimming pools, or whatever we can find, up on the roofs of buildings to catch rainwater. It's usually enough for cooking and drinking, but whether it's in our minds or for real, that water always has a funky, tainted taste to it. If I had to describe it I'd say it tastes dirty, although that can't really be the case. Either way, this bottled water is clean and pure and tastes of heaven. I wish I could take a bath in it.

"You hungry?"

I almost laugh at him, because we're always hungry. But I don't laugh because he's so darn sincere.

"Yeah, sure. I guess."

He reaches into a pocket and pulls out two Payday bars, handing one of them to me. I'm not certain, but I'm pretty sure I let out an involuntary squeal at the sight of it. If I did squeal he ignores it in gentlemanly fashion. We both rip open the wrappers and dive in, finishing them off in four huge bites between laughs. The salty peanuts are magic on my tongue and I close my eyes and tilt my head back in near ecstasy. Last night and this morning are turning out to be the best times I've had in months.

"Holy crap," I mumble around the last of the candy bar. "That was awesome."

My expression must have been something comical, because he laughs out loud, his face lighting up. When Singer laughs like that he leans his head back and his shoulders jump up and down, but very little sound comes out.

"My pleasure. I just wish I had some more."

I put the wrapper up to my nose, and drink in the wonderful, salty, peanut smell. Even with my eyes closed I can somehow tell he's still smiling at me. And that's okay. We both toss our wrappers in the fire. He turns toward me.

"Mind if I ask you a question? Well, two questions, really."

"Sure, I guess."

"I haven't known you all that long, but that entire time I've called you 'Scout.' Is that your real name? Maybe you've been asked this before?"

I grin at him. "Yeah, a few times. A few thousand times, actually."

"So what's the answer?"

My hand drifts to the rough leather cover of Hamlet. "Well, my dad loved to read. Did it all the time. Mom would get mad at him because he was supposed to be doing chores, or whatever, and instead he'd be parked on the living room couch reading. He'd completely lose track of time and then he'd be all apologetic and running around trying to get stuff done." I smile at the memory, but I can feel my eyes misting over. I wipe at them with my sleeve.

Singer gives me a moment. "So let me guess. His favorite book was *To Kill a Mockingbird*, so he named you Scout?"

I guess I shouldn't be surprised he'd be familiar with that one. "Actually, no. Mockingbird was one of his favorites, yeah, so he named me Jean Louise, Scout's real name in the book. Years later, when my mom saw the movie, she figured it out. From that point on, she's the one that started calling me Scout. My dad loved it."

He nods. "I figured it had to be something like that. When you meet a girl with the nickname 'Scout,' that almost has to be the reason. Now, how about your brother? Where did 'Lord' come from? That one I can't figure out."

"Yeah, no one ever does. Lord's real name is Jordan. But when he was a little kid, everyone called him Jordi, for short."

"Jordi? Okay, but I still don't get it."

"Well, I couldn't pronounce Jordi right. The Js came out as Ls," I continue, "so I called him Lordi."

"Lordi?"

"Yeah. After a few years that just got shortened to Lord, and that's what everyone called him. And you know, it kind of fits him. He was always a leader, among his friends, on whatever teams he played on, at school. Pretty much everywhere."

"And with you, too?"

I look out the window at the steady drizzle coming down. Even with my eyes open, images of the horrors we've survived play across my mind. I see a lifetime of nightmares condensed to several horrifying seconds. I wrap my arms around my knees and keep staring out the window.

"Yeah, with me, too. I would've been dead long ago without him."

I feel Singer's eyes on me. "Then thank God he's here. Right?"

I don't say anything, and the silence stretches out. I want to tell him that I'm not so sure about that, that I hate our new reality so much that perhaps surviving all this hasn't been the best endgame for me, or any of us. But I turn and look at him, and see how sincere he is, how serious this is to him, that I can't say that. Instead, I smile and I'm about to agree with him, when I hear footsteps coming toward us and Lord pokes his head into the room. I don't think he heard any of the Scout/Lord History 101 lecture, but it doesn't really matter if he did. He looks back and forth between the two of us with a raised eyebrow. "So you two spent the night down here together?"

I hadn't really thought of it that way, I guess. On top of that, it just occurred to me that Singer's arm was draped over me while the two of us slept side by side. Just the two of us. I look to Singer, who hasn't replied yet. I clear my throat.

"Uh, yeah. I was keeping an eye on the fire, and we fell asleep. Why?"

Lord's mouth twists into a quick, humorous smirk. "No reason. I hadn't seen either of you yet today, that's all. Come upstairs and let's get busy."

"Okay," I say, although I'm not anxious to get going. I'm feeling so very content and almost happy down here right now. Just me and Singer, the fire, and my book. Our book now, I guess. I know once I head back upstairs it will be the normal, pandemonium-based morning ritual again, and I'm not looking forward to that. It just feels so damn peaceful down here.

Lord starts to leave, and my heart clenches in my chest. I almost stop breathing When I can finally say something my voice is high-pitched and thin, jumping up an octave again.

"Hey, Lord," I manage to squeak out.

He was already down the hall, but he comes back and peers at me with a question mark on his face.

"Yeah? What?"

"Um, turn your head to the left for me, okay?"

It takes him a second that feels like a lifetime to me, but he finally does. What I see turns my stomach and I nearly puke up my Payday bar. I'm faint and shaky.

"What?" he asks, concern lacing his voice. I'm sure he can see how pale I've become. "What is it?"

When I can finally talk, my death sentence is uttered in a hoarse whisper. "It's started. Oh my god…"

I point a quivering finger at the side of his head, and next to me I hear Singer gasp. A thick lock of Lord's black hair has turned almost white overnight, and I know in my heart that my dear brother's days are numbered.

"Lord, you're going Gray."

What happens when one of our companions starts to change? Simple. They take a hike. We kick them out of the group. We all know it's a cheap way out, that we should just kill anyone going Gray, but none of us have the guts or ruthlessness needed to pull the trigger on a friend. Well, maybe Hunter could, but we've never asked him.

Since all this began, several of our friends have been forced to take a hike when their change began. The first was a cute Asian girl named Misumi, then a few months later an annoying, brash guy who for some reason wanted us to call him Flash. Misumi accepted her fate with what can only be called quiet dignity and grace, and took a hike the next morning. She left with a flask of water and some food, bowed to us, and walked off through the slop, her petite form quickly vanishing in the murky distance. We never saw her again.

Flash, on the other hand, was less than dignified and refused to leave. We ended up forcing him away at gunpoint, and even then Hunter had to send a few warning shots over his head to properly convince him. From a distance, he screamed and ranted at us for hours before his voice went out, and even then we're pretty sure he shadowed us for a few days. We never saw either one of them again. Unless, that is, they came back later as Grays and we had to, well, deal with them.

But this is different. This is my brother!

I'm nauseated and weak in the knees as we follow Lord. He hasn't said a word, even though I'm grabbing at his arm and trying to hold him back. Tears are rolling down my face and I'm babbling and begging; any pretense of dignity is long gone. The three of us head back up the stairs to the eighth floor where the kids are just waking up, and Annie is starting to cut up some candy bars for breakfast. All eyes turn our way and any chatter dies when they see us, and the shape I'm in. Dog is propped in the corner and wrapped up. He still looks like hell, but he's the least of my worries.

Lord grabs his backpack, two candy bars, and a few bottles of water and stuffs them into his pack. Hunter is still asleep and he goes over and kicks him, not nearly as gently as he did yesterday. Hunter jerks and sits up, looking ready to attack.

"What the hell?"

Lord's voice is flat, but the tone of command is unmistakable. He points at him. "You're in charge now. Take care of everyone and don't do anything stupid. Listen to my sister and Singer. They're smarter than you, but you're more capable. Got it?"

Hunter's gaze locks onto my face and he can see I'm crying. There's no noise at all except for my sobbing, which I can't hold back. From where she sits, Annie finally spots the gray swatch of Lord's hair and her hands fly to her mouth to stifle a cry. Dog sits up and the blanket falls away from his scrawny frame. His eyes are wide and huge, so big they even overshadow his nose.

Lord slowly pivots where he stands, looking at each of us. His face is flat and holds no emotion at all, except maybe tired resignation. We've all known this would happen sooner or later, but that doesn't blunt the anguish of it. Nothing else matters to me now, not my books, not the past, not Singer. Nothing. This is my brother, and he's about to take a hike.

Lord sighs, exhaling long and slow. He tries to smile but nothing that looks like that should ever be called a smile. It's strained and brittle, like his teeth are fragile, and if he clamps down hard they'll shatter in his mouth.

"I'd appreciate it if you'd give me a ride out of here. Just drop me off in the slop, okay? I'll take it from there."

I can't help myself. I launch myself at him and throw my arms around his sturdy frame, burying my face in his shirt. My cries become huge, aching spasms, and I'm pleading but I can't control it.

"No! No, don't go!" I scream between sobs. "We'll figure something out, okay? Maybe you won't change! Maybe you're different!"

My brother hugs me back, then easily but gently peels my arms away. He stares down at me. When he speaks his voice is so steady it makes me want to scream. How can he be so damn calm?

"Scout, it's time for me to go. We knew this would happen someday." I start to say something, to object, but he puts two fingers on my lips. "I have to go. Before I turn dangerous."

The others come to grips with this better and faster than I do, I guess, because as Lord walks towards the stairs they all follow him. I'm the last one, because I can't seem to move my feet. They're rooted to the ornate marble floor. Finally little Carly comes back and reaches for my hand. Her own hand is so tiny and warm as she grasps mine.

"Come on, Scout," she says in her little, serious voice. "It's time to go. We have to say goodbye to Lord."

She tugs, and I follow. We descend the dark steps in silence, all the way to the third floor where we broke the window to come in. The boats are moored just outside and one by one we get in and sit down. I'm normally in the front of the canoe, but I can't bear to be separated from my brother, so I sit next to him in one of the row boats. We push off and start paddling. The rain is coming down hard but no one notices or complains, and pretty soon we're all soaked to the bone, our hair matted flat to our heads. It's raining so hard even the mosquitoes have taken refuge elsewhere.

We row toward a distant tree line, and far too soon the bottoms of the boats start to clunk and scrape on unseen objects underwater, probably cars or the tops of houses, or whatever. I'm not looking and I really don't care. My tears are one with the rain now, silently augmenting the flood around us.

Ahead of us muddy ground rises from the water as we paddle between dead trees, a few chimneys, and the peak of a roof. I can see big brick houses through the tree trunks, and it looks like we're coming up on a once-posh subdivision filled with those large, newer houses we used to call McMansions. They were once high on the only hill around, and I'm sure they commanded a wonderful view. We get closer, and just a minute later we've gone as far as we can. Lord leans over and hugs me.

"Goodbye, Scout, my Firebrand," he murmurs in my ear. "Be safe and take care of yourself. Take care of everyone. I'm sorry I can't stay and help protect you any more. And always remember I love you, Jean Louise."

Before I can do or say anything else, he jumps out into the thigh-deep water and starts sloshing through the muck, his pack slung over his shoulder. My vision is blurred with tears, but I see that the white swatch in his hair has already spread. I want to yell out to him, to tell him that I love him, too. But I'm so choked up my voice won't work. He finally steps out of the water, and his rubber boots sink in the slop. The ground is so saturated with the constant rain that it's the consistency of wet cement. With some effort he starts walking, each step making a sucking, popping sound. That's why we call it the slop. Thirty feet away he turns and gives me a two-fingered salute, then continues on until he's lost among the houses and tree trunks. I feel my chest constrict, and I can do nothing but put my head in my hands and cry.

Hunter calls for us to move out, and we slowly paddle back to the office complex in reverent silence.

I'm less than worthless for the next few days. All I want to do is sit by myself down by the fire pit on the seventh floor and stare out the window at the gray sky, drowning in my own flood of pity and despair, my arms wrapped tightly around my legs. I can't think of anything but Lord, and what he must be going through now. I can only hope that he's all right, but I know that isn't possible. Singer checks on me once in a while, and even plays his harmonica a few times, but I barely notice he's there. I think he throws more wood on the fire now and then, but I'm not entirely sure of that either. One time he left a Payday bar and a bottle of water for me, but I'm not hungry. I'm not thirsty, either. I'm not anything.

On the third or fourth day, I'm not really sure which, I hear some small noises from outside the room. Out of the corner of my eye I see Carly's little head peering inside the room. Her head is tilted almost perpendicular to the floor so her black hair is hanging straight down. A spy she most certainly is not. Despite my foul mood I feel my spirits lift ever so slightly.

"Hi, there," I say, my voice stale and scratchy from inactivity. "What are you doing?"

Her head retracts like a scared turtle and disappears behind the wall. There's grit on the floor and it makes sandpaper noises as she nervously shuffles her feet.

"Uh, you okay, Scout?" she finally asks, peeking back out. Her round eyes are huge, the brown irises so dark they're almost black. "Everyone is kinda worried about you. Hunter said you were going bonkers, or something like that."

Hunter. He would tell them something like that. What an ass.

I pat the floor next to me and she walks over and sits down. I'm touched that she's worried about me, worried enough that she crept all the way down the dark stairwell and through the strange, foreign hallways and rooms to find me all by herself. That was very brave.

"So are you going bonkers?"

I reach over and gently rest my hand on her back. "No, I'm not going bonkers. I'm just sad about Lord, that's all."

She nods sagely, as if that's all she needed to hear. "Oh. We're all sad about Lord, too. He was a nice guy."

Was. She's already referring to him in the past tense. I press my lips together and try not to start crying.

"Yeah," she continues in her little girl voice. "Did you know, once, when I was real hungry and there wasn't much to eat, he gave me his dinner? Yeah, just gave it to me. I ate it then felt bad after, but he said it was okay. He said he wasn't hungry." She sighs. "I wish he was still here, too."

That sounds just like something Lord would do. I lean over and give her a big bear hug. She wraps her arms around me, her head buried in my chest. I stroke her smooth black hair, and begin to see what

I've never been able to see before, to understand why Annie holds these little ones so dear. I give her one more squeeze then stand up, brushing dust from my butt and legs.

"Come on," I tell her. "Let's go upstairs and check on everyone else. Okay?"

She smiles and nods happily, and in her young mind this crisis probably seems over. I carefully arrange some wood on the fire and we wait until it catches, then together we make our way up.

CHAPTER
SEVEN

We've been in the office building for almost three weeks now. Hunter and Singer go out scrounging each day, and for the most part they're able to find something to eat in the distant McMansions and businesses. In the third building just a few hundred yards away, they stumbled across a storage area they missed before, and inside a cupboard was a case of Kraft Mac & Cheese and canned goods galore. Vegetables, fruits, and other stuff that's a mystery to all of us (what the heck is okra, anyway?). Some of the cans are swollen and close to exploding, so, of course, we stay away from those, but most of the others are still okay. A yellowed note taped to the box said something about a food drive for a local children's charity. We were happy to accept everything on behalf of those kids, whoever they were. We've been eating like kings ever since. There's been no sign of Lord, not that we expected one.

The bottled water ran out a few days after we found it, so we had to resort to collecting rainwater on the roof again. We store some of it in the used Dasani bottles, but it's not the same. As Carly says, it tastes yucky. I agree.

But there always comes a time when we have to leave our temporary home, for one reason or another. Usually it's because Grays have found us, but other times it's because we've picked the area clean of supplies. This is one of those times. The guys have foraged farther and farther away, and after the third day of scrounging and not finding anything, we agree that it's time to move on. None of us are happy about it since this office building has far and away been the nicest and cleanest place we've seen in recent memory. I'm giving it six out of five stars. But besides that, it's also the last place I lived with Lord, so it has a special spot in my heart. Even so, the practical me trumps the emotional me, and I know we've got to go.

As we gather up our meager belongings I'm certain that little Carly is going to hate leaving, too. She's spent the last week decorating the eighth floor, using brightly colored hydraulic hoses the workers left behind. She's draped them all around like streamers, and hung thin, shredded pieces of plastic from them. They gently wave when you walk by, and make a light fluttering noise, like leaves moving in a summer breeze. I love that sound. Yeah, I'm going to hate leaving here, too. But we do, because we have to. We don't have a choice.

Dog is recovering slowly. His face looks like hell, but it's healing. Annie removed the stitches last week, and now he's sporting a long, puckered scar down his cheek. As it healed it pulled his lower eyelid down and now he looks like he's suffering through a bout of Bell's palsy or something. Poor guy. According to Annie, he was vomiting and sick the entire time I was by myself on the seventh floor, but he slowly recovered. We don't know if the expired antibiotics helped or not, but he's finally starting to act like his old self again. Which is good, because we'll need him and that amazing nose.

In the morning, as the rest of us are packing up our things, Hunter has a pretty bright idea to do some reconnaissance. He and Dog row out from the office complex and invoke his super schnoz, scouring the area for Grays. It pains me to think that Hunter came up with this idea by himself, since Singer or I should've thought of it first. On the bright side, the two of them are back an hour later, with Hunter looking extremely satisfied.

"No sign of any Grays," he announces proudly, hands on hips. "We're leaving in half an hour. Gather your crap up and let's move out."

The rest of us are basically already packed and ready, so while we wait on Dog and Hunter, Carly begs Singer to break out his harmonica. She's never experienced video games, or TV, or anything else like that. His music is some of the only entertainment she's ever known. He likes her, so it doesn't take much prodding before he shyly pulls it out. He buffs the chrome against his sleeve.

"Any requests?" he asks the group.

A few of them shout out their favorites, but with no consensus he soon holds his hands up for quiet. Their voices trickle to nothing.

"How 'bout I play one of my favorites instead?" he asks them. Carly looks at him dubiously, but he takes that as a yes, and begins. The melody is slow at first, almost mournful, but it soon picks up. I recognize it from the second or third note, and my heart almost stops, and without even realizing it I start to quietly sing along. Annie smiles at me and joins in, bouncing Tiny on her knee in time to the music. Her voice is very pretty, so much better than mine.

The lyrics and music come crashing back to me, so much so that I almost have to sit down. My throat is clenching, which doesn't improve my already shaky ability to carry a tune. The song is "American Pie," and dad used to play it nearly every day his freshman year in college. We would listen to it on trips in the car because it was one of the few we could all agree on. That, and it was long enough to keep us occupied for a while. He was a pretty smart guy.

I haven't heard it since long before the Storm. I was closer to Carly's age, if I had to guess. Lord and I would be sitting in the bench seat in the back of the SUV, and he'd pretend not to like it, but I know he did. I would always see him tapping his toe and mouthing the words when he thought I wasn't watching. My vision is clouding over as I fight back tears, but I can't stop smiling and singing along. I not only love this song, but I love what it reminds me of.

Carly loves it too, or at least I guess she does. She's dancing around and laughing as soon as the tune's tempo picks up. She's spinning around so fast she's wobbling around and getting dizzy. She bumps into Annie and they both laugh out loud as she tumbles to the ground in a heap.

Singer is laughing at Carly so hard he's having a hard time playing, and ends up missing more notes than he's hitting. No one cares. Annie pushes some of the furniture away to enlarge the size of our impromptu dance floor, then she joins in. On her hip, Tiny's eyes are huge, but he doesn't make a peep as she happily spins around.

Meanwhile, Hunter and Dog have finished packing and they walk up, a twisted grin on Dog's scarred face. His smile will forever be twisted, I'm afraid. Hunter frowns at Singer, then claps his hands a few times to get our attention and kill our fun.

"Okay, okay," he shouts. "That's enough screwing around. We've got to get moving. There's no telling where our next stop is, or when we'll find it. We don't want to get caught out in the slop. Let's go."

All of us moan, but the fear of not finding a safe place to hunker down is enough to sober everyone up and spur us to action. To be honest, that knocks the fun out of me, too. But I do take a second and walk over to Singer.

"Thanks."

"For what?"

"That song. "American Pie." It was a family favorite."

"Oh," he replies, dipping his head shyly. I'm beginning to like the way he does that. He can be so modest at times. It's very endearing. I lean forward and kiss him lightly on the cheek. His skin is warm to the touch.

We all hoist our backpacks and begin to head out, Carly whispering a mournful goodbye to the eighth floor. Singer slides his harmonica into his back pocket, where it fits into the familiar outline there, and we make our way down the dark stairs so we can gather the fire. I find that I'm humming the chorus to myself, and to my surprise I find that I'm feeling pretty good.

CHAPTER
EIGHT

Long ago, when the world fell apart and Lord and I fled the remains of Cleveland, we headed west. It was Lord's idea, but to be honest I was glad to blindly follow his lead because I didn't have a clue what else to do. I don't know if he knew where he was going or what he was doing, but it sure seemed like he did. I didn't care, we just needed to get out of there. What we left behind in northeast Ohio was so horrible that any destination was preferable to staying there. It took months of slow slogging through the slop and flooding to get us where we are now. Sometimes we could live in one place for weeks, sometimes only a day or two. We avoided any large cities, since that's where Grays tend to cluster. Along the way we picked up others, like Hunter and Annie, but we lost even more. In fact, we've lost so many people that I'm ashamed to say I can't remember most of their names. Now they're just blurry, indistinct images in my mind: that girl from Fort Wayne with the dirty blond hair, the wispy ghost of a smile on the face of that quiet boy from Detroit, or the kid with a Wisconsin accent. I'm pretty sure his name was Hank, and we would all eye-roll at the way he pronounced his Os in words like Minnesota. It came out as Minn-a-SOOO-da. Other hardy souls preferred to go it alone and left of their own accord, and a few like Misumi and Flash had to take a hike when they started to change. But if I had to keep track, I'd say most were killed by Grays. I have no desire to keep track.

For the past half a dozen months Lord had us heading south, following the big green highways signs down what used to be Interstate 75. We'd stay put when we could, and move out when we had to. We're somewhere around Lima, Ohio, according to the signs. The land here is pool table flat, which means the floodwaters are always about ten to twenty feet deep, except in places like the elevated railroad tracks by the Motel 6. I have to think it was Lord's plan to get here all along, but he didn't share, and there's no way I'll ever find out now. Hunter surprised us all one day by telling us that, up until the late 1800s, this portion of Ohio used to be called the Great Black Swamp. After being drained this whole section of the state became some of the most fertile agricultural land in the country. Some fun facts he picked up in Ohio history class, I guess. We'd been considering renaming it the Great Black Cesspool, or maybe the Great Black Toilet. The vote is still out.

There are always some areas where the land is

above the waterline, of course, like where Lord took a hike, but they're rare around here. This makes travel by water easy and preferable, because there aren't many Grays around. It also ensures that we've been able to locate safe places to stay, like our temporary home in the office complex. But we know this massive, putrid lake can't go on forever, and once we get farther south our luck is bound to run out. The hills and valleys will come, and we'll have to trudge through the slop more often. Worse yet, that means we'll be exposed to a lot more danger. We're not too keen on that, but it's a lot easier to make tough decisions like this when you're hungry.

This is one of those times. We've been paddling for several hours since we left the office complex. So far we've still been able to stick to what used to be Interstate 75. It's been easy going, relatively speaking, since all we have to do is follow those big green highway signs peeking out of the sludge every so often. But our easy going is coming to an end: up ahead we see dirty pavement easing up out of the brown water. The four-lane highway is crammed with abandoned cars, trucks, and SUVs, all covered in dirt and bird crap, their sides streaky with dark brown rust. And if anything, the smell here is worse than before. I find myself breathing through my mouth without even realizing it, because a breath through my nose is enough to make me gag. I don't know how Dog can stand it. My eyes are burning.

Hunter has his telescope out and is surveying the terrain. Unlike Lord, he looks nervous in command, unsure of himself and our next steps. He's new at this, sure, but he's not instilling confidence in any of us so far.

"Uh, you got anything, Dog?" he asks, the telescope still pressed to his eye. His voice is jittery, not the bold, cocky Hunter we're all used to.

Dog is leaning forward and sniffing deeply. He wrinkles his huge nose and his eyes close to mere slits, as if that helps him somehow focus his sense of smell.

"No, no, boss, I don't think so. But it's tough, you know, with everything else. This place reeks, boss, you know what I mean?" It stings a little to hear Hunter referred to as boss.

"Yeah. Well, we can't stay here for the night. How much more daylight we got?"

Singer and I look around. Just like forever, the sun is completely hidden behind a bank of dark clouds, but we figure it's late afternoon.

"We've probably got two or three hours until it's dark," Singer says, guessing.

"Damn it." Hunter collapses the telescope and looks around. "We'll have to keep going, that's all. I don't think any of us wants to sleep in these things. Right?"

No, we don't. We've been forced to bed down in them before, and it's always been an awful experience. Cramped, cold, wet, buggy, and uncomfortable.

And Carly hates it worse than we do. It's a bear to keep the fire going, too.

With no one objecting, we keep rowing until the hulls scrape bottom next to an overturned pickup truck that's half in, half out of the water. Its dirty exterior is shiny with rain and its tires are flat. The kids and Annie stay in the boats while the rest of us hop out and tug and pull them up onto the muddy pavement. We've all got tall rubber boots on, so we don't have to touch the disgusting water. On the plus side, it feels weirdly awesome to step on rock-solid pavement, since all the dirt is super-saturated and turns into pudding under your feet. But on the other hand, we're so exposed now that I'm about to jump out of my skin. Everyone is. We're as twitchy as if we were about to step into the climax of a Stephen King novel.

"Okay, here's what we're going to do," Hunter says, his voice just loud enough for all of us to hear. "Scout and I will go on ahead and see what's over the hill. Hopefully the floodwater will be back over there. If so, then we'll come back and carry the boats one at a time. If not, then we'll have to make do for now on foot, and scrounge for something else later on. Questions?"

There aren't any. We've gone through this exercise before, but that was with Lord in charge. Hunter's nervousness is infectious, but I'm trying to give him the benefit of the doubt. I mean, we don't have any choice, right?

"Singer, find one of these cars that isn't too skanky and shut Annie and the kids inside. Then you and Dog stand guard until we get back. If you get into any trouble start shooting and we'll come running. Okay?"

Singer nods. He's got the shotgun at his side, but he doesn't look too comfortable with it. Dog is armed with a pair of pistols on his hips that are way too big for his skinny frame. Annie likes guns as much as I do, which means not at all. And besides, she's got Tiny in her arms and couldn't do much anyway. I've got Chuck still strapped to my leg. Like most little kids I had a security blanket that I dragged with me wherever I went when I was little. That's how I feel about Chuck.

Hunter stares hard at Singer and Dog. "If you hear any gunshots from me, I want you to grab the kids, and haul ass back and paddle like hell into deep water. Don't worry about us. We'll have to play it by ear after that. Got it?"

"You got it, boss," Dog says, his head bobbing up and down vigorously.

Annie doesn't waste any time taking care of her charges. She and Singer carefully peek into some of the vehicles around us, and find an old Honda SUV that's unlocked and in better shape than most. And by better shape, I mean with no dead bodies inside, and with windows that aren't broken. She ushers Carly in, then follows them inside with Tiny and locks all the doors. A locked vehicle isn't absolute protection from Grays, but it's better than nothing. She gives us an okay sign once they're there and tucked in. I can see their thin faces and terrified expressions staring back at me through the dirty, rain-streaked glass.

Hunter taps me on the shoulder, and it startles me so much I'm afraid I yelped out loud.

"Let's go, Scout. You lead the way. I'll be right behind you."

Like air, clean water, and a newly scrounged book, boots are a necessity in my world, but not now, not here. Here boots are loud and squeaky on the concrete surface, and you can't run in them worth a damn, so I tug them off. I'm down to my Nikes now, which feels great. Hunter takes note of what I'm doing and follows suit. I cautiously move out ahead of him, and after I've gone about twenty yards he follows, keeping a constant buffer between us. All of the abandoned vehicles left here look like every disaster movie I've ever seen; they're scattered about at crazy angles, with no regard for white lines, lanes, or direction. Some have their doors open, others are crashed or half-buried in the muddy median. It's amazing how quickly the laws of the road went out the window when all hell broke loose. It's like some giant kid got pissed playing with his Hot Wheels and kicked them all over the place. I have to make sure broken glass doesn't crunch underfoot as I creep along.

To my credit, I really am pretty damn stealthy.

I've always been like this, able to sneak around people without making a sound, and small enough to easily hide when I have to. As a little girl I loved sneaking out of my room at night and tip-toeing downstairs to where mom and dad were, just to see what fascinating things adults did after we went to bed. I was so good that one time I managed to creep behind the big screen TV when my parents were in the same room. I almost gave it away because I was trying not to laugh out loud. Dad kept thinking the little snorts and snickers I made was something wrong with the sound on the show he was watching. This talent has come in very handy, that's for sure, even though I'm so scared now I'm about to pee my pants.

Slinking around your house for fun is a world away from creeping around a few zillion wrecked cars to avoid hungry Grays. Dog didn't sniff any out, but that doesn't mean they aren't nearby. I dodge around soundlessly, ducking behind each vehicle as I make sure we're alone here. I look under and around every car or truck before I move on, padding silently in a zigzag pattern. Right up in front of me there's a huge Winnebago that's half on and half off the road. Its side door is open, and the darkness inside creeps me out so much I steer well clear of it. Some distance behind me I can hear the odd shuffle and crunch as Hunter tries, unsuccessfully, to emulate me. I don't look into any windows as I pass, because I'm afraid of what I'll see. Any dead bodies out in the open are long gone, but those sealed up in cars haven't had the good grace to decompose as quickly or thoroughly, and they can be pretty hideous.

I crest the hill and find that I can see pretty well in both directions. I sigh with relief when I spot the floodwaters start back up again a quarter of a mile away, down the other side of the hill. The brown water extends to the horizon, where they become one fuzzy line. That's awesome. This means we can lug the boats over and get right back on the water, and hopefully still find a place to bunk down tonight. A shoe crunches glass behind me, and I turn to see Hunter.
"Check this out," I say quietly, pointing towards the welcome expanse of water to the south.

He walks up and stands close to me. Too close, really. I frown a little and inch away. He doesn't change position as he pulls out his telescope and extends it all the way. He puts it up to his eye and scours the water in front of us.

"Awesome. We need to get everything over here and keep moving."

I agree. We can't waste any time. Being out in the open like this is way too dangerous. I start to walk back the way we came, but Hunter doesn't move. He's staring out over the water, looking intently at something.

"Hey, check this out. What do you think that is?"

He hands me the heavy telescope and points

to a spot on the horizon. I put it to my eye and focus into the distance. All I see is a close-up of more water. I pan back and forth but can't spy anything out of the ordinary. I shake my head.

"I don't see anything. What am I looking for?" Then I jerk as I feel his head directly next to mine, his chin almost on my shoulder. His breath is hot on my cheek. I'm suddenly reminded how much larger he is than me, and that we're completely alone. Just the two of us. The hair on the back of my neck is standing straight out and my palms are suddenly slick with sweat.

"No, you're not looking at the right place," he whispers. His breath is stale and not pleasant, although to be fair I'm sure mine's not minty fresh either. "Look to the left more, and down."

His hand is now resting on my shoulder, exerting just enough force to twist me a little to the left. I resist for a second, then let him guide me. I'm more aware than ever of how close he is to me. Now he's pressing his chest against my back. I'm not sure what's going on here, but I'm not liking it. The telescope quivers in my hands.

"Good. Now see the group of buildings over there? They're a few miles away, I'm sure, but there's nothing else around them. Nothing but water. I say we head there."

Despite the fact that Hunter seems to be trying to merge into my spine, I look where he wants, and my heart leaps. Yes, I see them. It's actually one large building, with a few smaller ones around it. I can't make out any detail from this distance. The drizzle and dim light don't help either.

"Yeah," I say, and for some reason I'm whispering, too. "I see them. Let's go get the others and head out, okay?"

I turn around but Hunter doesn't move. We're so close that we're almost touching. I'm so much shorter than him that I'm eye-level with his chin. I can see some acne scars there, and a few stray whiskers. His freckles are bright red.

"So, Scout, we've never been alone before. Not the two of us."

I manufacture a smile and try to make light of the situation, forcing out a laugh that isn't fooling either of us. "Yeah, I guess you're right. Darn kids are always around, you know?"

He grins, but his face is all twitchy and weird. His hands are on my shoulders now, and I can feel his fingers holding on tight. His grip doesn't hurt. Well, not much.

"I've seen you staring at me," he says, and I want to correct him that, no, he's been the one staring at me. Instead, I force a hand to his chest and try to push away, still smiling, although it's a smile in name only. Then his fingers dig into my shoulders and he pulls me to him. His lips smash into mine and I try to pull away, but now his hands have jumped to my head and I can't move. Panic flashes white in my mind and I grab his arms and twist to break his hold, but he's too damn strong. His breath is coming harder and louder now, and he's making a low noise in his throat, almost a growl. His kiss is so rough I taste blood in my mouth, and I hope to God it's mine and not his. All I can think is *where's my brother when I need him?*

He pulls away. His face is flushed and his nostrils are wide, but he hasn't let go of my head. I start to push against him, but he spins me around and wraps his arms around me. He roughly gropes at my chest.

"Hey, Scout," he growls. His voice is hard, but I can tell he's smiling. "You've got a little something there after all. You're not as flat as I thought."

I struggle harder and manage to break his grip, pushing us apart. "Let go of me!" I shout, no longer concerned with being quiet.

His brow knits together and he swallows rapidly several times, and he pauses, thinking. Then he moves in to kiss me again. For a second, just before his lips smash into mine, he closes his eyes. And in that moment my fear is gone, just gone. Vanished. Anger, disgust, something wells up inside me, and for some reason all I can think about is Singer and it should be him kissing me, not Hunter. And not like this, either. This is not how it's supposed to happen! I pull back and swing the telescope at his head like a club, as hard as I can. The telescope is metal with thick brass rings, and the end connects with the side of his head with a crash. He barks out a yell and staggers backwards, his hands pressing against his temple. Blood starts to run down the side of his face and around his fingers, mixing with the rain.

"Jesus Christ!" he screams. He stares at the blood covering his hands in disbelief. Then he stares at me, and his face contorts into something awful, something a girl should never see. "You bitch. Look what you did to me!"

I stumble backwards, and I'm about to run somewhere, anywhere, when his bloody hand lashes out and grabs my arm. I'm once again conscious of the size difference between us, and I feel my anger draining away, replaced with a new breed of terror. I've never seen him look like this before. Of course, I've never smacked him with a telescope before, either. I try to jerk my arm away, but I can't. He pulls me close and I cower backwards, my head twisted to the side.

"It's Singer, isn't it?" he hisses. Blood covers the side of his face and runs into his mouth. Red droplets fly from his lips with each word and spray on my face. "You want to be with that son of a bitch, don't you? Admit it!"

I tug and pull, but I can't get away. He draws his fist back. I see it coming and move enough that his fist catches me above the ear, but the force of the blow is enough to send me crashing to the wet pavement in a heap. My head explodes in white light, and for a few seconds my vision blurs and goes dark at the edges. On my ass now, sitting in a puddle, I see him looming over me, a vein in his temple throbbing. His face is so contorted and red with rage he's almost unrecognizable. His freckles are nearly black.

"Listen, you bitch!" he shouts. "I'm the leader now. You're with me now, got it? You're nothing but a girl, and you'll do as I say!"

My head still ringing, I clumsily crab-walk backwards a few feet, but he advances with a snarl. Grit and glass scrape at my palms. He towers over me, straddling my legs, his chest heaving. He presses his bloody lips together and reaches down to grab me again. I'm about to scream when we hear a boom in the near distance. Then another. And another.

Hunter stops, and tilts his head in that way a dog does when it's confused. Then he snarls under his breath, grabs his rifle from the ground, and takes off running toward the noise. I watch his retreating back for a second before I can gather my wits, then I lever myself up. I catch glimpses of him as he's dodging around the abandoned vehicles in a full sprint toward the group, splashing through puddles. My head still ringing, I take off after him.

CHAPTER
NINE

Hunter's a lot faster than I am, and truth be told I'm still groggy from his damn sucker punch. I hear two more shots, followed by screaming. My fears are confirmed when I get close. Singer and Dog are on the roof of the SUV, and as I cautiously draw nearer I can see one of the Honda's side windows is shattered, glass strewn around the muddy pavement. Singer is shouting something and pointing, and Dog has both pistols out and is shooting as he screams. Four or five twitching Grays are on the ground already.

My feet stutter to a halt and I duck down behind a car. I can't help myself. The word coward springs to mind as I press up against the rusted fender, shivering and shaking. I'm trying not to freak out as I conjure and quickly dismiss next steps from my mind. I mean, what can I do? I'm only armed with a knife. I'm not a fighter. But above all, I'm terrified. I'm so damn scared I don't think I could command my legs to go an inch closer, no matter what the reason.

Peeking over the hood of the car, rain running

in my eyes, I see Hunter rushing headlong toward the fight, rifle up, shouting. This is his element, and it boggles my mind how he can be like this. But at the same instant he arrives, another wave of Grays dash out from behind the mass of wrecked cars. Dog sees them too, and screams out a panicked warning. Hunter's rifle is lousy for close up fighting, not like the shotgun, and he knows this. He stops where he is and plants his feet, methodically squeezing off several shots. Three charging Grays go down, and two stay there, flopping around as they die. The third jumps to its feet and doesn't seem to notice that it's got an exit wound the size of a grapefruit in its back. Black blood gushes from the ugly hole. Singer's shotgun blast to the head takes it out and it slams to the ground like it's been punched by the Hulk.

I watch in silent horror as one of those damn fast Grays sprints in a flash past everyone and leaps easily up onto the Honda's damp roof in one bound. It's so damn quick! Terrified, I watch as Singer turns with the shotgun, but the Gray is too close, and Singer, a mere mortal, is too slow. He shouts and reflexively pulls the trigger, but the booming shot misses as the Gray bats the barrel aside. Its hand blurs and it grabs Singer around the throat and lifts him completely off the roof, his feet kicking like he's treading water. He's hitting the Gray in the head with the barrel of the shotgun, but the swings are frantic and don't carry any force or menace. I think Dog can see what's going on, but he's got his hands full with Grays that are coming at him from the other side of the SUV. Hunter is still taking measured shots at the slower Grays.

No one is more surprised than me, but before I know it I'm running toward the fight, Chuck glinting in my right hand. In that moment I suddenly know there really is something that can make my legs take me toward the fight, and that maybe I'm stronger than I thought. I'm not worried about being quiet or subtle, not now. In fact, I'm not thinking of anything, not even the fact that I could be horribly wounded or killed. My single, overriding thought is that Singer is in terrible danger and I've got to help. I reach the front of the Honda and launch myself up onto the hood, then scramble onto the roof. The Gray's back is to me, and with an overhead, two-handed thrust, I sink my knife deep into its back, directly between its bony shoulder blades.

The Gray stiffens and spins around, ripping Chuck from my hands. I slip on the slick surface and fall backwards. My body bumps and slides down the windshield, the wipers scraping my back. Grays never make a sound, but I swear it growls as it lunges at me. I'm kicking backwards as hard as I can, but my pants are snagged on the damn wiper blade. I'm stuck. My whole field of vision is filled with its horrific, skeletal face. It comes at me with both arms raised and its mouth wide open. For some unreal reason, I see one of its front teeth is broken in half, and think how much that would have hurt a normal person.

A scream is clawing its way from my mouth when there's a deafening boom and the back of the Gray's head vanishes in red and black mist. It stiffens, too stupid to realize it's already dead. Its eyes roll back and it falls on top of me. Now I do scream, loud and long and heartfelt, and I flail around, trying to push the bloody, nasty corpse off of me. The thing is hotter than a car muffler, so hot that it has to be singeing me where it touches my bare skin. I'm still screaming as Singer shoves it off of me with a grunt. His face his full of concern and fear as he stares down at me.

"You okay?" he shouts above the commotion. "Are you hurt?"

I scamper to my feet and almost fall off the hood. My breathing is loud in my ears, and I'm shaking uncontrollably. He grabs me with both hands and makes me look him in the eye.

"Are you okay?" he asks again, saying each syllable clearly, one by one.

I finally manage to nod. He puts a hand to my cheek. Unbelievably, he smiles. Even more unbelievably, his smile flicks a switch or something inside of me. I feel my heart slowing, and the shakes start to fade.

"Yeah, I'm okay."

"Come on. We're not safe yet," he warns me.

With a powerful tug, he yanks Chuck out of the dead Gray's back. He hands it to me handle first.

I take it and stare at the black blood dripping down the blade. I quickly jam it back into the sheath and try to wipe some of the death off my hands, but my pants are soaked and all I succeed in doing is smearing it around. I'm about to thank him when Dog shouts again, and I feel terrible that I nearly forgot him. He's pointing at something.

"Two more fast ones, boss! Coming right at us!"

Singer and I swivel our heads to look, and sure enough we see two blurred figures darting between cars and trucks. They're so fast not even Hunter can get a clear shot. No one could. Singer has the shotgun up and firing, but he misses and blows the window out of a nearby sedan. One of the Grays smashes into Hunter and knocks him flat on his back, and the other sprints to our Honda. In a blur of movement it grabs the doorframe around the broken window, and tugs. There's the shriek of tortured metal, and the door is ripped free. It goes spinning through the air like a Frisbee and skips over the pavement twenty feet away. It thrusts its gaunt arms inside and grabs Carly, then it takes off running. Her tiny mouth is in a perfect O, and she's screaming. Her arms are outstretched toward us, pleading with us for help.

Annie tumbles out of the Honda, her red hair as wild as the contorted expression on her face. She runs after Carly but the other Gray intercepts her and takes her down. She jumps to her feet and launches herself at it, strange noises coming from her open mouth, sounds I've never heard a human make before. She crashes into the Gray and together they tumble to the wet pavement in a jumble of flailing arms and legs. Hunter and Singer both have their weapons up, but they can't fire without hitting her.

Before I even realize what I'm doing, I'm back on the ground and running after Carly. Chuck has magically appeared in my hand again. I suddenly realize how much that little girl means to me. I am not going to lose her! I'm not fast enough to catch them in a straight out sprint, no one is, but I'm not going to let that stop me from trying. I'm praying all the vehicles strewn around might slow it down and prove to be an equalizer. Plus, I'm hoping even the fast ones can't keep up such a blistering pace for long. In no time my chest is burning and water is streaming from my eyes, but I keep going. I can still hear her screams from up ahead, but to the right now, and closer, thankfully. I veer toward the sound and dig down deep, way down, and somehow find a hidden reserve. I increase my pace. I've never run this fast before.

"Hold on, Carly! I'm coming!" I manage to shout.

I'm thinking they've got to be close when the Gray silently leaps out from behind a delivery truck and smashes into me, sending me sprawling. I tumble and roll like I've just wiped out on my bike, scraping skin off my elbows and palms. I yell in pain. Chuck skitters from my hand and bounces away.

Then the Gray is on me. It still has Carly wrapped up in one arm, but she's limp and not moving. Before I can even blink, it grabs me by the throat and squeezes. For the second time in ten minutes, my eyes bulge as I'm being choked. I try to kick it off, but it's way too strong, and it feels like I'm battering at a concrete wall. I've got my hands wrapped around its wrist, and I can feel the heat coming off of it. My vision is starting to go black and I hear myself making strange, underwater gurgling noises, when I catch a glimpse of a blurry shape rushing in from the side. It crashes into my attacker, sending all three of us sprawling to the pavement, with Carly ending up on her back in a puddle. It's another Gray, but this one's bigger, more muscled. It hasn't been Gray very long. Wheezing and coughing, rubbing my bruised throat, I manage to push myself up on an elbow.

The fast Gray that attacked me is still down, but not for long. As it leaps to its feet the larger one grabs it and quickly wrestles it into a headlock. The big newcomer twists violently, and I hear a moist crunching noise as my attacker's neck is reduced to splinters. The larger Gray stands there for a moment, triumphant, then violently thrusts the dead one to the ground. It lands in a boneless heap the way only dead things can. The winner whips its head around. I shuffle back a few feet in terror. I'm about to run and throw myself over Carly to shield her when the Gray locks eyes with me, its head low. With difficulty, it lifts a jerky hand up and touhes a pair of fingers to its forehead. It's a two-fingered salute.

It's Lord. The new Gray is Lord.

CHAPTER
TEN

I'm more shocked than when Hunter sucker-punched me. I'm staring at my brother, at what he's become. I feel like all the air has been sucked from my lungs. He's gone Gray, but not completely. His long wet hair is almost white, his shirt hangs from him in shreds, but his face doesn't have that hollow look of a true Gray. And his eyes, his eyes still hold a hint of awareness and intelligence. I see a faint candle flame of Lord's essence flickering there. But…this doesn't make any sense. He started to change more than three weeks ago. He should be completely gone by now.

In the back of my mind I realize I haven't heard gunshots for a little while, but I do hear someone shouting. Whoever's yelling is calling out my name. Lord turns to the sound, then faster than I can track him he's towering over me and hauling me to my feet. I don't weigh much, I know, but he yanks me up like I'm an empty husk. He's standing there, staring down with those eyes that are his, yet not completely his. His mouth moves, and the sound of gravel being crushed is forced between his pale lips as he fights to form words.

"Scout...help me."

Then there's a gunshot. Lord's body jerks and a bloody hole the diameter of my finger appears in his side. I twist and see Hunter twenty yards away with his rifle aimed right at us. I scream and hold up my hand and I jump in front of Lord, shielding him.

"No! Stop!"

Lord winces at the wound, but the bleeding has already stopped. He spots Hunter and looks quickly between the two of us, like he's deciding his next move, trying to figure out whether to fight or flee. Before I can do or say anything else, he pulls my arm to his face and bites down hard, hard enough to break the skin. I scream and yank it away, and stare in confusion at the bloody teeth marks on the meaty part of my forearm.

"What the hell? You bit me!"

Then he drops my arm and looks at Carly. Thankfully, she's awake and sitting up. She seems to be okay, but she's whimpering, her black hair a tangled mess across her red, mottled face. He tilts his head at her and stares softly for a moment, then takes off in the opposite direction, away from Hunter and his gun. He's weaving between the wrecked cars and trucks and is out of sight before I can so much as blink. He's gone, and I'm left bewildered and shaking, cradling my bloody arm and holding back tears.

Hunter is the first one to me. He's reloading from the stash of bullets he keeps in his pockets. He may not be much when it comes to raising our confidence, but he's demonstrated again and again how amazing he is in a firefight. He stares daggers in my direction as pulls up next to me.

"What the hell, Scout? Why'd you tell me to stop? I had it!"

Singer isn't far behind. As he draws up to us, chest heaving from the run, I point a shaky finger towards Carly. She's crying now, that loud, choking cry of a child either very hurt, very scared, or both. He looks between us, and he's torn trying to decide who needs help more. At least, I think that's what makes him hesitate.

"Take care of Carly!" I order him, trying not to flinch as I move my injured arm. "I'm fine. Take care of her. Go!"

He rushes to her side and quickly kneels down next to her, his hands on her shoulders. I can hear him ask softly if she's okay, if she's hurt. Her sobs are so strong she can't answer him, but I can see her arm is skinned up and bleeding a little. There's a scrape on her cheek, too. She can't catch her breath. Her tears mingle with the rain.

"Jesus Christ, Scout, what the hell's going on?" Hunter shouts at me. He doesn't wait for an answer, but jumps up on the hood of a nearby car and scours the area for any remaining threats. I see him pat his pocket for his telescope, then stop when he realizes it's not there. He looks my way, and his face is unreadable. Still cradling my wounded arm, I quickly retrieve Chuck. I wipe the water from the blade on my pants, then slide it back into its sheath. Hunter is still on the hood, rifle locked to his shoulder as he sights around us in a full three hundred and sixty degree circle. I hustle over to Singer and Carly. She sees me coming and breaks away from him and runs into my open arms, tears coursing down her dirty face.

"Oh, Scout, it almost got me! I was so scared!"

I scoop her up and hold her so tight I'm afraid I might crush her tiny body. My mind blanks and I can't think of a thing to say, so I make soft, cooing noises, sounds I've heard Annie make. I stroke her tussled, sopping wet black hair, smoothing it down, and pull her face into my chest.

"It's okay, sweetie," I finally whisper to her, my voice filled with more passion than I thought possible. "I've got you now. I've got you."

Singer wraps his arms around Carly and me, and the three of us are still standing there when Hunter walks up. His face clouds as he stares at us.

"Come on, enough of this Kumbaya crap. We gotta go."

I jerk my head up and stare at him, furious that he's so insensitive to Carly and what's she's just gone through. I'm also still pissed at that shit he pulled on me, and what he said before the fight began. He may be the leader now, but there's no damn way that I'm his. He has no claim on me. But this is not the time or place, not with what's just happened. I tamp down my anger and tuck it away for later.

"Let's go," I say to Singer. "We need to get back before anyone else gets hurt."

Singer's expression melts, and he looks away from me, back to where we left the others. He rubs a hand down his face and I can see how haunted his eyes are. His mouth works for a second or two before he can manage to say anything. I don't know what's up, but it can't be good.

"Um, it's too late. Annie's hurt, and…" He pauses, but forces himself to continue. "And…we lost Dog."

My heart sinks in my chest, and I hold Carly even tighter as I feel her stiffen up in my grasp. Suddenly she's so very heavy, and I'm afraid my knees might give out under our combined weight. I stare back at him in disbelief as my eyes well up.

"After you took off, I jumped down to help Annie. She was guarding Tiny in the SUV," Singer says softly. "But then a Gray came at her, and she attacked it. I'm not kidding, she went all medieval on it. But there was no way she could beat it barehanded, even though for a few seconds she was holding her own. Honest-to-God, I've never seen anything like it before. She was insane."

It's Singer's turn to fight back tears now. He's

so upset he's still having trouble looking me in the eye. Hunter isn't saying anything, just standing conveniently far enough away to stay out of the conversation. He's still tense and alert, his head swiveling this way and that like a bird of prey, making sure there are no more pending threats. Fine. I don't want the bastard near us, anyway.

And Annie? Kind, sweet and motherly until you mess with one of her youngsters. I never thought she'd go so far as attacking a Gray by herself. Damn. Once again I've underestimated her. I seem to be good at that.

"I got close enough that I could use the shotgun, and when I finally got a clear shot, I took it. But one of the other ones wasn't dead yet. I thought it was, I swear it." He takes a deep, shuddering breath. "It took Dog down, on the other side of the SUV, and before I could do anything it gutted him and...and was eating him. Jesus, there was so much blood..."

His head falls, and he starts to cry in earnest now. Thick, gulping sobs, but silent, like someone turned his volume all the way down. His shoulders are shaking. Like with Carly, I'm not really the comforting type, but I end up letting him lean in and rest his head on my shoulder. I was afraid a moment ago that my knees were about to give out, and now with his emotional weight added, I'm certain I'll collapse. But to my surprise, I don't. I'm still standing.

I catch a glimpse of Hunter, and he's staring at

us, and for once he's bright enough to keep his mouth zipped and not mock Singer's tears. If he does, so help me, I'll give him a personal reenactment of that Gray and me on the SUV back there. Even so, I agree that it's time to go. We've been separated too long, and there may be other Grays around. It's not safe. Of course it's never safe, but that's the way it is.

"Singer, come on," I whisper into his ear. "We've got to go. You said it yourself, Annie's hurt, and she needs help."

He nods against my shoulder, and together the four of us hurry back towards the boats, with Hunter bringing up the rear. As we move out, all I can hear is the splashing of our hurried steps in the puddles, our heavy breathing, and the rustling of our plastic ponchos. Around us, the rain continues to come down, but it does nothing to wash away my crushing despair.

I glance over my shoulder. There's no sign of Lord, at least none that I can see. But if I'm being honest with myself, I knew he wouldn't still be there. I guess I was just hoping. I turn back and see Singer staring at me, one eyebrow raised in a question.

"I'll explain later," I tell him, tilting my head towards Hunter. Singer's raised eyebrow stays up, but he gives me a small nod and we keep going.

Soon Carly's sobs soften and she stops crying. Her breathing slows, and the tension melts from her body. Amazingly, I think the poor thing has fallen asleep. And even though I continue to whisper sweet nothings in her ear and stroke her head, my thoughts continue to revolve around Lord. What is he? What happened? Why hasn't he gone completely Gray? And most important of all, he wants me to help him. How am I supposed to do that?

My head is spinning. All I have are questions and not a single answer.

CHAPTER
ELEVEN

Singer and I tend to Annie. She's suffering from some gashes across her arms and neck, but they're not as bad as we feared. Four of her fingernails, her only real weapons, are broken and bleeding, and she wrenched her shoulder. She's also got a golf ball-sized knot on her forehead that could seriously use some ice which, of course, we don't have. Singer tells me she suffered that when the Gray threw her off and she bashed it against a truck bumper. That was right before Singer took out the Gray. In typical Annie fashion she doesn't care about herself, and won't sit still long enough for us to properly bandage her up. She's got her arms wrapped around Tiny and Carly at the same time, holding both of them so tight that Carly is starting to whimper. She's so worried about the kids that she won't let us properly check her out, until Singer gets stern with her. She grudgingly lets me hold the kids, but only if I stay next to her where she can keep an eye on them.

While Singer's checking her out, Hunter volunteers to take care of Dog. I'm so pissed at him that I can't even look in his direction, but at the same time I'm relieved that I don't have to see our fallen companion. Or see what's left of him, I guess. There's no way to give him a proper burial out here, so Hunter wraps him up in an old army blanket he found in the trunk of a car. We all take a moment to stare at the small, sad bundle stretched out on the muddy pavement, and I know that I won't forget him. Not like I've forgotten so many others. He was quirky, twitchy, and could get on your nerves once in a while, but he was a sweet guy who worked hard to be helpful and kind. I realize again how important simple kindness can be, and how much I appreciate it.

"Goodbye, Dog," I whisper.

Singer is standing next to me with his head lowered. "Paul," Singer says softly. "His name was Paul. He told me once."

I nod, and in my head I say a prayer for the soul of Paul, even though my faith in any kind of god or deity has long since vanished. I mean, what kind of god would put all of us through this sort of torture? If the Bible is to be believed, God flooded the world once before, but he also said he would never subject his people to this again, sealing the deal with a rainbow. Which means either he lied, or he checked out and doesn't care about us any longer. Neither option is very comforting.

Singer clears his throat and begins to sing. It's

"Amazing Grace", and his voice is more beautiful than ever. It's so perfect that, for the duration of the song, just that short while, my soul is eased and I'm almost at peace. I wish he would sing forever.

When he's done and we've said our goodbyes, Hunter and Singer lift the bundle and place it in the trunk of the car where he found the blanket. I gently close the trunk lid, hearing it click shut, completing our simple ceremony. At least Dog's remains will be safe from scavengers.

The others slowly drift away, leaving me standing by myself. A feeling of abject and helpless anger washes over me. I'm tired of losing people close to me. My parents. Lord. And now Paul. I reach out to touch the car, and I see that my hands are shaking, but not in fear. I curl my fingers into fists and slam them down on the dirty metal trunk lid so hard the entire car shakes and a huge dent blossoms, like I'd pounded on it with a bowling ball. Hunks of rust shower down from under the car and coat the ground, and one of the rear tires pops with a rush of air. The boom is loud enough to startle me, and I jump backwards a few steps, whipping my gaze back and forth between the dented trunk and my clenched fists.

"Scout, what was that?" Singer calls from where the others are gathered, getting ready to head out. He takes a few quick steps towards me.

"Uh, nothing!" I call back, waving at him, "on my way."

"Well, we need to go. It's going to get dark soon."

I walk toward them, still looking back in amazement at the car and huge dent.

I gather up my backpack and boots, check to make sure my book is still dry and intact, and look around for the cook pot holding the fire. When I finally find it, I forget about the car and need to choke back a scream of frustration. In the fight it somehow got knocked over, and the precious embers are scattered across the muddy, wet pavement. They're dead and extinguished, nothing more than soaked chunks of cold charcoal. We've got no fire. I've got the magnesium block to help start another one, but I've got no dry fuel. I slump down to the ground and pick the pieces up, one at a time, inspecting each, hoping and praying that it's not true. My fingers are black and dripping with cold soot, shouting out my failure for all to see. I feel the tears coming, and I can no more stop them than I can halt the rain from coming down.

A feel a hand on my shoulder, and I can tell it's Singer. He picks up the cold cook pot and inspects it with tight lips.

"Come on, Scout. We need to get over the hill and back on the water. We'll worry about the fire later."

I don't answer, but I know he's right. Of course he's right. I collect myself and stand, still crying softly, and together we carry the boats, one at a time. They're not too heavy when we all pitch in, but they're awkward as hell to transport. Hunter keeps watch while we transfer everything, including our supplies. In less than thirty minutes we're back on the water, but a man short, which means that we don't need the canoe for passengers any longer. We fill it with our dwindling supplies, tie it to the back of Hunter's boat, and tow it along behind us. Hunter, Annie, and Tiny are in one, and Singer, Carly, and I are in the other. The two Jon boats are plenty for our diminishing group, which is sad, when I think about it

Huddled under our own ponchos, we row for hours but don't seem to make any progress. I'm pretty sure that the hill behind us is fading, but it's too dark out to see what might be ahead of us. The building that Hunter and I spotted earlier is masked by the rain and failing light, and for all we know it was merely a mirage that vanished like a highway shimmer on a hot day. There are no lights or anything else to prove that it ever existed at all.

No one is talking. We're all too exhausted and upset. There's a lump and a circular gash on the side of Hunter's head where I bashed him with the telescope, and I enjoy a grim sense of satisfaction when I see him touch it and wince. Serves the asshole right. Singer keeps massaging his throat where the Gray grabbed him. His skin's too dark to see bruising, but I have to think it's there. I run fingers over my own throat. I can't comprehend why it's not sore or damaged. I mean, I was strangled twice in quick succession: once by Hunter, and a second time by a very pissed off Gray. It should be killing me, but it isn't and that doesn't make any sense. But right now I'm okay with that.

We keep paddling, the oars clunking against the sides of the boat as we clumsily soldier on. Hunter is staring at me with a cold, flinty look in his eyes. I'm depressed and tired, and I'm in no mood for his crap.

"What, Hunter?" I snap at him.

"So, Scout, you want to tell me about what happened with that big Gray? Why'd you stop me from taking it out? I had it!"

I involuntarily glance at the bite mark on my arm, but I'm shocked to see that it's gone. I check it out this way and that in the dim light, but no matter which way I look there's no trace of Lord's teeth. It's like it was never there. I rub my forearm. "It was Lord. I think that big Gray was Lord. He saved me."

Hunter and Singer stare at me in silence. They look back and forth from me to each other several times. Eventually Hunter screws his face up in disbelief and spits in the brown water.

"Lord? What the hell are you talking about? He took a hike over three weeks ago. We all know he's totally gone Gray by now. That's how it works, Scout. That's how it always works."

I glance back toward the highway where we

lost Dog, but I can't see it any longer. It's too dark and obscured by the rain. I fight back a bout of tears as Dog's final resting place vanishes from view.

"I know how it works, Hunter. But I'm telling you, it was Lord. And not just that, he…he talked to me."

Hunter shakes his head. "No way. Not possible. Grays don't talk."

"I'm serious," I bark at him, fed up with his bullshit. "He asked me to help him."

"Help him?" Singer asks, jumping in. "Help him how?"

I shrug. "I don't know. But for some reason, he could still talk. He's still aware. I mean, it's still Lord in there. Something about his change is different. It's slower, or it's something else completely. I don't know what."

"What else did you notice? Did he say anything else?" Singer asks.

I think back. "Um, his hair was almost all white, but he didn't have that starved, hollow look in his face or the rest of him. He wasn't all bony and skeletal, you know? At least not yet."

Singer's staring at me, but he's too deep in thought to see anything. "What else? Was he hot, like the others?"

I'm racking my memory. "I don't know. I wish I could remember, but it all happened so fast. But I don't think so."

The three of us talk about it some more, with Singer accepting my claims that it was Lord, and Hunter doing everything but calling me a liar. For some reason, he can't or won't accept that it was my brother. I guess to him you're either a Gray or you're not. There is no middle ground. It gets to the point where I'm mad enough at him that I just clam up, and we angrily agree to disagree. But now I'm worried that if we run into Lord again, Hunter will be Hunter and shoot first and ask questions later. I can't let him do that. I won't, no matter what.

CHAPTER
TWELVE

A little while later, I try to lift our spirts when I fish the block of magnesium out of my pack. There are a few damp sticks still in the boat. I pile them up carefully and shave tiny flecks of magnesium from the block into a pile under the kindling. Using Chuck, I make a spark on the block, but everything is too wet. I try and try to get something going, but after a while I get pissed off and give up. I'm sorely tempted to cannibalize my prized book for fuel, but I can't bring myself to do that. It's selfish, I know but there will be no fire tonight.

Carly is starting to whine about being hungry, and I can't say I blame her. Unfortunately, all we've got left are two cans of kidney beans and some packets of oatmeal we found at one of the McMansions. I dish out the cold beans to everyone, but it's just enough to blunt the sharp edge of our hunger. Annie mashes up some of the beans for Tiny, but he doesn't like the cold paste and keeps pushing them away. I don't have any clean water to mix up oatmeal for him, but magically a bottle of Dasani appears in Annie's hand.

"Here. Use this," she says, wincing as she hands it to me, sore from her bout with the Gray. I'm too tired to drill her about where this came from. I mix some oatmeal up and she feeds most of it to Tiny, and the rest to Carly. Hopefully in the morning I'll be able to get a fire started, and we can have a hot breakfast. Singer keeps insisting it's not my fault, but deep down I can't agree with him. I'm the Firebrand. Keeping the fire going is my job.

We can only row so long. Eventually we call a halt and tie the boats together, then do our best to get comfortable. We cover up with our stinky, damp blankets and manage the best we can. Carly decides to curl up next to me, and I'm thankful for her warmth. Singer is next to her. The only sounds are the boats clunking together and the buzzing of mosquitoes. It's an uncomfortable, nasty night, but not the first one we've endured. I'm sure it won't be the last.

It's tough to describe how miserable I am right now, both physically and mentally. I'm lying in half an inch of nasty brown water, with my head propped up on my backpack. I'm cold and wet, and thinking of Dog and Lord, and what's happened to us since all this began. I'm furious at Hunter and what he did to me. And I'm ashamed that I've let the fire die, even though Singer keeps insisting it wasn't my fault. More than that, I'm really afraid I'm about to snap and do something stupid, like jump to my feet and start crying and screaming blindly at the sky, but I'm even more afraid that if I start I'll never be able to stop. I'm a rubber band stretched to the limit, vibrating and just short of snapping.

But I know Lord would want me to keep it together. He'd want me to stay strong, and help care for the others. He'd push me to do and be more than I thought possible, to be granite when I feel like crumbling shale. I squeeze my eyes shut and hold back tears, silently promising my brother that I'll try, I'll really try to be strong. Even so, a sob catches in my throat as we huddle beneath our ponchos and blankets, and listen as the incessant rain hisses into the water all around us.

Then I sense movement, and a hand reaches for mine. I involuntarily stiffen and almost lash out, for a second flashing back to Hunter grabbing me. But of course it's not Hunter this time, it's Singer. Carly is between us, but she's so little I barely notice her small form. His warm hand curls around mine and he inches closer to me, our heads nearly touching. We're sharing the backpack as a pillow.

"You okay?" he whispers, his voice low.

I start to nod and say that, yes, I'm okay, but then I change my mind. I've come to find in my short life that honesty isn't always the best policy, but right now I believe it is.

"No, I'm not," I whisper back to him, my voice trembling. "I don't know if I can do this anymore. It's too hard…"

I wait for him to say something, but instead I sense him move closer and he kisses my forehead. His lips linger there, and then he pulls away, but our foreheads are still touching. His hair tickles my skin, just a little.

"You can, I know you can," he assures me. "You're tougher than you think, and I'll be here to help you. We're in this together. You and me, okay?"

I squeeze his hand so hard he gasps, but he doesn't let go. He can't see me, but I know he can tell when I nod back at him. I'm crying now, but the tension in my emotional rubber band has loosened up a little, to the point where there's no immediate threat of it breaking. Don't get me wrong, my tears are not of joy, but of relief that I'm not in this by myself, that Lord may be gone but Singer is here with me. At that moment I realize how very special he is to me. For the first time in my life, I may be falling in love.

"You and me, okay?" he repeats.

"Singer, I…" My voice trails off. I don't know if I can say out loud what my heart is telling me. This is all so new to me.

He kisses me again, but this time on my mouth. My face is wet from my tears, and I'm sure he can taste the saltiness of them. I kiss him back, softly but with feeling.

I can hear the smile in his voice when he whispers, "I know, Scout. Me, too."

Then he starts to hum. It's "Amazing Grace"

again, and it's the most beautiful sound I've ever heard. The tension in my mind and body melts away, and I realize how very exhausted I am. I drift away, our hands still clasped together, his song filling my head.

In the morning I wake up before the others. My mind is hardwired to check the fire, and it doesn't understand why we don't have one. It's still dark out, but I can see the faintest glow to the east where the sun should be. There are several shapes in the sky circling in the dim morning light. Turkey vultures. Besides the Grays, they've been some of the few creatures that have thrived in this soggy new world. They've had a field day with all the death, and they'll never go hungry. Good for them.

I hear a stirring next to us, and Hunter sits up. He looks like hell, but I can't judge because I'm sure that I'm far from senior picture perfect myself. His eyes are red-rimmed, and he moves like he's been blindsided by a truck, stiff and sore and moaning. Fighting Grays and sleeping in the bottom of a fishing boat will do that to you. Next to me Singer sees that I'm awake and he graces me with a small smile.

"Did you sleep okay?" he asks quietly.

"Oh, wonderful, thanks. But I'd like to complain to the management about the accommodations. And my teeth. What I wouldn't do for some toothpaste."

He smiles wider, a real one this time that touches more of his face, then he winces as several new aches spring to life in him, too. Next to us, Hunter curses as he rolls his head from side to side and cracks his back, trying to work out the night's kinks. I ignore him and look back to Singer.

"How about you?"

"Oh, you know, I'm wet, sore, and my throat is killing me where that Gray tried to pop my head off like a zit, but otherwise I'm good to go. Pretty much the standard stuff around here."

We talk quietly a little longer, enjoying each other's company as well as we can under the circumstances. Before I know it, it's light enough outside to see what I'm doing, so I get busy fixing some breakfast. I mix up the rest of the oatmeal with the water that's left in Annie's Dasani bottle, disappointed in how little it makes. Carly and Tiny hear us moving around and sit up, and I'm impressed at how rested they each look. When I'm done preparing the oatmeal, I share most of it with the two little ones, which means the rest of us only get a few mouthfuls each. It's not nearly enough, and almost serves to remind our stomachs how little food they've enjoyed lately. It sucks, but that's the way it is.

We break out the oars, and I'm pretty sure I hear Hunter and Singer both suck in sharp breaths when they grab them with hands that are blistered and sore. I inspect my own and notice that they are unmarked. I flex them a few times and they don't hurt at all. I think back to Lord's bite mark that vanished almost instantly, and I wonder again what's happening.

We don't have to paddle much longer before the darkness lifts completely and we can tell what's around us. Off to our left I can see a sliver of land rising above the waterline, complete with skeletal trees and a scattering of houses and buildings. It's a small town, one of a thousand dotting this part of Ohio. Of more interest to us is a building on a hump of land a mile or so away. From here it looks like a church, complete with a steeple, some outbuildings, and what's probably a large copse of trees. The flooding has cut it off from the town. And there's something else.

"Do you guys see that?" Singer asks. "Is that smoke?"

I squint and I'm pretty sure he's right. Once again I see Hunter pat his pocket for the telescope and frown when he remembers why it's not there. I smother a satisfied smile at his reaction, even though we could really use it. We'll have to scrounge for binoculars or something as soon as we can. Not having one puts us at a serious disadvantage.

"Yeah," he admits, peering into the gray distance. "That's smoke, alright."

Singer looks back at him. "And smoke means fire. And that means it's decision time. Do we head into town and scrounge for food and take our chances? Or do we trust that whoever's in that church will be willing to help us?

We've never been a democracy before, not when Lord was in charge. He would ask for our opinions, but then he would decide, and that was that. But if we're going to vote, then I'm punching my ballot for the church. I'm hoping that whoever is there knows they've taken refuge in a house of God and might have a streak of humanity left in them. That's probably irrational pre-flood thinking, but at the very least the smoke means they've got fire, and maybe they'd be willing to share that. And since Grays don't like fire, the possibility that the place is harboring any should be remote. All positives in my book.

On the other hand, we're out of food, and we might be able to scrounge some in town. But we've had horrible luck lately, and the thought of sneaking around in a strange place right now is creeping me out, especially coming on the heels of yesterday. This is the kind of circumstance where I really miss Lord. He would make up his mind, and the rest of us would follow.

"What do you think?" Hunter finally asks all of us. I detect a nervous flutter in his voice. I'm beginning to realize that he likes wearing the mantle of leadership, but isn't too keen on the nitty gritty responsibility that comes with it. It's a tough lesson to learn.

Annie's been silent this entire time, but she finally speaks up. "We need food. We're going to starve pretty soon if we don't get any. The kids need to eat. I say we take our chances and check out the town."

Hunter nods and looks at Singer. "You?"

"The church. They've got fire, and maybe more. They might be willing to let us crash there for a little while. We could go into town from there later and scrounge."

For a moment I don't think Hunter's going to ask for my opinion, but he finally looks my way. My first inclination is to head to the church, too. But at the last second I change my mind: I have a feeling that no matter what I say, Hunter will choose just the opposite.

"Town. I agree with Annie. We need food and supplies right away. There's no other choice."

Hunter works his mouth for a moment as he thinks. "The church. We're heading to the church," he finally proclaims, ignoring Annie's low growl of displeasure. "Like Singer said, they've got fire, and whoever's there has gotta know all about that town. We're going there."

Okay, so that worked out well. It doesn't take much for me to manufacture a withering glare at Hunter. He stares impassively back at me, his face thick and impossible to read. I pretend to look away in a huff, and out of the corner of my eye I swear I can see him smirk. This once again confirms his status as a complete dick.

Being forced to deal with Hunter takes me

back to yesterday. I haven't told anyone about what he did and said to me, not even Singer. I'm not really sure why. I tell myself it's because we need to stick together if we have a prayer of survival, that we can't be fighting among ourselves. I keep telling myself that's why, but I'm not a hundred percent sure of that. One thought keeps scratching at the back of my mind, an annoying sensation that won't go away: I'm embarrassed. I don't have any reason to feel that way. I mean, he's the one who assaulted me, groped me, choked and hit me. Even now I can feel his hands pawing at my chest, taste his blood in my mouth. I can barely look at him. What the hell do I have to be embarrassed about? But if I'm not, then why haven't I said anything to Singer? I absently rub my throat again and wonder for the millionth time why it doesn't hurt.

Obeying Hunter's order, we start paddling. It's amazing how unbearably challenging it can be to paddle one of these Jon boats any distance, especially now that Dog's gone and we're another man short. They're awkward and made for a small motor to push you merrily along, but motors and fresh gasoline are a thing of the past. So we row, and we row some more, and the building slowly becomes less ghostly, its finer details growing more distinct. And still we row, and even though we've been doing this a lot lately, I can see that the others are starting to struggle. But I must really be getting used to all this physical stuff, because I'm not tired.

We're close, and yeah, it's a church for sure, not that there was any real doubt. The first thing that jumps out at me is the bright red door. It's big, and if I had to guess I'd say it's at least fifteen feet tall, a grand entrance for a majestic structure. The large building itself is brown brick, with tall, narrow, stained glass windows that are as thin as gun slits. It's traditional, picture-postcard stuff, right down to the white steeple with a gold cross on top. There's a chimney at the back where the smoke escapes, and the whiff tickling my nose reminds me of an old chest at my grandma's house where she used to keep blankets. It's cedar. Whoever is inside is burning cedar. I love that smell and breathe it in deeply through my nose. I irrationally like these people already, whoever they are.

Carly claps her hands together. "Look, Annie, it's a church island! Neat!"

I look at Singer and lift my hands in a "why not?" gesture. Church Island is as good a name as any, I guess. Annie shushes her and makes her and Tiny lay down low, out of sight and hopefully out of any potential danger, too. Tiny doesn't protest, of course, but Carly fusses and complains because she doesn't like missing the action.

Hunter calls for a stop twenty yards from shore, and we wait for some sign that we've been spotted. We've learned many useful bits of info since the Storm, and one biggie is that, unless you want to be shot, stabbed, or otherwise attacked, you never sneak up on someone without a damn good reason.

"How about a whistle," Singer recommends to Hunter, who obliges by putting two fingers from each hand in his mouth and blowing. The volume of sound that he can generate with those four fingers will probably rattle the stained glass windows.

The high-pitched screech blasts across the water, rolling away until it fades to nothing. We sit there and I watch the light drizzle dapple the brown sludge around us. Then I hear a muffled clunk, and half of the red door opens. Out steps a girl, probably around my age, no older, I guess. She's wearing a green robe that extends to her feet and is belted with a yellow rope. Her long brown hair is pulled back in a ponytail and shows just how thin her face is. She almost seems to glide down the steps as she approaches the water's edge.

"What do you want?" she calls out, her voice steady and firm, the sound easily traveling to us across the open water. Her tone is stern and not what I'd call friendly.

Out of the corner of my eye I catch a glimpse of Hunter's hand moving toward his rifle and pulling it onto his lap. We all look at each other, not sure how to proceed. I'm waiting for Hunter to say something, but for some reason he doesn't, so I sit up straight and decide to take the lead.

"Um, we're just looking for a place to crash, and maybe something to eat," I yell to her. I'm happy and surprised how strong my voice sounds. "We don't mean you any harm or anything. We're just tired and hungry, that's all."

She tilts her head a little and stares at us. There's a shadow on the left side of her face that I didn't see before. "Why would we help you? We have our own problems."

"Please. We…we lost one of our companions to the Grays yesterday, and we're out of food. I don't know what we'll do if we don't eat soon. Please help us."

"I'm sorry, but I can't. Be on your way."

I can feel myself getting pissed. I'm tired and hungry, and I just spent the night sleeping in a damn row boat in the rain. I'm sore and my ass is soaking wet from lying in a puddle. "No, wait. Please let us land so we can rest for a while. Then we'll go."

She points away from the island. "No. We're done here. Go away."

Now I'm fully pissed. I'm about to argue some more but I see Hunter bring the rifle to his shoulder. He aims the gun roughly in her direction.

"Screw this!" he yells. "We're gonna land, whether you like it or not. Got it?"

The girl doesn't move, but from out of no-where there's a hissing sound and an arrow whizzes past my head and crashes into Hunter's boat, landing right between his legs. Then another flies past and thunks into the first aid kit near his feet.

"What the hell?" he shouts, his gaze whipping around as he tries to locate the source. I'm not sure, but I think they came from the stained glass windows. "They could just as easily kill you," the girl yells. "Now put down your gun and go away!"

But Hunter won't drop his rifle. He's done trying to locate the archer, and instead he's targeted the girl. I can see his finger turning white as he puts pressure on the trigger. I open my mouth to yell at him to stop, but another arrow comes zipping from the direction of the church. I catch a glimpse of it in flight as it arcs toward us, but then the weirdest thing happens. Suddenly everything around me seems to stop moving. No, that's not quite right. Nothing stops completely, but everything's gone into extreme slow motion. I can actually see the arrow arcing toward us, see how it flexes and spins in flight. The shaft is dark metal, and the yellow fletchings gently ripple as they hold the projectile on course. All sounds around me are oddly muted and thick, like I've got cotton stuffed in my ears, or I'm underwater. Then I blink and time snaps back to normal, and the arrow hisses past me, smacking into Hunter's shoulder with a moist thud. He screams and the rifle clatters to the bottom of the boat. The bloody arrowhead is sticking out the back of him.

"The next one will kill you. Now go!" she yells at us. Then she turns and walks calmly back towards the church, her robe moving gently with each step.

Next to me Carly jumps up. "Hunter! Hunter! Are you okay?"

He doesn't answer, just cradles his wounded shoulder and moans as he rocks back and forth. He's sucking air through his gritted teeth and he's gone ghostly pale. I quickly glance back toward the church and I see that the girl has stopped and is looking back at us.

"You have little children with you?" she asks.

"Yes!" I shout desperately, waving and pointing at Carly and Tiny, sensing an opening. "Yes, we have little ones. Two of them! A boy and a girl!"

She turns and puts a knuckle up to her mouth, thinking. After a moment she gestures to us.

"Come ashore. But know that if you do anything else stupid, you'll be killed on the spot."

I've already dismissed the slow motion vision, or whatever it was. It was probably caused by stress and lack of sleep. We don't waste any time, especially since I don't want to give her a chance to change her mind. Singer and I row in, while Annie has to manage hers alone, which she does with great difficulty. I jump out into the knee-deep water and tug both boats up onto the squishy land. The canoe is still tied to the back of Hunter's craft, but I figure it should be fine. I turn and find the girl standing right in front of me.

The first thing I notice is the purplish birthmark covering most of the left side of a face that is astonishingly pretty. That must be the shadow I saw earlier. She stares at me without so much as a blink, as if daring me to say anything about the birthmark. And being this close I can see that, like me, she's quite petite, which the robe effectively hides. But unlike everyone in our group, she doesn't suffer from that half-starved, malnourished look that's all the rage these days. Her skin is darker than mine, or like mine when I used to lounge around the pool basking in the sun.

"We need to help Hunter," I tell her. "We've got to get that arrow out of him."

"He shouldn't have threatened me," she states matter-of-factly.

"He wouldn't have done anything," I counter, although that's certainly a lie. I know him, and that's just the kind of stunt the idiot would pull. "He's just looking out for us."

She stares at me for a second without a change in her cool expression, then nods. "Bring him in and we'll see what we can do."

I look to Singer and together we convince Hunter to stand up, although moving has to be the last thing he wants to do. We each grab him around the waist and help him out and into the water. His shoulder is a bloody mess. He yelps a few times and almost passes out as we ease him toward the red door. If he pukes on me I'm going to be really pissed off. The girl walks next to us, on our left, effectively shielding us from her birthmark. Did she position herself over there on purpose? We take the church steps one at a time, pausing between each one so Hunter can catch his breath. Above the door, etched into the stone, are the words Cedar Ridge Lutheran Church. We cross over the threshold and step inside.

It's darker inside than I thought it would be. We're in the sanctuary, and while the stained glass windows let in some light, it's not much. After my eyes adjust I can see that the pews are gone, but the large space isn't empty. It's filled with beds and bedding in neat rows from one end to the other. Up against the walls along the windows there are ladders and scaffolding, and on top of each one is a boy or girl staring down at us. They're armed with bows, which they've got trained on us. There must be a dozen of them. Suddenly I'm feeling horribly exposed and uncomfortable.

"Stand down," the girl in the green robe tells them, and slowly they obey. "Jacob, come here and help."

A younger, stout boy of no more than a hundred and twenty or thirty months jumps down from his perch and steps up to us. There's a compound bow in his right hand and a quiver of arrows across his back. His blond hair is so fair it doesn't even look like he's got eyebrows.

"Take him downstairs so we can look at the wound. You," she says, pointing at Singer, "help him. Go with Jacob.

"I'll go too, if that's okay," Annie says, stepping up. "I can help."

"Fine," the girl replies. She looks around and calls out, "Mim, come and take care of the little ones. Get them something to eat."

Annie and I are both about to object, but the girl's face softens. "Mim will take good care of them," she assures us. "She'll feed them and get them cleaned up. I promise you, they'll be in good hands."

A girl slightly younger than me steps out from behind the altar. She's also in a green robe with a yellow rope belt. She's got short dark hair that's so curly it's almost an afro. The robe is a little long for her and she's got to be careful not to trip as she walks. She has a round, kind face. She kneels down in front of Carly and smiles.

"Hello, there. What's your name?"

Carly presses herself into Annie, but finally whispers, "Carly."

"Well hi, Carly. That's a very pretty name. Would you like to come with me? We can get something to eat, and maybe play some games. Would you like that?"

"Can we paint or draw or something too?"

Mim smiles. "Sure. I've got paper and crayons and all kinds of stuff." She holds out her hand.

Carly looks up at Annie, who nods. "It's okay, honey. Go on. I'll be there in a little bit. I have to take care of Hunter first."

Permission granted, Carly grasps onto to

Mim's robe. Then Mim takes Tiny from Annie and holds him tightly on her hip, and together the three of them exit through a door at the other end of the sanctuary. I can hear Carly open up and start chattering away in her happy voice, the thought of paper and crayons taking center stage above all else, even food.

Singer and Jacob help Hunter and slowly make their way through the same doorway where Carly and Mim went. I can hear his moans as they move away. The girl stares after them.

"Martin will be able to help. He's very good at this. And I'm pretty sure the arrow didn't do any permanent damage. At least I don't think it did. Jacob is a very good shot."

We stand there in silence while her people on the ladders and scaffolding watch us quietly. Now I'm feeling exposed and alone. When the girl looks at me I notice she still keeps the left side of her face slightly turned away, hiding the birthmark in the shadows.

"What's your name?"

"Scout. I'm Scout. What's yours?"

"Scout? Interesting. Mine's Evelyn. But everyone here just calls me Eve."

I nod. "Thanks for taking us in, Eve."

"Yeah. So what brought you here, to Home? How did you know we'd be here?"

Home. That's what they call this place. I give her a condensed version of the last few months. I keep my composure and stay strong when I talk about Lord and what happened to him, and I wrap up with our fateful encounter with the Grays, and what happened to Dog. She doesn't interrupt, but wrinkles her brow when I talk about Lord.

"So you just let your brother go? Why would you do that?"

I'm not really sure what she's asking. "Well, we couldn't let him stay with us. He was going Gray. We…we let him go. That's what we do when someone's about to change. They take a hike."

She's still confused, I can tell. Her brow is knotted together and her head is tilted. "Why would you do that? You know he'll change, and then he's one of them. A mindless killer. Why would you let another one of those out into the world?"

Now it's my turn to be confused. "What else are we supposed to do? Just kill them?"

"Yes. That's exactly what we do. What's the difference between you killing them out there, and us killing them in here?"

CHAPTER
THIRTEEN

I can't believe what she just said. How can they be so heartless? To simply kill someone, someone you've known, a friend, or a relative? A brother. How could these people be so cold-blooded? I grab at the sleeve of her green robe.

"You kill anyone that's going Gray? How can you do that?"

She stares at my hand on her robe, and after a few moments I let it fall back to my side.

"It's our way," she says finally, like she's telling me that ice is cold or that Grays are dangerous. "If you don't want to follow our rules, there's nothing keeping you here. Get back in your boats and be on your way." She points outside.

I think back to when Lord took a hike, even though it kills me to go back there. My heart clenches when I see him trudging away through the slop and disappearing between the houses. I try to imagine what it would be like if we had that rule, if we killed our people before they changed, and I can't. There is no situation I can imagine where I could let that happen, or worse, do it myself.

But now is not the time to push Eve on this. We desperately need food and medical attention. Not to mention that I'm completely alone in a building full of total strangers, most of them armed. She's still staring at me, waiting, and after a few moments I nod my head and look down at the floor.

"Okay then," she says, and I can see that in her mind the discussion is over. "So tell me, what's it like out there these days?"

I'm more than a little relieved to change the subject. I continue where I left off, telling her about Singer, Annie, and Hunter, and where we found them and how long we've been together. I already told her about Lord and Dog, so I fill her in about the rest of us, Carly, and Tiny, and especially how Tiny is different and never makes a sound but otherwise seems fine. I talk, and she listens. But all through my little history lesson, I can't come to grips with what she told me about how they handle someone going Gray. At some point I realize that I stopped talking, and Eve takes that as a cue to share her own past with me.

"When the floods came and people starting changing, my parents and a lot of others brought us here," she tells me. "They loaded the place with food and supplies, and when the water got high enough that you could only get here by boat, they all left. They knew what would happen if they stayed. They told us this was our new home, and they were right."

"How many of you are there?"

She starts to walk away, always keeping to my left, and I follow. I hadn't noticed before, but the floor is sloped gently downward, auditorium style, originally designed so the folks at the back could see the altar better.

"We had a lot more, at first. More than a hundred. People from town brought their kids here and left them. But over time we've lost some to sickness, a few to accidents. The rest went Gray and we had to deal with them. We're down to less than fifty now."

"You've been here the entire time?"

"Yes. Sometimes we'll go into town for more supplies and food. We're lucky. There's a grocery distribution center on the other side of town we raid but we don't like leaving Home. It's too dangerous."

We reach the door and step into a wide hallway. There are five steps leading up to another room. She goes up and I follow. At the top of the stairway is a large open room, dimly lit by candles. There are more beds there, all neatly made with different colored blankets and sleeping bags. Near each bed is a small pile of each kid's personal possessions. I see dolls, some stuffed animals, a black and white soccer ball that could use some air. Next to one bed is a shrine of pictures of a smiling family enjoying a day at some amusement park. In the background I can see the Eiffel Tower, so it might be Kings Island, an amusement park outside of Cincinnati. We went there as a family long ago, and I fondly remember their small scale Eiffel Tower. Then I stop so fast I nearly fall over.

"Wait," I say, as I stare through another doorway. I thought I was in shock before, but that was nothing. They just keep coming and coming. "What's that? What's in there?"

Eve stops and looks where I'm pointing. "That? That's our library. Why?"

I'm pretty sure she's still talking, but my mind has blocked her out. I hurry to the open door and step in. Like all the other rooms it's pretty dark in here. But a window on the far wall lets in enough light that I can look around.

Holy crap, it's a real library, with wooden shelves along all four walls, completely filled with books. Most are old and dark with cracked gold print on their spines, but a few are newer and jump out at me, their colors bright and inviting. I stand in the middle of the room and slowly spin around, not sure where to start. My mouth is open. I hope I'm not drooling.

Eve steps up next to me on my left, and her cool, business-like manner has eased. She almost looks like she could smile, something she hasn't done so far.

"This is amazing," I whisper, afraid to speak

too loudly, as if it were a real library before the Storm and I might get shushed by a stern librarian. "I haven't seen this many books in good shape, well, forever."

I walk to the nearest shelf and touch a fingertip to a dark brown, ribbed leather spine. It's the theology section. I see books about something called the Reformation, Martin Luther, and all sorts of texts about modern and ancient religions. There are also newer books with brightly colored spines and with titles like The Holy Spirit: Communication or Confusion? To be honest, I'm not all that excited about the subject matter here, but I can't help but sense a feeling of reverence when I trace my fingers over the covers of these wonderful books. I breathe deeply and catch the scent of old paper and leather. This is what heaven has to smell like.

Then I spot a small, newer bookcase off to the side. Above it is a hand-written sign that reads "Lending Library," with a small caption below that says "Keep it clean, please!" There's a yellow winking emoji face printed below there, as if it's saying "You know what I mean, people". I hurry over, and I'm pretty sure I've broken some sort of record for not breathing.

The titles and authors are all over the place, spanning genres from science fiction to documentaries, and everything in-between. In the first row there's something called *The Foundation Trilogy by Isaac Asimov*. Then one that even I've heard of, George Orwell's *1984*. Books by a guy named Dick Francis, thrillers by another known name, James Patterson, some more science fiction by Larry Niven. A bright orange one called simply *The Martian*, three copies of *The Hunger Games*, what looks like the entire Harry Potter series, and hundreds more. I could settle down in this room for months, probably until I go Gray myself, and feel like I might actually have lived a full life. I would lose myself in these wonderful worlds, these normal times, for the rest of my abbreviated existence.

"I can't believe how many books you have here," I whisper to Eve, who's moved next to me. "They're all in such awesome condition. It's amazing."

She straightens up some that have tipped over. "We keep it because our parents asked us to. But honestly, there's very little time to enjoy them. We're too busy trying to stay alive and taking care of each other."

Knowing what I do about survival in this world, I can understand that. But I'm still a little envious knowing that they're here, untouched and unloved, ignored while they quietly turn yellow and stiff with age. I pull out *1984* and I'm slowly thumbing through the pages when I hear a scream. I nearly drop the book.

"What was that?"

"Don't worry," Eve assures me, looking casually over her shoulder. "That's your man having the arrow removed. I'm sure it hurts like hell." She crosses her arms and her voice cools. "Maybe next time he won't be in such a hurry to aim his gun at people."

I quickly slide *1984* back. "I should probably see him. Make sure he's okay."

She shrugs under the green robe. We leave the library and go back into the main room, then out another door on the far side. We head down a long flight of steps into a basement area and enter a small room lit by electric lights. It's so bright I have to blink a few times and let my eyes adjust. Electric lights?

Eve sees my bewildered expression. "There are solar panels on the roof. It takes forever to charge the batteries with the cloud cover, but we'll have enough juice for a few more minutes."

It may have been a Sunday school classroom before, but it's a hospital room now. The white fluorescents hum softly overhead and clinically show just how filthy and disgusting we really look. We're caked with dirt and mud, and like birds may have been nesting in our hair. To say we're gross would be charitable. Around us there are at least a dozen shelves filled with books on anatomy, first aid, surgical techniques, holistic and homeopathic healing, and much more. Singer is leaning against a wall, watching us with his arms crossed. He's staring at me, waiting, and I share a small smile with him. He visibly relaxes, his arms unfolding, and I realize he's been worried about me, which I find very sweet. He steps up to me, standing close, and lays a hand on my arm. Hunter is sitting up on a bed, and Annie and a quiet young boy with black-framed, taped up glasses are bandaging Hunter's shoulder, busily wrapping it this way and that. The bloody halves of an arrow and a large pair of bolt cutters are on a table next to him. Hunter's face is nearly as white as the sheet he's sitting on, but the stiff way he's holding his body and his icy glare show how pissed he is, which means he's probably going to be okay. Honestly, he looks like he could pop and go nuclear any second. I'm glad he's no longer armed.

"You okay?" I ask him. I can't bring myself to make it sound like I care, but I should at least ask. Deep down I hope it hurts like hell.

His stare could melt steel, but he doesn't say a word. Annie doesn't take her eyes from the work at hand. She cuts the gauze and tapes it up, pushing the adhesive down. He winces at the pressure, but she's clinically blind to his pain.

"We had to cut the arrow in half and pull the rest out. It was the only way. He didn't care for it."

"Yeah, I don't doubt that. Any long-term damage?"

"I don't think so, but there's no way to know yet," she answers, still focused on her work. The boy with the glasses nods. He must be Martin. "It went through the outside fleshy part of his shoulder," she continues. "Probably nicked the bone. Whoever shot him was either very good, or he was lucky, or both. Either way, it's going to hurt for a while. It'll be stiff, too."

I nod in her direction. Looking at Hunter's bloody shoulder reminds me to inspect my arm where Lord bit me. Even in this light, I can't see a trace of the bite mark. Nothing. How can that be?

Eve touches my sleeve, motioning with her head back the way we came. I'm not completely convinced Hunter won't snap and go all medieval, so I ask Singer to stay and keep an eye on him. He doesn't look pleased, but I think he understands. Eve and I walk out of the room and across the hall and step into a large space with a very tall ceiling. It's a gymnasium, complete with a painted floor and basketball hoops at either end. There are kids of all ages scattered around, and while I don't see any as young as Tiny, there are a few close to Carly's age. Some are sitting in a group and working on something that I can't see very well, a large map or something, while others are playing with younger ones. A few are eating. Many of them stop and stare at me as I step inside, and the steady hum of multiple conversations drops a few decibels. I'm guessing they can't be used to seeing new faces here. I spot Mim and Carly sitting at the far end, with Tiny snuggled on Mim's lap. Carly's face is down and she's intently working on something using brightly colored markers. I have to say her name loudly twice before I get her attention.

"Scout, look at what I made!"

She holds up a piece of paper and grins ear to ear. It's a colorful drawing of three boats with all of us, including Dog and Lord, smiling and paddling along on blue water.

"That is some very nice artwork, Carly," I tell her, and it really is. She's got quite the talent. In the old days it would be refrigerator-worthy, for sure.

Then she points to a bowl at her feet. "And look! They've got peaches! Real peaches!"

In front of Carly there are bowls and plates of food, including sliced peaches in syrup, just like I remember from school lunches. Next to my budding artist, Mim is busy spooning real oatmeal into Tiny's wide-open mouth. He's happily gobbling it down as fast as she can shovel it in. I find that I'm smiling at both of them, relieved that they're finally being taken care of. Annie did the best she could with what we had, but there's no substitute for good food and proper shelter. Then my own stomach rumbles as I realize how hungry I am. It's loud enough that Eve raises an amused eyebrow in my direction.

"Would you like to grab a bite?"

I can't say yes fast enough, and together we leave the gym and I follow her down the hall. We go through another door and into a section of the building that was likely more Sunday school rooms. It's cooler down here, and very pleasant. As we walk down the hall and I look into each open room, I'm stunned at what I see: hundreds of clear bins of boxed food, rows and rows of free standing shelves of canned goods, and stacked cardboard boxes neatly labeled with their contents: cereal, cornbread, rice, and much more.

"So what would you like? There's no fresh produce, of course, but we've got just about anything else you might want."

"Oh my god, where did all this come from?"

Eve turns and surveys the storage area in pride, her hands on her hips. "Like I said, our parents saw what was happening and set all this up. What we don't have we can still find in town, for the most part. Going hungry is not one of our worries, not for a long time, at least."

She gathers up some cans and carefully rummages around in several of the larger boxes until she finds whatever it is she's looking for. We head back toward the gym, but before we get there we take a detour to a large kitchen that's located behind it. As we walk in, the first thing I see is a huge fireplace complete with an impressive cooking fire, and the smell of cedar permeates the room. I know it's irrational, but I'm so happy to see the fire. I involuntarily take a few steps toward it, then quickly retreat when the heat smacks into my face. It feels like a thousand degrees in there. Three teenage boys, all dripping with sweat, are rushing around adding fuel to the blaze, stirring a large pot, mixing ingredients into bowls, wiping off countertops, and more. The oldest of the three shoots a hurried glance our way.

"What?" he asks, not unkindly. "Cleaning up from breakfast and getting ready for lunch. Kind of busy here."

"Mind if I step in? Our guests are hungry."

He dismisses us with a wave and goes back to work. "Guests? Whatever. Just stay out of the way."

"No problem. Thanks, Harold."

In less than fifteen minutes I'm sitting down in the gym and eating peaches, some sort of hot au gratin potatoes that Eve whipped up from a box, and beef jerky from a vacuum packed bag, like the kind I used to see next to the cash registers in gas stations. I'm aware how fast I'm wolfing all this down and how completely wild I must look, but blind hunger has assumed control and any sense of civility is gone. Thick, sticky peach juice is running down my chin and my jaw muscles are starting to ache from chewing the tough beef jerky. Eve has left me alone while she took plates of food for the others in our group. She's back about the time I'm wiping my mouth on my sleeve and trying not to throw up from inhaling my meal like a velociraptor. I recall my social graces enough to carefully muffle a burp with my hand. She sits down with her face angled to her left, hiding the birthmark. Port stain. That's what that kind of birthmark is called. I remember now. It's the sort of thing kids probably made fun of her for her whole life.

"Your injured man isn't very happy."

"Hunter? No, I'm not surprised," I admit. "But to be honest he's rarely happy."

"But he didn't have a problem taking our food."

"No, none of us would. We've had a rough time lately, and our last meal was yesterday. And even that wasn't much. Thanks for everything. But I'm still wondering why? Why did you decide to help us?"

Eve nibbles on a cracker she produces from a pocket in her robe. She points at Carly and Tiny.

"Your little ones. Long ago we decided we had to take care of as many kids as possible. It's what our parents would have wanted. If we didn't step up we knew no one else would. If we have any chance of surviving this, we'll need them. They're our future, it's as simple as that. That's our mission now."

I stare at the little kids all around us. There are dozens, and they look well fed and happy. I'm so pleased there's some humanity left in the world. We've seen so little of it since the Storm began.

"Have you ever taken others in? Other kids, I mean?"

"Yes," she tells me. "Although only a few. We accept all children. Little kids are such easy targets for the Grays, and there just aren't very many left out there."

It's not the first time I've thought of that. Is anyone having babies now? It's certainly possible,

I guess, but besides Tiny we haven't seen any. What happens to us, to humanity, when everyone turns Gray? The only upside, and I mean the only one, is that a handful of months after the last person turns, the Grays will die and the world will be empty of them forever. It's a satisfying yet terrifying thought.

"Yeah, I know," I eventually say, my voice quiet in the noisy gym. "Have you seen any other signs of civilization? Heard any rumors? Anything?"

She thinks for a minute, surveying the activity around us and still munching on crackers. She sees three young boys arguing over something, and her face tightens up, ready to dish out some parental discipline, but she doesn't move toward them right away. After a moment they split up and go their separate ways, laughing and carrying on, slapping each other on their backs. Her expression softens. She's always on guard, I'm finding. Always watching, and aware.

"No, not really. We turn on the radio once a day when we've got power and listen for broadcasts of any kind, but we haven't heard anything for years. Just static. Several months ago a few young boys thought they saw something in the sky, but they didn't know what it was. Probably a vulture or some bird, even though they insisted it wasn't. Besides that, we haven't seen or heard of anything. How about you?"

She's waiting for me to answer her, but something just occurred to me, something I haven't considered before, and I pause. Tiny is only six or seven months old. I just realized it's so incredibly unlikely that he should be here at all. I mean, the timing varies person to person, but we've seen people go Gray when they're anywhere from a hundred and ninety to two hundred and forty months old. I guess it could be possible that someone could time a pregnancy just right, but the thought of that just boggles my mind. Accidents happen, of course, but would anyone intentionally have a baby these days?

Unless that's not what happened at all?

I sit back against the cool wall, my mind spinning. Could it be? Why haven't we thought of this before?

"What is it?" Eve asks, her voice louder and her eyes narrowing. "You just thought of something, I can tell."

I find myself staring at Tiny, sitting so comfortably in Mim's lap as he smiles at Carly. She's poking him playfully in the stomach and laughing at his surprised reaction.

"It's Tiny," I say, and explain to her what I'm thinking, about how little time there would be between when a girl could get pregnant and when she changes. "People can go Gray as soon as one hundred and ninety months. The timing would have to be almost perfect for a baby to be born. But maybe that's not it. Could it be possible that his parents, or at least the mother, were immune and never went Gray? Could that happen? Have you ever heard of anyone being immune?'"

Eve shakes her head, and when she answers I can tell this potential revelation is new to her, too. "No, never. And why do you use months when you're talking about someone's age?"

I have to think about that for a moment. "My brother started it, I think. It was a way of keeping better track of our ages, which is pretty important, as you know. He always thought it sounded better, too. Saying you're sixteen years old sounds a lot worse than saying you're one hundred and ninety two months, I guess. He thought the bigger numbers helped. He started using it, and we went along. And he had a good head for numbers, and kept track of the calendar."

She sits back. "That would take some getting used to. I'd have to keep a calculator handy. But back to your point: no, we've never heard of anyone being immune, not even in the beginning. It's not possible."

Despite her insistence to the contrary, it's quite likely that she's wrong. It may have happened, at least once. The proof is sitting right in front of me, giggling as Carly plays "got your nose" with Tiny.

CHAPTER
FOURTEEN

We stay in the gym for a while, just talking and relaxing, something I'm not at all used to doing. We're so accustomed to being on guard that it's weird chilling out and not constantly watching your back. Eventually Eve stands, brushing off and straightening her robe.

"We should get your beds set up. I think there's enough space in the library. That way all of you can have some privacy."

The library? It takes all my control not to break out in a happy dance. Eve instructs some younger boys to get bedding out of storage. They obediently hustle off without a word, and we head upstairs. Moments after we get there they show up, each one loaded down with a cot and blankets. I catch a whiff of something musty, like an old farmhouse cellar with a dirt floor, and I realize it's the cots. It's not a bad smell, if I'm being honest. It's kind of homey. Two other boys bring in an ancient wooden crib for Tiny, complete with a crinkly mattress and clear plastic wheels that squeak on the wood floor. It takes them a little muscle, grunting, and arguing to get it set up, but eventually they've got it. Eve is quietly supervising the operation from the doorway.

"We've got plenty of cots now," she says, and there's a distant look in her eyes like she's thinking back to an earlier time. "When we first got here we had to sleep on the floor, on pews, wherever we could find space. That's not the case any longer. There just aren't that many of us now. And anyway, we chopped up and burned the pews for firewood a long time ago."

The library is easily big enough for the five cots and the crib, with room to spare. We're surveying the arrangement when Hunter walks in, his arm in a makeshift sling, leaning heavily on Singer. He's still pale, to the point where his freckles are subdued and washed out. Without a word he gruffly shakes Singer's arm off and collapses with a grunt onto the first cot he comes to. His eyes are closed and he's faced away from us. He's in a lot of pain, but I can't bring myself to care.

Eve turns to me. "Isn't he the pleasant one?"

Singer's face clouds, and he takes a step toward Eve. He tops her by at least six inches, but she doesn't budge. "Hey, that's not fair. He was shot with an arrow, in case you don't remember. Your man did it."

I admire Singer standing up for one of our own, I really do. But deep down I can't stand that he's defending that bastard. My mouth opens halfway, and

I'm tempted to scream the truth to everyone, to curse and yell and pound my fists on Hunter's bandaged shoulder, right where it would hurt the most. But I don't. I force my mouth to stay shut. I'm not sure I'll ever be able to talk about what he did, but I do know that now's not the time.

I catch Eve looking at me. I glance away, but the weight of her stare presses on the back of my neck. After a moment she pushes herself away from the door and begins to leave. "And if he screws up again, I'll make sure he gets more of the same," she coolly replies to Singer. As she's walking away she calls out over her shoulder, "Rest up now. You'll hear the bell when it's time for dinner."

Singer watches her retreating back, then turns and comes up next to me. We're alone for the first time, except for Hunter. We wrap our arms around each other, and I bury my face in his chest. We stand that way for a long time, and it's a wonderful moment, one of those special times I'll cherish forever. There aren't many of them. Eventually we pull apart, but his hands are still on my waist. I'm looking up at him. I never noticed before, but there are flecks of gold swimming in the brown of his eyes.

"Everything okay with you?" he asks.

"Yeah, why?"

He places his hand gently behind my neck. "You're just a little quiet, that's all."

I pull him down and kiss him on the cheek.

He's got a patch of stubble there that tickles my lips. "I'm fine. Just tired, I guess." I smile at him, trying my best to look and sound convincing, but I'm not sure he's buying it. Instead of giving him a chance to dig deeper into what's bothering me, I turn and point to the cots. "Here's an idea. Let's claim those two by the window, and push them together. Like a big bed."

He likes that suggestion as much as I do. As we're moving them around I fill him in on what I've learned from Eve, the history of the place, and what's been going on. The bed moving and conversation do what I'd hoped and steer him away from what's bothering me. When I'm done he tells me what he's picked up, but it's not much.

"I was in with Annie and Martin most of the time. Martin's not much of a talker. But he seems like a good kid. And he's smart, I'll give him that. He and Annie did a nice job on Hunter. Right, Hunter?"

Hunter doesn't budge or say a word. He's either asleep, or pretending to be. Singer shrugs, excusing his behavior.

Then Annie comes in with Tiny in her arms and Carly in tow. The little girl runs up to me with more papers in her hands, drawings of us, the Motel 6, and a self-portrait of her smiling with a bowl of what has to be peaches in her lap.

"These are so good!" I exclaim, full of praise. I bend down to her level and tussle her hair, which makes her giggle. "If I can find some tape, we'll hang them on the walls, okay? Art should be enjoyed by everyone."

She claps her little hands and giggles. I wish I could record that happy, innocent laugh and listen to it over and over. Annie puts Tiny in the crib, and he rolls onto his stomach and watches us in silence. I guess he's happy, too, but how would we know?

We catch up with Annie, but she doesn't have anything to add. The bulk of her time was spent with Hunter and Singer, although she did get to spend a little while with other kids Carly's age in the nursery. That made her day.

A very young girl ringing a handbell walks past our door, one of those pretty gold ones I've seen in churches before. The sound is pure and deep, a note I'm sure Singer could identify if I asked. We see movement outside the library, people walking toward the steps. Dinner time? All of us except Hunter make our way downstairs, following the aroma of food. This time it's mac and cheese, and some corn bread cut up and served out of baking dishes. The gym is loud, the voices and laughter bouncing all around the ceramic walls, but it's organized chaos, and everyone waits their turn for food without a fuss. Eve is sitting at a table nearby, and when we're almost done she stands and holds up a hand. In seconds the talking stops, and all eyes turn towards her.

"We have guests, as I'm sure you've noticed." She introduces us one at a time, and doesn't miss a beat when she doesn't see Hunter, who I'm assuming is still lying down in the library. We each wave when she says our name. She gives a very brief history of our travels so far, spending additional time talking about Carly and Tiny and how we saved them. After she's done there's a warm round of applause, and I feel my face flush at the unaccustomed attention. She raises her hand once more, and the applause abruptly stops again. She's got them well trained, I'll give her that.

"As many of you know, we've got a raid scheduled for tomorrow. I already have a few volunteers, but we could use a couple more. Only older ones, please. See me afterwards if you'd like to join."

Singer leans over to me, his mouth close to my ear, so close I can feel his warm breath. "I'm going to sign up," he says.

I spin to face him. "No!" I say, louder than I had intended. Heads turn our way at my outburst.

"Keep it down. Yes, I am. We need to pull our weight around here. Plus, I want to check out that town. We need to know the area in case we ever leave."

Visions crowd into my head, visions of Singer hurt, Grays attacking, him getting separated from the group. Him never coming back. Me by myself. I shudder.

"Singer, no, you can't go. Please. Something could happen to you."

"Don't worry. I'll be with the others, and from the sound of this they do raids all the time. I'll be fine."

I sit back in my chair. "Okay. If I can't talk you out of it, then I'm going, too."

He holds his hands up. "Whoa. No, you can't go."

"Why?"

"Because it's too dangerous."

"Too dangerous for me, but it's fine for you?" I needle him. "No, I don't think so. We're both going."

Our argument continues through the rest of dinner, but eventually we realize we're both too stubborn to back down. As everyone else is leaving the gym we step up to Eve.

"We'd like to volunteer," Singer tells her. Her eyes widen a bit, but otherwise she doesn't react. I'm struck again how pretty she is.

"Both of you?"

I step forward, now even with Singer. "Yes. We'd like to help, and we're pretty good in a fight."

She glances back and forth between us. "Well, you wouldn't still be alive if you weren't. Go see Jacob. He'll be leading the raid tomorrow."

We follow her directions and go in search of Jacob. We find him in the sanctuary of the church, standing guard up on a platform by one of the thin windows with his compound bow by his side.

"We want to volunteer for the raid tomorrow," Singer informs him.

Jacob considers us for a moment, then jumps down from his perch. "You're sure about this? Did you ask Eve? What did she say?"

"She knows. She told us to find you."

"Okay, good. We can use the help, especially from someone older and with experience out there. We'll be leaving right after breakfast. Do you have your own weapons?"

Singer points outside. "We've got a shotgun, and some handguns. They're still in the boats, along with our ammo."

"I'll send someone to gather them up. You sure you want to do this?"

Singer and I both say yes at the same time, but I'm already starting to question my decision. I'm voluntarily leaving the safety of this place and heading over to the town? But I see no hesitation or fear in Singer, and I just can't stand to see him go without me. So I do my best to stay strong, but inside my stomach is churning. What have I done?

It's been a very long and tiring day, so it's no surprise that not long after dinner I'm stumbling around like a sleep-deprived zombie, bumping into things and losing my train of thought. If I don't get some sleep I'm going to hurt someone, probably myself. The others aren't doing much better. Hunter is still out cold. Annie is sitting crossed-legged on the floor, dozing, her head bobbing around like her neck's made of rubber.

Carly has passed out in Annie's lap, curled into a tidy ball. Tiny is asleep on his back in the crib with his arms and legs sprawled every which way, a little drool dripping down his cheek. As I'm watching him sleep, I'm reminded of my discussion with Eve. I nudge Singer, who's laying out a blanket on our cots.

"What's up?"

I point to Tiny and recount what Eve and I talked about, whether or not it's possible for someone out there to be immune to going Gray. He pauses in his very precise, detailed bed-making, then gently smooths the blanket out with the flat of his hand.

"I don't see why not," he finally replies. "I mean, there were over seven billion people on the earth when all this started. Out of all those billions, you have to think that someone, somewhere, is immune. Even if less than a tenth of one percent of the Earth's population is immune, that still leaves…seven hundred thousand people. Or is it seventy thousand? I don't know. Math was never my strongest subject, but either way, that's a lot of people. I'm sure they're out there."

We've never talked about this before. I have no idea where he's getting the tenth of a percent figure, if he pulled it out of thin air or what. But for some reason his belief that there could be that many people out there, living their lives and not turning Gray, gives me an odd sense of hope. Deep down I know it could be nothing but wishful thinking, but it's something to cling to.

"Just because we haven't found them yet, doesn't mean they don't exist," he continues. "The world's a big place. If we keep moving, I'm sure we'll run across someone. It's just a matter of time."

I like the way he thinks. This might even help explain what's happening to Lord. I wouldn't mind talking about it some more, but we decide we'd better get Annie up off the floor and help both her and Carly to bed. We wake her with a gentle nudge, and pick Carly up off her lap. The little girl moans softly and smacks her lips as I transfer her to a cot at the far end of the library, tucking her in. Annie checks out Tiny, then lies down and is snoring in seconds.

Singer and I both climb into our joined cots. It doesn't really work as one big bed since the hard sides of the cots get in the way, which is a bummer, but we're close to each other, and that's a start. We cover up and lie there, our noses about a foot apart. It's not quite dark outside yet, and the window is a gray square against the deeper darkness of the library. There's enough light that we can see each other's eyes, just a little bit.

"Night, Scout," he whispers to me softly, his voice full of sleep.

"Night, Singer."

We move close and kiss, then pull apart. I'm on my stomach and he drapes an arm across my shoulders. I'm thinking how nice all this feels, how warm and secure, and so different from the night before. I'm still thinking this, and then I'm not, because I'm asleep.

I wake at some point in the night. Of course I have no idea what time it is, but the room is pitch black and the window is no more than a pale outline, so faint that I can only see it in my peripheral vision. I'm on my back and staring into the nothingness. Singer's arm isn't draped over me any longer, but I reach out a hand and my fingertips brush against his side. I can hear soft breathing around me, but nothing else. There are no other sounds, not even the patter of rain. At first I'm not sure why I woke up, and then it dawns on me; old habits die hard. My body may be exhausted, but somewhere in my mind an alarm went off so I could check the fire, the fire that doesn't exist. I don't have a manual override in my brain to turn that off, unfortunately. But that's okay, because this is one of those rare occasions when my stomach is full, my clothes are dry, and most of the people I care about are safe and sound and right here with me. Tiny moves around in his crib, and the plastic covered mattress crinkles. I smile in the dark.

After a while I close my eyes and relax, ready to fall back asleep. But as I'm lying there with the blanket pulled up to my chin, my brain refuses to shut down. I start to think back to the day before, when we first arrived, when Hunter had his gun up and was ready to shoot. I can still clearly see the arrow soaring at him in that weird super slow-motion, like something from a movie, or a football replay on TV. I can't wrap my head around what I saw, can't understand how I could see the arrow as it serenely flew past me, fletching fluttering gently, before it smacked into Hunter's shoulder. It sounds crazy now, even to me. Was it some sort of hallucination? A waking dream? A vision? And the sounds were so strange, so deep and thick, like all the high notes had been lopped off. I'm afraid I may never understand what the hell that was.

Just then Singer grunts and his arm flops over and lands across my chest. I flinch and nearly jump off the bed, breathing fast, because all I can think about now is Hunter and how he pawed and groped at me. I shudder, and hate how that son of a bitch has damaged me. When my anger and shakes finally subside and my heart slows, I gently move Singer's arm back to his side of the cot. Then I roll away from him and face the other direction, staring blankly into the dark.

FIFTEEN

The next morning we eat a huge breakfast of waffles and syrup (waffles and syrup!), and wash it down with some watery orange drink that may have been Tang. I'm not used to all this food, but I'm sure as hell enjoying it while I can. When the meal is nearly done, Eve raises her arm and in that magical way that she has, everyone in the room falls instantly silent. She instructs all volunteers to assemble outside. Singer and I swap a glance and follow a group of older boys toward the exit. Hunter and Annie see us and he calls out.

"What the hell are you two doing?" he asks. His sharp tone comes across like we're in elementary school and we're trying to ditch him. He's still a little pale, or green around the gills, as my mom would say, but other than that he appears to be feeling better. I'm ignoring him, but Singer stops and turns around.

"Scout and I are going on the raid."

"Oh, no you're not. Not without me. I'm the leader here."

Singer shakes his head. "You really want to

go? In your condition? I don't think you'll be much good out there, do you?"

"It doesn't matter. I'm going, and you can't stop me."

"Come on, man. You can't even hold your rifle. Just stay here and get better, okay? There'll be more raids."

They argue back and forth, and eventually Hunter relents and stalks away, still muttering under his breath. Singer watches his back and purses his lips in thought. Almost to himself, he says, "That boy's got some serious anger issues."

I don't say anything, but I couldn't agree more. We hustle to catch up with the boys, up the stairs and out a side door. We pull on our ponchos against the drizzle that gathers on everyone's eyebrows and the hair of uncovered heads. It's warm out, but I feel a deep shiver coming on, like my guts have been locked in a refrigerator. I'm scared already, and we haven't left Home yet. What am I going to do when I get there?

Jacob and another boy step up to us, their arms loaded down with weapons. I recognize our shotgun and a few of the handguns. Hunter's rifle is there, too. "Here's your stuff. We brought it all in yesterday to keep it out of the rain. Take what you want, and we'll haul everything else back inside."

Singer chooses the shotgun, which is no shock. It's got a strap, so he slings it across his back. He also gathers up as many shells as he can carry, loading up until the pockets of his pants are bulging. Before the flood kids our age used to laugh at cargo pants and their ridiculous number of pockets, but not any longer. The more pockets the better, I say. Then Jacob holds the remaining options out to me.

"Your choice, Scout. Pick."

I hold my hands out, palms up. "No way. I'm no good with those things. I'd probably shoot myself in the leg. I've got my knife, thanks." I pat my thigh.

Jacob doesn't argue. He carefully hands the rest to a few younger boys and instructs them to store everything downstairs, along with our heavy box of ammo. They obediently hurry off, waddling under the weight. Not for the first time I'm impressed how everything and everyone work together. I'm beginning to understand that there's a strict and orderly code here at Home, one that everyone follows. I half expected small societies like this to collapse into chaos, like some rehashed Lord of the Flies, and maybe some places are like that. But not here. There are rules, and a chain of command, and it seems that everyone knows what's expected of them. Circumstances like ours can mature you before your time.

All told, there are nine of us going. Everyone has a gun but me. I'm the only girl, and some of the boys are giving me a sideways look and nudging each other. One snickers with his hand to his mouth. They probably think I'm not up for this, and I'm doing my best not to show any fear and prove them right. Another group of boys hands each of us a large backpack. I take mine and heft it. It's light, and when I peer inside I see it's empty. Once everyone slings theirs on, Jacob directs us to three battered canoes tied to the bumper of a rusting white panel van. One of the canoes has a huge floating platform tied to the stern. I have no idea what it's for. I'm sticking so close to Singer that I'm a tripping hazard. We climb into the canoes and take our seats. Singer's behind me, and a boy I haven't met is in the bow. He's small, almost my size, and the rifle across his lap is huge. I can't believe he'll be able to pick the damn thing up.

"Most of you know the drill," Jacob says from his place in the middle canoe. His voice is loud and controlled. "We go close to shore and wait. When we're sure there's no threat, we'll dock and haul ass to the warehouse. We stay together until we're inside, then we break off in groups and fan out. Don't spend any time at the front of the warehouse, in sections A through F; we've already picked those areas clean. We'll have to go deeper inside." He pauses and waits for questions. There aren't any. Well, I have a million, but I hold my tongue.

"When you've got all you can carry, regroup at the entrance and we'll hustle back to the boats. All good?"

Singer holds up his hand. "What do we do if we spot any Grays?"

Jacob holds up his handgun. I don't know

guns, but it's huge and silver and looks like it could take out a rhino. I guess for raids like this he leaves the bow behind. "Two quick shots. Boom boom. We'll all come running. Any other questions? No? Let's roll."

People on shore shove us into the water, and we're on our way. Jacob's canoe is the one with the big platform tied to it. It's heavy enough that all three guys strain as they row, trying to keep up. Singer and the boy in front have paddles, but I'm simply a passenger. We're about a hundred yards from shore when Singer asks him what his name is.

"Joseph," he says, expertly swapping the paddle from the left to the right to maintain our heading. "You guys are Singer and Scout, right?"

"That's right."

We keep rowing, but have to stop once in a while so they guys pulling the floating platform can catch up. It's very quiet out here. There's not much chatter from anyone, with only the clunk of an oar and the slap of the soupy water on the hull breaking the silence. As we float along, I look down and I see plastic wrappers, water bottles, six-pack holders, and whatever else hasn't already disintegrated. Anything paper is long gone, but plastic doesn't rot and will be here forever. There must be a million of those flimsy plastic bags they used to hand out at grocery stores floating just beneath the surface, twisting like ghostly apparitions. Mankind's legacy in all its glory.

"How many of these raids have you been on?"

Singer finally asks.

Joseph doesn't answer for a moment. "Three. No, four. Three went okay, but the fourth...didn't. We lost guys on that one."

I stare at his back. "But you keep going out?"

He flips the oar to the other side. "Yeah. My little brother's back there. We all need food and supplies. So yeah, I keep going out. Someone's gotta do it."

They paddle for a while longer, and before I know it we're closer to shore than we are to Home. We keep going until I can make out details of the town. The white frame houses on the water's edge are half in and half out of the water and collapsing on themselves. The main road aimed toward Home that vanishes into the channel. Dead trees line the streets, their naked arms lifted to the gray skies. The shops on this once-quaint street are now left with broken windows gaping at me like black mouths filled with jagged silver teeth. As I stare at this corpse of a town, my inner chill expands and begins to engulf my entire body. I can't stop shaking. I wrap my arms around myself, but the shivering won't stop. My teeth start to chatter. Singer senses something and stops rowing for a moment. He rests his hand on my shoulder, and his touch warms my freezing soul a few degrees.

"This place is awful," I whisper, more to hear myself talk than to pass judgment.

"It was nice once," Joseph says softly. It doesn't

sound like he's upset at my statement. "I grew up here. My house was right over there. Behind the theater."

He points to the right to a tan brick building with the words "State Theater" in neon letters above a marquee sign. At some point the building burned. The front of it is charred and black, the doors blasted out. Windows above the marquee are shattered and soot-stained. Joseph doesn't elaborate; he's a man of few words.

The other two boats draw alongside us. No one is talking at all now. They're too overcome with emotion as they're confronted once again with the desolate remains of their town. We sit there for what feels like hours, drifting a little. Finally Jacob sits up.

"Anyone see anything?"

One of the boys has binoculars up to his eyes. He's looking left and right, pausing here, going back and forth over certain areas. Eventually he drops them down and proclaims the landing zone safe. Jacob nods at him. Damn, I wish Dog were here. His nose wasn't always right, but relying on sight alone is no great comfort to me. That talented beak of his was a thing of wonder.

"Okay, everyone. You know what to do."

The guys paddle like mad and we practically fly up to the submerged street. The canoes scrape bottom and before I know it I'm standing on the road with Chuck's leather handle slippery in my sweaty hand. Everyone else bails out and together we pull the canoes up far enough that they won't drift away. Jacob points at two of the younger guys.

"You two, get to work."

Those two scamper alongside the shore, fighting through the thick, muddy slop. They come to a clump of tall bushes full of brown needles and pull saws from their packs. Immediately they get busy taking down the bushes. Jacob sees the confusion on my face.

"They're cedar trees," he explains quickly. "We need the fuel for the kitchen."

"But you've got trees on the island. Why don't you use those?"

He's already moving away, but over his shoulder he says, "We do, but only if we have to. This place is thick with cedar trees. They're easy to cut and transport. We save the trees on the island in case we really need them. They'll load them on the flatbed so we can haul them back."

And that explains why I smelled cedar when we first arrived at Home, and what the floating platform is for. But I don't have any time to think because Singer grabs my arm and pulls me along.

"Let's go," he says. We fall in behind the others and start running up the road toward downtown.

CHAPTER
SIXTEEN

The street is slippery with mud and trash, and I'm thankful for Singer's steadying hand pulling me along. There's standing water everywhere. We dodge around a few derelict cars, the clumping of our boots loud in the bleak silence. The others are breathing hard already, but I'm barely winded. My nervous shakes are gone and I'm only focused on watching for trouble. This kind of open, full throttle assault is not my style. I prefer my subtle ninja method, sticking to the shadows and sneaking around. But I don't have a choice. Everyone is running, so I'm running, too.

We're coming up on an intersection where four mangled cars once tried to occupy the same space at the same time, and Jacob slows, furtively glancing each way and making sure the coast is clear. When he's certain there's no threat, he motions us on and we take off again. We do this three more times, and each time I'm grateful for the short break to try and calm my nerves. At one point he motions for us to huddle up. The guys are all sucking wind, and several of them have their hands on their knees, their heads down and panting heavily.

"Two more blocks up, then we turn right at Maple. You'll see the warehouse dead ahead."

Break time is over. We run up next to a derelict delivery truck and I catch a movement out of the corner of my eye. I stop so fast I nearly wipe out as a white and brown cat shoots across the street, streaking past us and quickly vanishing into a ruined store window. I haven't seen a cat in months, and as we pick up the pace I give it credit for not ending up as a furry Scooby snack. Grays aren't particular what they eat, and the rat and mice population seems to have dwindled drastically.

We careen around a corner, and at the end of the street I spot the warehouse. Wow, it's big, three stories tall at least, white with beige trim. There are loading docks along the left side, with several semitrucks backed into their slots. Those slots are completely filled with greasy water. There's a big sliding door directly in front of us, big enough to drive one of those trucks into, with a regular door next to that. The sliding door is open, and from here the interior is dark and forbidding as hell. If this were a horror movie the audience would be covering their eyes and screaming at the red shirts not to go inside by themselves, knowing that's where Freddie or Jason was waiting to puree them. Dammit, why did Singer have to go and volunteer?

We split up when we get close and converge on the big doorway in two groups, one to each side. We've all got our backs against the steel siding, pushed up tight against its corrugated surface. I'd like to say it makes me feel better when I see the fear on everyone's faces, but it doesn't. In my quivering hand Chuck feels small and outclassed, as useful as a butter knife. But it doesn't matter now, because Jacob is pointing inside. It's time to move.

We step over the threshold, sliding from the dim outside light into an even dimmer inside light. Foul smells assault my nose. Rotten food, wet cardboard, mildew, dead and decaying things I'd rather not think about. The interior is a single huge room that stretches all the way from one end to the other, at least the size of a football field. My dad loved *Raiders of the Lost Ark*, and it looks like the warehouse at the end of that, except where theirs was neat and tidy, this one is a soggy, stinky mess. There are dirty skylights overhead, so we're not as blind as I feared we'd be, but it's still pretty dark. Singer nudges me and unglues my feet and we take a few more steps inside.

"Hello, mama," he whispers, his mouth dropping open in awe. Despite my jangling nerves, I stifle a laugh because his jaw has dropped so low it's almost comical. It's all I can do not to reach out a hand and gently push it closed. "It's the damn mother lode…"

The shelves before us are at least twenty feet high, and there are more than a dozen aisles all packed with boxes and crates of all shapes and sizes, like a Costco on steroids. The nearest containers have been rummaged through, that much is clear, but farther on back much of it looks untouched. A few abandoned forklifts are rusting between the tall shelves. One is toppled over. There's some fluttering overhead, and if I squint I can see a nervous, undulating blanket of leathery wings and squirming bodies dangling from the metal rafters. Bats. The entire ceiling is thick with them. Honestly, I don't mind bats. They eat mosquitos, and I'm okay with that.

Jacob starts pointing to each of us. "Pair off and get moving. Remember, we've already hit this front area and picked it clean, so go beyond that. Start somewhere around F. Only grab cans that aren't swollen, and boxes that are dry and undamaged. Go!"

Singer grabs my hand and we take off. He acts like taking my hand is the most natural thing in the world, and maybe it is, and I'm okay with that, too. We head to the right, past a small room that was once an office. The biggest immediate threat is tripping on the trash that's strewn all on the floor. We fly around the office and turn left and sprint between two towering shelves. Overhead there's a metal sign with a big A on it, and about ten feet farther on there's another one with a large B. It's barely bright enough to see the big cardboard boxes on pallets with numbers printed on their sides, some with a cryptic word or two that make little or no sense. Most that we see have been sliced open enough to spy what's inside. I can barely make out things like Tupperware bowls, hand mixers, windshield wipers, and a thousand other random objects that do us no good. They were once valuable to someone, but not to us. Not now.

Singer slows, so I do, too. He's staring at the sign high overhead, and I can faintly see the letter F on the dangling sign above us. The boxes here haven't been touched before. Even so, some are sagging and split open with their contents revealed, while others are whole. He points up.

"Give me a hand. Let's check those out," he whispers. I slide Chuck into its sheath, lace my fingers together, and give him a leg up. He quickly climbs, and I'm left down below to wipe my hands clean of whatever gross, slimy crap was on the bottom of his boots. Yuck. He clambers up higher and I hear him grunt and tug at cardboard that puts up a much tougher fight than it should. As I stand there by myself, I can hear the bats twittering and fussing overhead. Up above, Singer mutters something.

"What is it?" I whisper in his direction.

"Damn. Nothing but cheap garden tools in this one. I'm going to keep looking."

I'm down here for a little while longer, nervously tapping my feet and furtively glancing every which way, and I realize that the only thing worse than being in this stinky warehouse is being in this stinky warehouse by myself. So while he's still ten feet up and rummaging around, I grab hold of the thick vertical support and pull myself up. I must be filled to the brim with adrenaline or something, because before I know it I'm climbing faster than a monkey. In seconds I'm up there next to him. It's dark enough inside that I can't see much besides his eyes and teeth, but if he's surprised to see me up here he doesn't let on.

"Let's keep moving," he says quietly. "I'll check out these, and you look at those."

I nod, not realizing right away that he probably didn't see that, but he gets the point. I shuffle between the huge boxes and crates. I can't stand up straight or I'll hit my head on the shelf above me, but I'm small enough that maneuvering around is a lot easier for me than it is for him. I squeeze between a few larger crates and settle on four smaller boxes that are lashed together with plastic strapping. I pull Chuck out and slice through it, then cut along thick tape holding the box shut. There's really very little light here so I have to grope around in the dark and determine by touch what's inside.

From a few boxes away Singer whispers, "Anything?" This place has a mausoleum quality that makes you want to whisper.

I pull something from inside, and hold it up. It's a beer glass with an Ohio State logo on it. "No, just a bunch of glassware," I reply, blowing off white packing peanuts. "I'm moving on to the next."

Four boxes of useless stuff later (electric razors, dog toys, skateboards, and some power tools that I don't recognize), I cut open a tall narrow one and Chuck clanks against something hard. I tear open the box and I'm rewarded with neatly stacked cans of Bumblebee tuna in those squat little cans.

"Score!" I exclaim loudly, belatedly tossing a hand over my mouth. Singer hurries over and I display a can proudly, shoving it in his face so he can see it. He flashes a huge smile and gives me a hug, an embrace I'm happy to return.

"Nice job! Let's load up."

We whip off our packs and start throwing in cans, but almost immediately he stops. He reaches into the bottom of his backpack and pulls out two cloth bags. No, not bags, but pillowcases, thick, heavy ones. We grin at each other and don't miss a beat, tossing in cans until the makeshift bags are bulging. When they're almost full he leans in close.

"That's plenty for now. Let's see if we can find some fruit or other stuff. We know these are here for the next trip."

Bent over low so we don't crack our heads, we shuffle down to the next section and do it all over again. In my first box I discover about a zillion bundles of colorful party napkins, and the one after that is filled with stacks of cheap little plastic champagne glasses, the ones with the removable bases. I shuffle over to the next, and my heart leaps when I find three crates of boxed powdered milk, but there's a leak in the roof somewhere above us and water has ruined the whole batch. That bums me out, thinking how awesome milk would be for cooking, drinking, and especially for Tiny. But we don't pause and move on to the next one, very aware that we've been here quite a while.

I'm about to slice open the one in front of me, when something catches my eye. On a box a few feet away I can barely make out a word in familiar script: Crest. I scuttle over to that one and slice open the top, then reach in and pull out a plastic bag about ten inches long and half as wide. It's a toothbrush and miniature tube of toothpaste, plus some dental floss and a few other odds and ends. The box is filled with the bags. This is amazing! I hold it out for Singer to see.

"Check this out. Remember those bags that dentists used to give away after your appointment? The ones with the toothpaste and stuff? I just found a thousand of them!"

He takes the one I'm holding in his direction. He rips open the plastic bag and inspects the contents, then hands it all back to me. He's not nearly as excited as I am, which baffles me. Clean teeth. Fresh breath. What more could a girl want?

"Cool," he says. "You want some, go ahead and load up."

I don't need to be told twice. I stuff a dozen or so into the pockets of my backpack. I get that they're not food and aren't totally essential, but they're pretty damn essential to me. I can't wait to get back and try one out. I run my tongue over my teeth and wish I could do it now, but Singer taps me on the shoulder.

"One more? Then we should get going, I think."

I agree with him, and we move back to the other box. He's seen how easy it is for me to slit these open with Chuck, so he watches from a few feet away while I get busy. I slice a huge X across the box's face, and we're quickly rewarded with the crinkle of cellophane as dozens of tiny bags slither around our feet. He reaches down and grabs one, holding it up to the dim light. When he realizes what we've found, his voice bubbles with excitement.

"Mixed nuts? Oh, hot damn, we found mixed nuts."

It's an entire crate of those little travel bags of peanuts, cashews, and almonds. I remember blue bags like these lining the racks of convenience stores and gas stations on family vacations. Lord and I would beg and grovel for ice cream or candy bars, but mom would only let us have healthy treats like these. I'm a lot more excited about these now than back then. These small bags are a gold mine of protein and salty goodness. We snatch up crinkly handfuls and hold them out, shaking them in each other's face and laughing. Singer rips one open and dumps the contents into his mouth, smiling and chewing at the same time. He starts to laugh again and a few nuts fly from his mouth and bounce to the floor. He covers his mouth, momentarily embarrassed at his food faux pas, which I find incredibly endearing. A wonderful aroma of peanuts fills our tiny space. We start cramming those little bags into our packs and pillowcases until there's no more room, then we start on our pockets. His cargo pants come in handy for the second time that day, and I cross my heart and hope to die and swear that I'll never make fun of them again.

When our pockets are so full I'm afraid we won't be able to walk, much less climb down, we know it's really time to go. We carefully make our way to the floor and grab our bags and backpacks. Filled as they are with so much tuna, they're heavy, so heavy I'm afraid they're going to burst open. Clumsily, we manage to swing the backpacks on. We take a few steps and stop, then turn and look at each other and grin; the bags of nuts stuffed in our pockets crinkle so loud we'd be quieter clanking around in suits of armor. But there's no helping it, so we shrug and keep going. Singer leads the way and is a few steps in front of me. I'm relieved when I see the hazy outline of the office in the distance. I can't see the big open door, but its glow throws some thin light onto the office wall and we head toward it like it's a beacon.

I'm about to catch up to Singer when something scorching hot wraps itself around my throat. My skin burns. I feel my feet leaving the ground. My scream is a muffled gurgle that travels no farther than my mouth. The bags slither from my grasp and I snatch at the unyielding fingers crushing my throat. I try to shout out Singer's name, but he's already twenty feet ahead of me and is oblivious to what's happening back here.

The grip on my neck tightens. The edges of my vision are going dark. The irony isn't lost on me that I was terrified of something happening to Singer, but instead it's happening to me. There's a blast of searing hot air on the back of my neck that makes my skin crawl.

Oh, shit. I'm going to die in this stinking warehouse.

CHAPTER
SEVENTEEN

My vision is tunneling, going dark like an iris slowly closing, but I can still make out Singer's fuzzy shape up ahead. He's walking stiff and funny because of all the bags of nuts stuffed into his pants. I try a final scream, but I have no breath and vocal chords need air to work. I only have seconds left before I end up like Dog and so many others. I am not going to let that happen. The others need me. Singer needs me.

I reach down and scrabble blindly at my thigh for Chuck. I swat around and miss completely my first few attempts, but on the third try I manage to grab the knob on the end of the handle. I fumble it from its sheath and nearly drop it, then finally get a good grip. Wildly and without any real plan, I thrust low and behind me. I hit something yielding and the blade turns in my hand, but I don't let go. I yank it out and thrust again. Over and over, sometimes connecting, sometimes not. Hot liquid splashes against my back and thighs, running down my legs. The Gray's got both hands around my neck, its grip scorching my skin. With my left hand I reach back and latch onto its wrist, and I squeeze. I squeeze as hard as I can, gritting my teeth with the effort. To my shock and surprise bones in its wrist crunch with the dull, muted sound of wet sticks snapping. I shattered its wrist. Did I just do that? I roughly rip its useless hand from my neck, but I don't let go. I must have really injured it because it can't hold me up in the air any longer with only one hand. My feet thud on solid ground. I've got its mangled wrist in my left hand, and Chuck in my right. It pulls me closer until our faces are only inches apart. Even in the near dark, I can clearly see its dim, witless eyes, eyes that at one time may have held compassion and warmth, but now only reflect hunger and rage. Its hair is long and wild, matted with sticks and dirt. The thing's steamy breath is the putrid stench of road kill mixed with hot summer landfill, and the smell is so horrible it makes my stomach turn. I gag and throw up a little in my mouth. The taste is nasty and bitter.

I haven't let go of its wrist yet. In fact, I'm gripping it so tightly that the tips of my fingers are nearly touching my palm. If it were a regular person it would be on its knees in agony. But it's still got me around my neck, so I snap its arm like a whip and the remaining hand is torn away. I twist ferociously, sideways and down, and the Gray face-plants to the floor. How the hell did I do that? I stare at its shadowy outline squirming before me. Blood is pouring from a dozen Chuck-induced gashes in its side, but it's not done yet. I know I should run. I should run like hell toward the door and hope that Singer sees what's happening and blows its damn brains out. But I don't. Why don't I?

Instead, I set my feet, spin, and with a grunt I hurl it away from me. It cartwheels towards the second row of shelves, up high, near where we found the tuna. Limbs flailing, it careens into the boxes. The impact is so extreme that the stacked boxes explode like they're on the receiving end of a bazooka. I stand there staring where the thing disappeared, while all around me mangled cans of Bumblebee tuna tumble to the ground and roll around my feet in tidy circles.

I don't wait to see what happens next. I scoop up the pillowcases of tuna and sprint for the exit. Little cellophane bags of nuts trail in my wake as they tumble out of my pockets, scattered behind me like a trail of breadcrumbs.

"Singer! Gray!" I shout.

The explosion of cans must have already gotten his attention, because he's turned back and staring at me, his eyes wide with the realization that I'm not directly in his wake. Singer throws down the bags and flips the shotgun off his back. He aims it at the ceiling and squeezes off two quick booming shots that echo throughout the building, then hauls ass towards me. The bats overhead react to the shotgun blasts and take flight, swirling in crazy patterns in and around the metal rafters, their leathery wings and squeals splitting open the silence. Singer and I almost collide, but he grabs my shoulder and slows me down.

"Scout! Jesus, I thought you were right behind me. What happened?"

I spare a harried glance over my shoulder. "A Gray, back there. It attacked me. We've gotta go now!"

He doesn't hesitate, although his expression is filled with questions, like how in the hell I managed to get away, or why I don't have a scratch on me. But we both know that where there's one Gray there are certainly more, so instead of wasting a precious moment he snatches up his bags on the fly and we sprint to the end of the aisle and bolt around the corner. The others are there waiting for us at the open doorway, guns up. But no, not all of them. I do a quick head count. There are only four there, plus the two of us. I don't see Jacob. Singer and I slide to a stop, our breath coming in harsh rasps. Joseph grabs my arm. He may be small, but damn he's got an impressively strong grip.

"What's happening?" he barks out.

I point backwards, still panting. "A Gray. It attacked me. Where the hell is Jacob?"

"Not back yet. He went off on his own."

"Shit! We gotta go get him."

Joseph doesn't let go of my arm. "No, everyone stay here. I'll go."

He doesn't wait for confirmation from anyone, but speeds away into the bowels of the warehouse.

He's got that huge rifle up and aimed loosely in front of him, tracking it back and forth. In seconds he's lost in the gloom, and only the muffled thudding of his boots gives us any indication of his location.

As soon as he's gone I look at Singer. He's still wide-eyed and panting, but he looks calm and relaxed compared to the other three boys. They're whispering to each other in low tones, and they can't keep their hands or feet still. They're almost dancing in place. One of them is so nervous his head's spinning around like he's possessed, trying to see every direction at once. They're so twitchy I hope they don't shoot any of us by accident. I keep forgetting that they're just kids, even younger than I am.

We hear sounds from deep inside the building, followed by panicked screaming. Three booming gunshots from the darkness make me jump and I grab at Singer's arm. He gently removes my hand and levels the shotgun towards the noise. His rapid, warm breathing is loud in my ear. Singer's got his shotgun up and ready. He steps close to me until his head is over my shoulder and he's staring into the darkness. I turn to warn the other three to get ready, but there's nobody there. It takes me a second to figure out what the hell happened to them, but then I spot their backs down the street, their boots pounding away through the slop at high speed. I curse them under my breath and nudge Singer.

"What?" he asks, then his mouth tightens and

his lips almost vanish when he sees we're alone. He takes a moment and loads several more shells into the shotgun. His hands are shaking. I'm about to ask him what the plan is when we hear another yell, closer this time. I grab onto his arm and peer into the darkness. Seconds later we see Joseph running full tilt toward us. His rifle is gone and his arms are pumping fast and hard. His hair is swept back. I've never seen eyes so wide and filled with terror before.

"Grays! Dozens of them! Run!" he manages to scream.

He's only thirty or forty feet away when he trips and goes sprawling face first. He jumps to his feet and keeps coming. Seconds later I see movement behind him, coming toward us fast. It's Jacob. He's sprinting too, but unlike Joseph he hasn't dropped his gun. That huge silver pistol is still gripped in his hand. Jacob skids to a stop and spins around and fires behind him twice. Bam! Bam! Then he spins back and continues toward us. He sees us framed in the open doorway and waves his free hand in a sideways motion.

"Shut the door!" he commands. "Now!"

And then I can see why. Behind him there's movement, lots of movement. Shadowy, terrifying figures dashing towards us, snapping at his heels. Five, ten, maybe as many as fifteen Grays are right behind him. If they get out of the warehouse we'll never get away. They're too close, and there's too many of them. Out in the open like this we won't stand a chance.

They'll tear us apart. Singer snaps a look from Jacob to me. He understands, too.

"You heard him. We've got to shut this door!" he yells, almost pleading.

"No! If we shut it now they'll die."

He grits his teeth and I can see that he gets it. "I know. But if we don't do it, then we'll all die!"

He grabs the rusted handle and tugs, but the big sliding door doesn't budge. He's straining, but it's not doing any good. Then Joseph crashes into us. He's so out of breath he can barely stand, but he throws his strength into the door, too. With the screeching of an angry cat, the big door lurches closed a dozen feet, then stops. The opening is still about five feet wide. Five feet too many. That won't even slow the Grays down.

"Help us, Scout!" Singer shouts. The muscles in his shoulders are straining, vibrating with the effort. Tendons in his neck are popping out. Joseph throws himself into it again, but his feet slide on the sloppy ground and he goes down. He screams in frustrations and jumps back up, teeth gritted.

I run to the back of the door and grab the edge. The thing is heavy, made of thick steel and meant to keep determined thieves out. Singer and Joseph are still struggling, but I wait. I remember how I tossed the Gray up and into the shelves, and the huge dent I put in the trunk of the car. I don't know why, but for some reason I'm strong now. Really strong. Singer and

Joseph are grunting and crying out in fear and anger, but I still wait. It takes every bit of control for me not to help. Survival instincts dating back millions of years are screaming at me to push now, to slam the door shut on the horrors flying at me, but I fend them off and wait. And I wait. I am not going to leave anyone to those things!

Then Jacob dives through the door, literally dives through. He hits the ground and rolls, his gun skidding away into the muck. At that second I summon up all my strength and I shove! With a deafening screech the huge door jumps forward and slams home just as the first Gray is partially over the threshold. The edge of the door catches it just above the waist and doesn't slow, shearing it almost completely in two. Black blood and guts explode as the half on our side thrashes in manic, grisly silence; mud and gore splatter us, the door, and the ground. The thing flops around for a few long, terrible moments in quiet agony, its chest heaving in irregular spasms. Blood pours from its mouth and skeletal nose, and its lips are pulled back to reveal stained teeth. Purple guts dangle from its severed torso and trail into the warehouse. Despite the fact that it's been sliced in two and is seconds from death, its shaking fingers are still reaching out, grabbing at us, and as one we take an involuntary step back. Finally they curl into arthritic claws and drop, and its head thuds down into the mud. Its eyes are open, but they'll never see anything again.

Jacob stares at us for a full ten seconds, panting and winded, hands on his knees. His blond hair is thick with sweat and his face is a messy, splotchy red. Then he looks down at the dead Gray. From the other side we hear the rest of them scratching and pounding on the door in frustration. If they had the ability to make sounds they'd be howling like a wolf pack. He steps around the dead Gray and slams home a huge latch, securing the door. Finally, he picks up his gun and wipes some of the gunk off of it. He exhales long and hard.

"Thanks. I mean, I don't know what to say besides thanks. I owe you one. Now we need to go."

Soundlessly, we gather up the bags of loot, then begin a fast jog towards the boats. I catch Singer glancing sideways at me as we run.

CHAPTER
EIGHTEEN

When we get back, I sit on my cot and shiver while Singer holds me. I don't know how much time passes that way as I rock back and forth. I can't get the image of that Gray out of my mind: chopped in half and thrashing in the mud, its guts pinched in the door, blood spewing from its mouth and nose. I don't know if the others noticed or not, but that Gray was a girl before it changed. It was so emaciated its breasts were almost completely gone, but I could still tell. Seeing that thing is seriously creeping the hell out of me, and hitting way too close to home.

It takes a while, but I finally settle down and the shakes fade away. We scrape off the muck and blood and clean up as well as we can, because there's a celebration going on in the gym and we should be there. Together we make our way downstairs.

When I arrive I see Eve leaning up against the wall by herself. When she notices me she manages a grin. The normal worry lines clustered near her eyes have diminished now that the raid is over and she's had time to relax. I go up to her and lean against the wall. I'm pretty sure I can talk now without my voice quivering.

"Jacob told me all about the raid," she says, watching everyone as they gather in the gym. "He told me what happened, how you all saved him. I want to thank you for that. I'm…fond of Jacob, and losing him would have been terrible."

I nod and smile back at her. "You're welcome. I just couldn't stand the thought of losing someone else, especially not so soon after the others. Please tell me all the raids aren't like this."

She takes a moment to answer. "Yeah, this one was rough, but the one before was even worse," she says, although the admission seems difficult for her, as if any past failure is a blemish on her leadership. "We lost three people and came away empty-handed. We needed this win."

"So it's a good day?"

"Yes," she agrees. "You all came back alive, with supplies. So yes, it's a good day. Or as good as they get."

We watch as more people arrive and fill up the gym. We're not talking, but just taking a breather and learning how to relax in each other's company. I'm happy to be doing anything to distract me from what happened earlier. But like any horrific incident, that's going to take time. The memory of that dying female Gray is a deep mental scar that may fade in time, but never completely disappear. I wince when I remember that all of these creatures were once normal people, just as normal as me and everyone else in this room, which in turn makes me think about Lord and what he's become. I start to shiver again, and cross my arms to ward off the chill. Anxious now to do anything to derail that train of thought, I turn to Eve.

"Those three boys, the ones who ran. What happens to them?"

Her face turns cool. "They'll be punished."

"Yeah, I figured as much. How?"

"Kitchen duty, extra sentry time, and more. And they're blackballed from any further raids."

"That's not so bad, I guess. Just try and remember that they're just kids, you know? It was a terrifying situation. I was scared to death."

"Yes, but you stayed. You didn't run. You could've all been killed because of them."

I don't have an argument there, because she's right. After a few minutes of silence, I watch Singer as he moves around the gym. He's milling around talking to people, shaking hands, introducing himself. A younger girl points to his back pocket, and he nods shyly at her and pulls out his harmonica. He breaks into the first verse of American Pie. Everyone claps and one or two people start to sing along, and many more chime in during the chorus. The unyielding brick walls of the gym ring with their voices. Eve doesn't join in, but from what I know of her so far, she's not what you'd call the sing-along type. I lean my head closer to her.

"If you don't mind my asking, what's with you and some of the others and these green robes? Is it a religious thing or something?"

Eve doesn't look away from her people enjoying themselves. "No, not really. Remember when I said that our parents stocked this place with everything we'd need?"

"Yeah, sure. They did a heck of a job. I'm impressed."

"Well, they thought about basically everything. But they were so concerned with loading up on enough food for the long haul, that they didn't have room left over for other stuff, like clothes. I had my own clothes back then, but that was a long time ago. I was much younger, and smaller. I've outgrown everything and there's not enough to go around." She shrugs. "The robes were here, so we use them."

"Choir robes?"

"Yes. And to be honest, I've gotten so used to them that I don't know if I could go back to pants and bras and everything else. Too restrictive."

"What, so you're commando under that thing?" For some reason I'm a little embarrassed at this, although I don't know why. Annie and I have seen each other naked before, sometimes out of necessity, but mostly because we just didn't care.

She stares at me, unblinking, her head cocked to the side. "Yes. Does that bother you?"

I give a little laugh that sounds annoyingly fake, even to me. "No, not at all. I mean, why would it?"

For some reason Eve's stare makes me uncomfortable, and I feel my face flush. Instead of continuing with this awkward conversation, I turn away and watch Singer perform. He's got the entire room singing along and swaying. I can't believe what a crowd-pleaser he can be. I'm smiling wide and silly before I realize it, and tapping my foot in time with the music. I'm getting into it when she leans in and our heads touch.

"So what are your plans?" she asks me. "Can I assume you'd like to stay here?"

I nod. "Well, we haven't really talked about it as a group yet, but I have to think we would. If you'll have us, that is."

"We don't usually take in older people, but you were taking care of children, like we do, so that should give you a pass. I'll talk to some of the others, but I wouldn't worry too much."

Interesting. Eve doesn't have the final word here? I've wondered how this place is ruled. The fact that she needs to discuss this matter with others is new information. Does this mean it's a democracy of some sort?

"That's awesome. Thanks."

"But I'll have to assign you jobs. There's no free ride."

"I understand. I'll have to clear it with Hunter and the rest, but I can't imagine they'd want to leave." I think for a moment, before I add, "Well, Hunter might have other ideas, but that would be his choice."

She doesn't say anything for a few moments, then, "At first I thought you were the leader of your group. But later I found out that Hunter is. Why is that? You've got so many more leadership qualities than he does. In my opinion he's more likely to get you killed than keep you safe."

I laugh under my breath. "No, I'm no leader. I'm what my brother called the Firebrand."

"Firebrand?"

"Yeah, I'm in charge of the fire. It's a title he made up for me. You know, finding fuel, keeping it going, making sure it doesn't go out. Without its heat and light, we wouldn't have survived this long. Being in here I'm not sure you understand how important having a fire is out there. Trust me. It's a big deal. I'm the Firebrand, and I took the job very seriously."

"You know, don't you, that that's not the real meaning of Firebrand, right?"

"Sort of, I guess." I'd heard or read the word in the past, but I can't dredge up its true definition. To be honest, I'm a little pissed that she knows what it means and I don't.

"A Firebrand is someone who is passionate about a cause, to the point of taking radical action. A change agent, or something like that. Does that sound like you?"

I almost laugh out loud. A change agent? That doesn't sound like me at all. "No, not really. I'll stick with Lord's definition. That's more fitting." We watch everyone milling around for a minute. "But back to Hunter, he's the leader. He's helped us more than I care to admit. And when my brother…took a hike, Lord picked Hunter to be in charge. Really, when the time came, I thought it would be Singer, but I was wrong. I think Lord chose him because he knew we'd need someone more, well, ruthless." My voice momentarily hardens. "You know, someone willing to make hard choices. That's necessary outside of this place. You've been on raids before, right? Then you know what it's like out there."

"I have. But it's ruthless everywhere. Not just out there."

She's standing on my left, the port stain on her pretty face hidden from me, as usual. She slides closer and rests her hand on my shoulder, and I think she's about to say something else, but she doesn't. She leaves her hand there, her fingertips lightly on my neck. I'm not really sure what's going on. She dips her head toward me so close our noses are almost touching. When she speaks, her voice is just above a whisper.

"Singer. Are you and he…together?"

I'm not always quick on the uptake, and slowly it dawns on me what she's getting at. I don't know what to say. I'm also more than a little confused. I mean, I've never thought of myself as anything but a plain Jane at best. But in just the last month Singer and I have fallen for each other, Hunter made that ridiculous claim, and now Eve is hitting on me? This is proof positive that the world has, in fact, gone crazy.

"Yes, we are," I tell her.

She drops her hand to her side. "I thought so, but I wanted to make sure."

"I'm flattered, I really am. I don't get it, but I'm flattered."

She turns to me, and our eyes meet. For once she's unconcerned with me seeing her birthmark. In fact, I think she wants me to see her just the way she is. I look at her, I mean I really look at her. The cool, detached leader I've come to know these last few days has withdrawn, and in her place there's a lonely and scared young girl, one full of weakness and doubt. It tugs at my heart, because I can see how difficult it must be for her here. In another life she'd probably be getting her driver's license, worrying about grades, considering what college she should attend. But that life drowned with the rest of the world. Now she's in charge and responsible for so much, for keeping everyone alive, just like Lord when he was in charge. I can only think that she sees something in me, something that reminds me of her and that she can't or won't share with anyone else here.

Worst of all, she's at least as old as I am, and we both understand what that means and how little time we might have left. I almost lean in and hug her, but I'm sure that would send the wrong message, so I don't.

"Don't sell yourself short," she assures me after a minute, her brown eyes locked on mine. She runs a finger through my hair and flips it over my ear. My hair is growing fast lately, and for some absurd reason I make a mental note to have Annie hack it short again. "Maybe in another life, another time, it would be different."

At this point I'm convinced that anything I say now will sound lame, but I try anyway. "Yeah, maybe. I…I don't know. Thanks." Yeah. Lame.

She manufactures an unconvincing smile and walks away, out of the gym. She seems to float away from me, a ghostly vision in green, her head lowered. For some reason I want to go after her, to apologize for something I haven't done. But my feet are one with the concrete floor, and I do nothing as she vanishes through the doorway.

Singer sees me standing by myself, and he motions for me to join him as he continues to lead everyone in song. I shake my head, my eyes wide in mock terror. He grins and weaves his way through the crowd and stands next to me, placing his arm around my shoulder and pulling me close. In no time at all the confused thoughts of Eve's advance are gone, and I'm singing and smiling along with the rest of them. That night Harold and the kitchen crew outdo themselves with the influx of new supplies and we eat like royalty, assuming royalty enjoy something bordering on tuna-noodle casserole. When we finally head to the library to crash for the night, I'm full and happy. I'm even happier when Singer kisses me goodnight.

CHAPTER
NINETEEN

The next morning I wake to a bright light in my face. I crack one eye open carefully and see the sun streaming through the filthy library window, little dust motes floating in the still air. The soft yellow rays illuminate the room in a way that candlelight can't. All around me the colorful bindings of the books blaze, their knowledge burning and begging to be explored. It's such an odd, novel sight that it takes me a few moments to understand what's going on. Once I do, though, I nudge Singer, who's gently snoring a few inches away from me, his face partially obscured by the pillow.

"Hey. Hey, check this out," I whisper, giving him a firmer nudge.

He blinks a few times and sits up, rubbing his eyes. The sunlight makes his black hair glisten as he holds a hand up to shield his face from the sun. He smiles wide, his teeth white and even. Somehow he looks good even first thing in the morning.

"Wow. The sun? That's something new and different."

I shake my head and move to the window, pressing my nose against it, feeling its novel warmth. He stands next to me on my right, and I'm aware how close he is. He's taken to doing that lately, which is fine by me.

"Since before the Storm?" I ask.

"Maybe. Probably."

"It feels so good. I've missed this."

Behind us Hunter sits up in bed, wincing as he jostles his shoulder inside the sling. He gets up and stands by the window, squinting. I take a step away from him, giving him plenty of room. He's moving his tongue inside his mouth like something died in there.

"Damn. Check that out," Hunter says, pointing with his good hand. "What a cesspool."

The window is facing north. In that direction we see nothing but dark brown, sludgy water stretching until it melts into the dreary horizon. It undulates slowly, reminding me of a monstrous vat of tar warming over a fire. This is the first time we've been able to see this far, and it's depressing witnessing firsthand what the world's become. In our hearts we knew it was like this, but seeing it with our own eyes is different.

Before long the three of us turn away, and we're all a little sad and melancholy. You'd think the sunshine would cheer us up, but instead it reminds us how everything used to be. We silently make our beds since we've been told that's a requirement here. Singer lends Hunter a hand, and Annie makes hers after she does Tiny's crib. Carly insists on doing her own, which makes me smirk. Honestly, it looks worse when she's done tugging and pulling at the covers, but she's obviously proud of her work so we all congratulate her on it. We're getting ready to head down for a bite to eat when I see Singer on his hands and knees searching the bookcases on the far side of the library. With the sunshine beaming in, it's so bright that details are truly visible for the first time.

"Hey, Scout," he says after a minute, holding up a large brown book. "Check this out." He hands it to me. I'm shocked at how heavy it is.

I read the title and smile wide. *The Tragedy of Hamlet–With A Modern Translation*. I start to flip through the pages and see all the familiar names and places, but for once I can actually understand what they're talking about.

"Now you can read it on your own," he says.

I laugh, but make a mock pout, my lower lip out. "But I like it when you do it for me. That's so much more fun. And I don't have to work so hard."

Annie is up now and is standing there, listening to our exchange. With an exasperated roll of her eyes and a smile, she mutters, "Oh, Jesus. Get a room, you two."

Singer dips his head and looks away, embarrassed at her insinuations. I ignore her and enjoy the moment, feeling the pleasant heft of the book in my hands and the warmth of the sun on my back. Right now I'm probably as content as I've been since the Storm. We're finally safe from Grays. I'm surrounded by hundreds of books, and for once we know where our next meal is coming from. With a few exceptions, I'm in the company of the people I care most about in the entire world. I look at each one in turn: Annie is like a mother to all of us; Carly and Tiny are our children; and Singer is my…well, husband is a little too much for me to wrap my head around, but he's topping the short list. I don't want to think about Hunter, but for better or worse, all these people are my family. I lean against the windowsill with the book clutched across my chest, and feel a kind of satisfied warmth spread through me that has nothing to do with the sun, and I remember that this is what love and family feel like.

Then the moment is over when we hear a call from the next room that breakfast is ready. All of us follow the noisy crowd downstairs to the gym and stand in line, where we're handed a plate and heavy silverware from the church's kitchen. Today it's cornbread and powdered scrambled eggs, along with more Tang. We gather in a corner and park ourselves on the floor and prepare to dig in. Halfway through the meal Eve steps up, looking down on us. There's no hint of anything in her stoic manner that might betray how she feels about me, or our earlier conversation.

"I've been talking with some of the others, and if you'd like to stay here, you're welcome to do so. But if you do you'll have to start pulling your own weight around here." She looks at all of us one at a time, ending with me. Each person in turn nods yes, even Hunter.

"Good. Annie, you can help take care of the young ones. I'm assuming you'll be okay with that?"

Annie beams, her smile brighter than today's morning sunshine. Nothing could please her more, and I'm happy for her.

"Singer, head into the kitchen and work with Harold and the others. We only let the older ones in there. It's hot and demanding, but I'm sure you'll do fine. You'll probably be on dish duty."

Singer gives an enthusiastic thumbs up. "Sure. Happy to help."

"Hunter, until you're healed there's not really much you can do. But I want you to go to the church sanctuary and work with Jacob. He's in charge of security, which means dealing with any threats, inside or out. I think that should be right up your alley. Both of you can learn from each other."

Hunter just stares at her and doesn't say anything, and I'm afraid he's going to be a jerk and blurt out something stupid. But after a moment he nods, and goes back to chowing down on his eggs. His verbal skills really could use a reboot and an upgrade.

"Scout, I thought about what you said the other day. We've got the library but we don't use it. I've decided we need to have more education here. I want you to take the oldest ones upstairs and start teaching them to read. Some know how already, a little at least, but others have forgotten or never knew. It's important for everyone to be more proficient in case the world ever comes back."

I don't have a problem with that at all. Working in a library? Reading? Talking about books? That's right in my wheelhouse.

"Perfect. Thanks."

"Okay. As soon as you're all done and cleaned up, get busy. There's lots to do. Scout, I'll send your first batch of students up in a little bit."

As she walks away, I glance over and see Hunter staring after her. I try to read his face, but I can't. His verbal communication skills may suck, but his nonverbal ones are even worse. Most times I'd have more luck reading a statue.

"What are you thinking, Hunter?" I ask him with a stern, sideways glance.

He pushes his plate away, confident that Annie or Carly will take care of it for him. He grimaces as he stands up.

"Wonder who died and made her boss?" he says to no one.

I feel my face flush. "Dammit, we're their guests here. Don't do anything stupid, okay?"

He waves me away with his good hand. "Don't worry, princess. I'll behave."

But he's Hunter, and where he's concerned I'll always worry.

After breakfast we all head to our new jobs. I'm pleasantly full again, and I realize it's a sensation I can get used to in a hurry. Singer dutifully hurries off to the kitchen to work with Harold, while Annie rushes off to the main sleeping area that doubles as a nursery for the little ones. Hunter takes his time and walks toward the church sanctuary to see what Jacob needs. I'm so excited that I'm back up in the library before I even realize it, and barely remember how I got there. I may have floated up the steps.

While I wait for someone to show up, I pick up Hamlet and start leafing through the heavy pages, wishing Singer was here to enjoy it with me. One line jumps out at me, one Singer and I have read before. It takes place in the first act, when Polonius says to his son Laertes, "To thine own self be true." Singer told me that Laertes has pretty much had it with his father by then, and hops on the next boat to Paris so he won't have to listen to him ramble on any more. In a normal world getting away from your annoying parents is what any teenage kid wants to do half the time, and Laertes is no different.

I've learned from reading with Singer that Polonius is a bit of a pompous ass. In fact, in my mind I always refer to him as Pompous Polonius. Lord would've called him a douche. But I can't discount the meaning behind his simple phrase "To thine own self be true," and I wonder how it might play into my own life. Am I being true to myself? How would I know? I'm lousy at introspection, but something here is bothering me, like a splinter just under the skin, or that feeling that you've forgotten something import-ant. We've been so busy simply trying to stay alive that there's rarely any time to just sit and think. But this place, this Church Island, has given me that opportu-nity. So now I wonder: who am I, really? I'm Scout, yes, but I was Jean Louise first. I can't forget that I'm the Firebrand, too. I'm also Lord's sister. But, if I'm all these things, then what else might I be? Or is this it? It's hard to be true to yourself when you're not really sure who you are.

This confused circle of thought is cut short when two boys and a girl step into the library. They're younger than I am by a few dozen months at least. Their playful chatter stops when they see me standing by the window, Hamlet in hand. I haven't had time to plan anything, and I have no clue how to get started or what to do.

"Hi, there," I start, figuring this is as good as anything. "My name's Scout."

The girl smiles at me, an open, sincere smile that does wonders to ease my nerves, and introduces herself as Tanya, and the boys as Carl and James. As warm and friendly as Tanya is, Carl and James treat me like I've got the flu, keeping their physical and emotional distance and not volunteering anything.

I'm assuming from their cool looks that they're here under orders and they'd rather be somewhere else. Now I know how my math teachers felt when I was younger.

I bite at my lower lip, still at a loss how I should proceed. I have no idea what I'm doing. But I think back to my shared time with Singer and Hamlet and how much I enjoyed that, how I loved him reading to me, and quickly glance around at my literary options. As all three stare at me I run my fingers over some bindings in the Lending Library and pull out the book I'm looking for.

"Just make yourselves comfortable, okay?"

Tanya plops down, but the two boys treat the floor like it might be lava. They continue to stare at me as they slowly slink down. I'm aware that I'm still standing, so I sit on the edge of my bed and face them. I clear my throat.

"Um, well, I really don't have much prepared, but I thought I'd start by reading out loud today, just to get us going. You know, to break the ice."

Tanya's face lights up. At first I thought she was the same age as the two boys, but on closer inspection I'm thinking she's actually a little younger. Younger, and a little more open-minded.

"Cool. What's that book?" she asks, pointing at the book in my hand.

I hold it up proudly, feeling its inherent wonder and magic. "Harry Potter and the Sorcerer's Stone.

Have you heard of it?"

They glance back and forth between themselves, but I can't detect any awareness. I would have gotten the same reaction, I'm pretty sure, if I'd asked them about global warming or internal combustion. I really thought some of them would have been old enough to remember Harry and the gang, but apparently not. I guess not even magic has survived our world falling apart. Before the Storm every kid I knew had either read the books or seen the movies, or both. I know that if I can't get them interested in reading through the magic of Harry, Ron, and Hermione, then I'm sunk.

"So that's a no? Okay then. Let's get started."

James and Carl exchange a dubious glance with each other, but Tanya settles herself more comfortably on the hard floor, her eyes willing and ready. I'm liking her more by the minute.

"Chapter one," I begin after clearing my throat. My voice starts off a little squeaky, but soon mellows out. As soon as I begin reading about the Dursleys and how nasty they were, and how badly they treated Harry, the story all comes back to me in a soothing rush, the fine hairs on the back of my neck standing at attention in excitement. The familiar words and growing sensation of wonder is still there, as if it had never really gone anywhere, and simply needed the smallest of nudges to make me take a step back into that amazing world. This is why I read. This is why I love books that carry me away. Honestly, at this point I don't care if these three like it or not. This is a gift that I'm sharing with them, and they can take it or leave it.

I keep going. A few pages in and I'm pleased to see that I've got Tanya and James pretty well hooked. Carl, on the other hand, fidgets and keeps shifting around, clearly not taken with the story so far. I have to muffle a laugh when a description of him comes to mind. *Muggle*. But I continue reading out loud, my voice gaining in strength and confidence as I go. When I get to the point where Mr. Dursley is out driving and beginning to notice an abundance of people in cloaks, Eve slips into the library and eases herself to the floor by Tanya. Her green robe rustles ever so slightly as she sits. I pause and look at her, my head tilted.

"Go on," she instructs. "Please continue."

So I do. I'm not sure if she's there to monitor me or is here as a student. I pause, tempted to start over, but I don't want to interrupt the flow of the story. She'll just have to catch up.

I read for over an hour, until my voice is getting raspy and my throat is dry. I'm thinking of taking a water break when church bells start ringing. My students all look around and stand up, Eve included.

"That's it for now," she tells me. "Class is over."

I find a scrap of paper and mark our place in the book. I won't deface it by folding over a corner of the page. I hate it when people do that.

"Okay. So what's next?"

"Next? Your second class. They should be here any minute."

Another class? I stare at Eve's back as she leaves, the other three in her wake. Say what you will about Eve, she might not have much of a sense of humor or seem to enjoy herself, but she's a wizard of organization. In Harry Potter's world, she'd be the minister of something. Probably banking.

True to her word, in a few minutes four more students come in. This batch is younger than the first, but are more eager than Jim and Carl were. I'm feeling more comfortable in my role this time around, too, so I kick off the class the same way. Harry Potter and I are quickly becoming fast friends. Conversely, my dislike of the prissy Dursleys ratchets up with each reading.

I repeat this routine five more times, with a break for lunch. By the time afternoon is pushing toward evening, I finish up with my last group and get ready for dinner. My throat is raw from talking so much, and I realize I need to drink a lot more water if I'm going to keep this up day in and day out. But my physical discomfort pales next to my joy at this latest turn of events. This is the sort of thing I was born to do.

At dinner our original group sits together in a clump, still more comfortable together than with the others, except for Carly, who is chattering away with some children her age not far from us. She casts cautious glances our way, as if making sure we're still here. Singer looks exhausted. His shirt is soaked in sweat from a scorching day in the kitchen, and he can barely keep his eyes open long enough to eat. Annie is bubbling and so happy that at one point Hunter tells her to shut up. Hunter doesn't say much else besides that, but he doesn't look too unhappy, either. For him, that's a bonus.

But even with Hunter being a jerk, I can tell we're all so very happy to be here. I hope and pray that we can live here forever, at least until the inevitable happens.

When we're back upstairs Singer smiles and presents me with a toothbrush and small tube of toothpaste from our raid. I snatch them from his hands and clutch them to my chest, laughing. I thought we had lost them all running from that Gray! For the first time in a dozen months I go to sleep with smooth, clean teeth, and icy cool breath. The kiss I lay on Singer that night is long and hard, and feels so right. Singer doesn't notice, but Hunter is staring at us with narrowed eyes, and his face is red and flushed. But I'm not going to worry about him, even though I probably should.

CHAPTER
TWENTY

We spend the next several weeks settling into our routines and getting used to our new lives at Home. I'm amazed how fast this place is making the fantastic and wonderful seem almost commonplace and ordinary. Three meals a day, a safe place to sleep, a roof over our heads, and no threat of Grays. This is our new normal, and it's amazing. It's no exaggeration when I say that we couldn't ask for better.

My classes continue. I truly have no idea how to teach these kids to read, except for what little I remember from my early elementary school days. I recall my first grade teacher at Forestview Elementary, Mrs. Haberer, smiling and reading patiently out loud to us while we followed along with our own copies. But those were short and simple sentences, Dick and Jane stuff, not the complex material I'm sharing with these kids. And they don't have copies to follow along with, either. I don't know if I'm making any progress at all, except that they seem to be enjoying the story, which is a plus. Harry Potter throwing curses with his wand beats seeing Spot run, that's for sure.

I continue reading out loud, and eventually I hand the book to each student in turn. Some of them have no clue how to read and stare blankly at the pages, while a few of the older ones actually seem to recall lessons learned in the past. Tanya is one of my better students, and after a few weeks she gets to the point where, with some patient coaching and a lot of grit and determination, she can actually fight through a full sentence. She's so happy when she holds the book that she's almost vibrating in place. A girl after my own heart.

A few days later a whiteboard appears in the library, along with dry erase markers that defy all odds and still work. Now it's become a staple in the class, and I can't imagine teaching without it. By the end of each session, the whiteboards are overflowing with words and names in a rainbow of colors. So many of these kids are visual learners, and the whiteboard helps them to see the words as I parse them out. I'm shocked and more than a little pleased when I realize that I'm making progress and this might actually work.

But we're about to hit a milestone in all the classes: tomorrow we're set to finish the first Harry Potter book, assuming everything goes to plan. Everyone's excited, even some earlier holdouts like Carl. The adventures of young Mr. Potter and his friends have them hooked, and I couldn't be happier. I've got Book Two waiting in the wings and ready to go. I try not to rub my hands together like a mad scientist when I think about what's waiting for them in Harry Potter and the Chamber of Secrets, but I can't help myself.

There is one odd thing: Eve never misses a class. She won't attempt to read when I ask, so I'm not sure if she can't, or doesn't want to. She's been content to sit and listen, even during the rough patches when some of the really bad readers take a turn, stuttering and stumbling painfully over each syllable. On the plus side, she hasn't said anything else to me about us, or me and Singer; I don't handle those awkward situations well. Even after all these weeks, I don't get her. How's that saying go? She's a mystery wrapped in an enigma? Yeah, that's what she is.

I'm up as the first dim light fogs the dirty glass of the library window. Everyone around me is still snoring and stirring gently. Someone farts softly, and I wrinkle my nose and grin. We've been together so long now that something as benign as a fart doesn't even bother me. Unless of course it really smells, which it doesn't, thankfully.

I'm in full Scout mode, which means I'm so stealthy that I don't make a sound and could probably stroll out of Alcatraz if I wanted to. I step around the beds and carefully pluck Annie's cherished brush from the stand by her bed. My hair is still growing like a weed and is longer than it's been since before the Storm. It's all the way down to my shoulders and needs more tender loving care than I'm used to. I run her brush through it a few times, then slide on a rubber band and make a ponytail.

I'm fully dressed and ready to go when the dull, outside light is strong enough that others begin to stir. Hunter rolls over and groans as he puts too much weight on his shoulder. It's healing pretty well, and he only wears the sling later in the day when it gets sore, or if he's been moving around more than he should. He'll have a nice scar there at the entry and exit wounds, but he reminds us daily that chicks dig scars.

Singer sits up and stretches, his one blanket falling off and to the side. The several weeks of steady meals and decent rest have treated him well. He's filled out through the chest and shoulders, and doesn't have that scrawny look about him any longer. The muscles in his arms are well defined. There's a darker shadow on his chin and above his upper lip. He's a young man now, and I'm torn between something that I'm sure is good old-fashioned lust, and dread that he's this old already. I'm seriously okay with the whole lust thing, but I can't bear that this physical change means he's getting closer to the end already. I just want to crawl into bed with him and wrap my arms and legs around him and try to hold off the inevitable.

"Morning, Scout," he says with a smile that

makes my pulse jump off the charts.

I can't match that gorgeous smile of his, but I try. "Morning, Singer."

Everyone else is starting to move about. I realize I've still got Annie's brush in my hand, so I quickly dart back and set it on her nightstand. Singer grins at me, and I give him a tight, thin-lipped look of warning; he knows not to mess with her kids or her brush.

The last one to wake up is Carly. Everyone else is quietly taking care of their individual morning routines when she finally sits up in bed. Her black hair is completely covering her face. She blows at it half-heartedly, and when that doesn't work she fumbles it aside. Her eyes have that groggy, half-asleep puffiness about them, and she's not focusing on anything in particular. She doesn't really "do" mornings, I've found.

I take a few steps to her bedside, and gently move her hair all the way out of her face. Her bleary eyes slowly track up and lock onto mine. Not for the first time, I realize how much this little girl now means to me. Not more than a month ago I was convinced that having little ones like her around were a detriment to our survival. I saw them as little more than slowing us down, getting in the way, and consuming valuable supplies. They were an unnecessary drain, nothing more.

But now? Now I can't think of life in this place without them. In the big picture, if humanity has any hope of surviving, if we have a prayer of existing as a species, then we need all the Carlys and Tinys we can find. Honestly, why bother going through the motions if we can't ensure a better life for them? My parents probably felt the same way about Lord and me.

I continue to stare at her. She rubs sleep from her almond shaped eyes, and yawns for what has to be at least sixty seconds. It's all I can do not to hug her and hold her close, to try and protect and shield her from the outside world.

"Good morning," I tell her softly.

She blinks a few times. "Morning, Scout," she mumbles.

I ruffle her hair. "Up and at 'em. Another day on Church Island, okay?"

She smacks her lips together slowly, then nods. As I ruffle her hair once more, I hear footsteps outside the library, running footsteps that are coming closer. Jacob bursts into the room. He's out of breath and hanging onto the door jamb with one hand. His head jerks side to side until he spies Hunter.

"Damn, there you are," he almost shouts between gulps for breath. "Hurry! Come quick! We...we don't know what to do!"

Hunter's up and off his bed in the blink of an eye, all concerns surrounding his shoulder momentarily banished. I can see potential threats and hazards running through his mind. Are there enemies at the gate? Are we under attack? Did Grays somehow make it to the island? Jacob is in charge of security, and he's been working with Hunter for weeks now. Hunter is bigger, stronger, and older. I think Jacob admires and looks up to him, like a big brother. No wonder he came here seeking him out.

"What's going on?" Hunter yells.

"It's Eve!"

My heart falls into my stomach, and I involuntarily put a hand to my mouth. I take a step, reaching out to him. "What do you mean? What about Eve?"

He gulps again. "She's changing. She's going Gray!" He turns away and runs back the way he came. Hunter and I exchange quick glances. "Oh, shit," he says, and the two of us take off after him.

We follow Jacob down the steps and into the room with the fluorescents. They're on again, and the bright light makes me squint for a few moments until my eyes adjust. When I can finally see clearly, I spot Eve calmly sitting on the edge of the bed, still in her green robe and yellow sash. Her hands are clasped in her lap. She's not wearing a ponytail today and her long brown hair is fanned out around her shoulders. There's an inch wide strand of white hair on the left side of her head, starting at her part and flowing all the way down to the ends. The white strand is hanging over her shoulder and practically pulses in the strong light, to the point where I can't look away. It's mesmerizing. Martin, the young boy with the taped up glasses that helped out with Hunter's wound, is standing behind her with his eyes wide and his hands hanging limply at his sides. He looks as helpless as anyone I've ever seen. I know that feeling.

Eve looks up at us. "So you've heard already, I see. News travels fast."

I can't look away from the white streak. It's the slashing mark of a death sentence, and not because she did anything wrong. It's just because she aged. Nothing more. It's so damn unfair.

"Oh, Eve," I whisper. "I'm so sorry."

She reaches up and pinches the white streak, peering at it quizzically, as if it doesn't belong to her. After a few moments she lets it fall. I look up at Martin and he stares back at me with a helpless gaze, like any doctor through the ages delivering a terminal diagnosis to a patient. I know there's nothing he can do. There's nothing any of us can do.

"It's not like we didn't know it was going to happen," she says softly. "I just wasn't, you know, expecting it so soon, that's all. I'm not that old yet."

I hesitate, then sit down next to her. The bed creaks under our combined weight. There are no tears from her, no anger, just quiet resignation, which shouldn't surprise me, not from her. I put my arm around her and pull her towards me, and she leans her head on my shoulder. Hunter looks at the two of us and cocks his head to one side, puzzled at our closeness. I never told anyone how she feels about me, especially not Hunter. Let him wonder.

"What can I do?" I ask softly.

She doesn't move her head from my shoulder. When she finally talks her voice is soft, but unwavering, like she's got this all planned out. Which, knowing her as I already do, she probably does. "We've got procedures in place when this happens. After that, they'll take me down to the furnace room, and that's where I'll stay. Until the end, that is."

Singer comes in and stands behind me, a little out of breath, not saying anything. I'm glad he's here. He lays a reassuring hand on my shoulder. The room is deathly quiet, the only sound I can hear is Eve's breathing and the hum of the lights. After a few moments, Martin clears his throat to get our attention. The noise is louder than a slammed door in that small space.

"What do you want to do?" he asks Eve, his voice low. "Standard procedure, you said?"

Against me, Eve sighs. Then she sits up and smooths her robe and adjusts the yellow belt. Just like that she's all business again, like she flicked an internal switch and is back in "Eve mode." She's amazing that way.

"Yes, of course. Go get everything ready, please. Get whatever help you need."

Martin nods and starts to turn away, then stops. He looks back, but his gaze isn't on Eve this time, it's on me. He adjusts his taped up glasses and squints at me in the bright light. He reaches out a hand toward my head.

"May I?" he asks.

I hesitate, not sure what he's asking permission to do. But before I know it, I'm nodding for him to go ahead, even though my terror meter just spiked off the charts. I find that I'm not breathing. The buzzing of the fluorescents is loud in my head, a beehive located in a spot between my ears. He tenderly takes a lock of my hair in his hands. He runs it through his fingers and holds it up. I want to scream at him to let go, to stop it, to leave me alone! But I don't.

"Jacob, come here and check this out," he says. Jacob grimaces and looks like he'd rather be anywhere else, but after a moment's hesitation, he obeys.

"What do you think?" Martin asks.

He scrunches his face up, his blond eyebrows scrunching together. "I don't know. I've never seen anything like that before."

Eve is staring at me now. They're all staring at me now. Martin reaches behind him and picks something up. It's a mirror with a purple handle. My mom used to have one just like it on the counter in her bathroom. She'd use it to check out the back of her hair in the big mirror behind her. He gives it to me. I take it with a hand that feels detached, like it belongs to someone else and I'm just borrowing it. Fingers that aren't mine close around the cool plastic handle.

"What's going on?" I finally ask, my voice up an octave. I look at Hunter and see that his gaze is fixed on my head, not my face, and he's gone white as a sheet, his freckles a dark band against his pale skin. I can't believe it, but for once he's not being an ass or saying something snarky. That terrifies me even more, since it takes a lot to shut him up. Singer's hand is on my shoulder, and he's squeezing so hard it's starting to hurt. I slowly raise the mirror and look at my own ghostly reflection, and I suck in a great lungful of air, finally remembering to breathe. The humming noise in my head grows in volume until it's a buzz saw that blocks out all other sounds.

Oh my god, my hair is shot through with flecks of white, like I just ran through a cloud of talcum powder. No one could tell before because it was too dark in the other rooms, but under the fluorescents it's clearly visible. Like Jacob, I've never seen anything like this before, but we all know what it has to mean. It means two death sentences in one day – one for me, and another for Eve.

Oh my god, I'm going Gray.

The angry buzzing in my head abruptly stops, and the mirror slips from my grasp. The room goes dark, and I pass out.

CHAPTER
TWENTY-ONE

When I wake up, I'm still on the bed, but the bright lights are off and the room is lit with a few candles. I sit up and see that the only other people here with me are Singer and Martin. They're leaning against the wall and talking in soft voices. When they see me stir they hurry to my side.

"Are you okay?" Singer asks, his melodic voice thick with concern. His hand is on my shoulder again, steadying me. He's so close to me I can see tiny dark streaks in the brown irises of his worried eyes.

I nod, but I'm not so sure that I am. My head feels thick and stuffed with cotton. The room is blessedly quiet. The buzzing noise has stopped, thank God.

"What happened?" I ask, placing my fingers on my brow and massaging it.

Martin steps in front of me. "You passed out. You looked at yourself in the mirror, then you passed out. Do you remember why?"

I do. I saw my hair. We all saw my hair.

"Can I look in the mirror again? Please?"

Martin hesitates, and I think he's about to say no, but in the end he hands me the mirror. There's a crack running through the glass, which I'm guessing happened when I dropped it. My image is oddly distorted now, the cracked glass making my face look even narrower than before. One eye is higher than the other in my reflection. The light from the candles isn't very strong, but now that I'm looking for it I can see how shot through with white my hair is. Before the Storm, when men reached a certain age and their hair and beards started to go gray naturally, they called it "salt and pepper." That's how mine looks now, although to be honest it's more pepper than salt. I shakily hand the mirror back to him.

"So what does this mean?" I ask the two of them. I'm trying to keep it together. "Am I going Gray? I've never seen it happen this way before. It always starts out like...like Eve's."

Martin glances at Singer, and shrugs. "We don't know either. This is new to us, too. I've never seen anything like it. We've never seen anything like it."

I swing my feet down and stand up, Singer's hand sliding down to the small of my back. My head is clearer now and I'm starting to feel normal again. But the small room is making me feel claustrophobic and I want to get out of there. I head for the door.

"Take it easy, okay? I don't want you passing out again," Martin calls after me.

I ignore him and leave, Singer right at my side. I pass by the gym and see lots of activity going on in there: people arranging tables in neat rows, dishes being carefully placed just so, silverware being set up. I hurry past the door and find the stairs, Singer in my wake.

"Where's Eve?" I ask him, a little harsher than I mean to. "I need to talk to Eve."

"Scout, wait." He grabs my arm to slow me down, and turns me towards him.

"What?"

He looks furtively up and down the steps, making sure we're alone. He's one step below me, and for once we're looking at each other eye to eye. "I was talking to Martin back there. I found out what happens next. I know what the 'standard procedure' is they were talking about."

"Yes, I heard that too. What is it?"

"Remember when we first got here? Eve said that when someone goes Gray they don't let them go."

"Yeah, I do." I remember it vividly. I can almost see her statement floating in the air in front of me.

"And do you remember what Eve said they do when someone changes? They kill them, that's what. Scout, they're not going to let you take a hike like we do. They're going to kill you."

I close my eyes and inhale deeply. "I know. I heard her."

Singer keeps his voice low and takes both my shoulders in his hands. "They're going to have a party for you and Eve tonight, a going-away party or something like that, then they'll lock you in some room in the basement until you change all the way, then they'll kill you. They'll kill you, Scout!"

I look up the staircase, then back at him. There's moisture rimming the underside of his eyes, and I realize he's holding back tears. I put my hand on his cheek.

"I know," I repeat. "That's why I want to talk to Eve. Help me find her, okay?"

He hesitates, then wipes at his eyes with the back of his hand. Water glistens across his cheeks.

"Sure, okay," he finally says. "But why?"

I don't answer him, but continue up the stairs into the main room. As I walk in I see a few people standing around, and as a group they stop whatever they're doing and stare at me. A few of them whisper and point. None of them says anything to me or takes a step closer. I see some of my students but they don't look my way, either. That hurts. But like Eve said, news travels fast around here. Especially bad news.

"Has anyone seen Eve?" I ask loudly, trying to make eye contact with those who don't look away. "I need to talk to her." No one answers. "Please, I just want to talk to her."

I wait a few seconds, but no one volunteers any information. I don't wait around, but move quickly down the short flight of steps into the sanctuary. I spot a few more people, mostly guys, up on the scaffolding as they stand guard. Others are doing odd jobs here and there.

"Has anyone seen Eve?" I ask, loudly this time, my voice bouncing around the large room. Still nobody answers. Like the others, they stare and say nothing, or look away. This is getting extremely frustrating. Any composure I worked up earlier is slipping away.

I'm about to scream at them all when Jacob steps up behind me. He motions to the guards and they go back to staring out the windows, keeping watch for outside threats. Everyone else looks away and continues doing whatever they were before. Jacob's got his bow with him and a quiver of arrows across his back. He's no taller than I am, maybe an inch shorter.

"I want to talk to Eve," I demand. "Where is she?"

"She's getting ready for the going-away party," he says. I see his blue eyes slip across my face to my hair.

"Where? I just want to talk to her."

"She's busy, Scout."

Behind me I sense Singer stepping forward. He grabs Jacob by the arm and pulls him forward roughly. This isn't like him at all, but I appreciate his presence and support.

"Take us to her," he says through gritted teeth.

Around us we hear some noises. I look up and the guards have bows trained on us, the wicked looking arrows pointing directly at Singer. From here they can't miss. Jacob doesn't move for a moment, then motions with his free hand and the guards lower their weapons. Singer slowly releases his arm and steps back.

"She's getting ready for the going-away party," he repeats, rubbing his sore arm. "She asked not to be disturbed. But I get it." He thinks for a moment, then, "Follow me."

He turns and heads toward the main door of the sanctuary where we first came in weeks ago. There's another door back there that leads down a steep, narrow flight of stairs to the basement. We pass by the storage rooms and turn down a dark hallway I hadn't noticed before. At the end is a thick steel door with an imposing metal lever connected to weights via chains. He grunts and the chains rattle over pulleys as he lifts the lever, unlocking the door. He pulls hard and it groans open. We follow him inside, the thick door clanging shut behind us.

I immediately wrinkle my noise. Inside it smells like an old mechanic's garage, one where oil and gas and chemicals have been spilled and rarely cleaned up. But there's another smell there, an underlying odor of sweat, piss, and blood. And fear. Bad things have happened here. There are some stout steel brackets mounted to the far concrete wall. The only illumination is from a glass block window ten feet up, and it lets in a few tired, hazy beams of light that shine down at crazy angles and die before they strike the far wall. As my eyes get used to the darkness, I see two huge tanks off to my left. They're marked Boiler One and Boiler Two. This is the furnace room someone mentioned before. I don't like this place, not at all.

"Where's Eve?" I finally ask. My voice falls flat in here, and I realize the place must be larger than I thought. There's got to be quite a bit of space behind the two boilers.

Jacob is about to answer when we hear the door clank open, and Eve walks in. She's carrying an old paper shopping bag. She sees us waiting for her but doesn't slow down. The port stain on her face is almost invisible in the low light, but the streak in her hair burns like a white flame. I can already tell that it's wider and more prominent than it was just a few hours ago. Shit, she's changing fast.

She stares at me, ignoring the others. "Hi."

I take a step towards her. "We need to talk."

Eve looks away, down toward the floor. "I thought as much," she answers. Her voice is tired and flat, absent of the determination and purpose I'm accustomed to. She sets the bag down and starts to go through it. She withdraws a picture in a frame, a brown stuffed rabbit, and some other items. Carefully, she arranges them on the floor near the wall, under the metal brackets. The last thing she digs out is Harry

Potter and the Sorcerer's Stone. I remember then that we never had a chance to finish it, that we were set to do that today. That makes me sadder than I thought possible.

"Can we talk alone?" I ask again.

For a moment I don't think she heard me, but then she looks up. "Jacob, please wait outside. Take Singer with you."

Singer starts to object, but before he can, I assure him it's okay with a pat on his arm. With a frown that I can barely make out in the low light, he walks stiffly out after Jacob. I spot the pale outline of the harmonica in his back pocket as the heavy door slams shut behind them.

Once I'm sure we're alone, I turn to her.

"We've got to get out of here. You and me."

She shakes her head. "Impossible," she says, pinching her white hair between her fingers and twisting it. "If you hadn't noticed, I'm going Gray. And so are you. At least, we think you are."

"I know. That's why we've got to leave. Remember what I told you about my brother, how his change wasn't the same?" I grab a handful of my own hair and shake it at her. "If you haven't noticed, it's pretty clear my change isn't the same either. Something is going on, and I have a…a feeling that there may be a way to save both of us. But not if we're locked down here and left to die!"

She shakes her head again and her eyes hard-en. "No, that's not the way we do it. I told you, we don't let anyone go who's about to change. We're not letting more creatures out into the world. Remember the raid? We're not putting more killers out there." She thumps her chest with a fist, and for a moment the hard edge of her determination is clear to see again. "I won't permit it."

My frustration is bubbling up, and I want to grab and shake some sense into her. My voice jumps up an octave, but I don't care. "No, dammit! That's just giving up. This is your life, my life, we're talking about! Down here we're dead. Out there, we may have a chance. It's the only chance we've got."

"I'm sorry, there's nothing out there. For any of us. We're not leaving here. Ever."

I'm so pissed I could scream. What is wrong with her? Here I am giving her a way out, giving us a way out, and she won't even consider it. I take a step toward her with my hands out. I want to grab her shoulders, to yell at her, to do something to change her mind, when she calls out for Jacob, an edge to her voice. The door opens fast and he takes a determined step in, and then the weirdness happens again.

Time freezes. Nope, scratch that. It doesn't exactly stop, but it goes into that super slow motion just like before, back when we were in the boats and I could track the flight of the arrow as it hurtled towards us. Jacob is nearly frozen in place. The only motion I can detect is the velvety movement of his eyelids closing as he blinks. To me, in my timeline, it seems to take several seconds for that simple action to take place. I stare at him and frame him against other objects, and I can tell that he's still making his way into the room, but so slowly.

Sounds are weird again, too. The loud rattle of the chain as the door opens is gone, and in its place all I can hear is a slow, drawn-out clunk…clunk…clunk as each link tumbles ever so gently over the pulley. My dad had a pair of headphones he used to use when cutting the grass, and I tried them on once. They were big, bulky things, like something a DJ would wear. They were comically huge on my little head, and they made everything sound deep and far away, and cut out all the higher frequencies completely. That's what this is like.

My hands are still out in front of me. I will my right hand into a fist, and it obeys, but slowly and with some effort, like I'm squeezing a balloon filled with wet concrete. I try to take a step, and I may as well be pushing through a room full of Jell-O. I can move, but slowly.

What the hell is happening to me? Am I losing my mind?

Singer is behind Jacob, and he's looking right at me. Even in this near freeze-tag moment I can easily see the worry in his face at Eve's sudden call for Jacob. I wonder how I look to him.

And then, snap, just like that, the super slo-mo is

gone and everything reverts to regular speed. Sounds are normal again, the rattling of the chain over the pulley is back, and Jacob steps into the room, Singer's head visible over his shoulder.

"Yes?" he says to Eve.

"Show Scout out while I get ready. We'll have the going-away party in an hour. For both of us. Tell Harold."

Jacob nods, and tilts his blond head at me, motioning me toward the door. I take a cautious step, not sure what to expect, but my legs operate as nature intended and move me toward the door. He looks a little surprised that I'm going so easily and without a fight or argument, but with what just happened I'm still too stunned to resist. I look at Singer and try to read his expression, but I can't. Jacob leads the way and we head back toward the steps.

Singer takes my arm and slows down, letting our guide move ahead. He puts his mouth to my ear.

"What the hell was that?" he whispers. His grip is tight on my arm.

"What? What did you see?"

He glances ahead to make sure we can't be heard. "Back there. Something happened to you. You, I don't know, blurred for a second. You moved so fast I could barely see it."

I'm so relieved my knees almost buckle. So it's not just me? He saw it too!

"I don't know," I whisper back at him. "That's

the second time it's happened. I've been thinking a lot about it." We're almost to the base of the steps, and Jacob is waiting for us. "I think it has to do with Lord and something he did to me. I'll have to explain later. No time now."

"Yeah, you will. But for now I wouldn't say anything to anyone else. Not even to anyone in our group, okay?"

I nod, and in the dark I hope he can see that. But for the moment I'm so damn happy that he saw it, too. That means I'm not going crazy. At least, I hope not.

We silently climb the steps and enter the sanctuary again. A few curious faces peer our way, then go back to work when there's nothing to see. Jacob turns to us.

"You heard Eve. We'll have the party in an hour."

He goes back to whatever he was doing before, and Singer and I make our way to the library, where Annie and Carly are sitting on her bed. Somewhere Annie found a copy of *Oh, The Places You'll Go* by Dr. Seuss, and she's reading it to her. They pause and look up as we walk in. Carly rushes over to me and hugs me around the knees. I feel my eyes welling up and I press her tight against me.

"Oh, Scout, not you too!" she cries.

For the next hour we talk quietly while she sits on my lap. Annie doesn't say much, and seems more

concerned about my proximity to Carly than anything else. Maybe she thinks I'm going to suddenly
change and go nuclear or something? I don't know.
After all we've seen, I can understand why she's so
worried, I guess. I want to talk to Singer about what
he saw down in the furnace room, but we haven't had
a second alone yet.

When the hand bells ring, Jacob and some
others come and gather us up. Quietly, we follow them
down to the gym, Carly latched onto my hand the entire time. Her hand is tiny and she's only grasping a
few of my sweaty fingers. As we get closer the noise
level increases. I hear talking, laughing, and chairs
screeching as they move across the concrete floor.

I walk in with the others, and see that the
gym is filled with orderly rows of tables and chairs,
like something you'd see at a wedding or an awards
banquet. People are milling about, chatting, smiling,
and a few laughs bubble up here and there. It's certainly not a sad affair, that's for sure. Jacob is there.
He gently takes my elbow and ushers me to a table at
the head of the room. Eve is already there too, looking her usual proper self again. I glance around and
there are only the two chairs there, one for me, and
the other for her. Singer, Annie, and the others are directed to another table nearby. Eve pulls mine out and
motions for me to sit. Still a little numb with all that's
happened in the last few hours, I plop down. There's a

bottle of red wine on a table, and two glasses. She fills both of them.

"Drink," she orders softly. She nudges the glass towards me.

"Wine? I don't like wine." Well, I don't think I do, that is. I can't remember ever having any before. She spins the bottle around and points to the label. "It's really pretty good. It's soft red table wine, whatever that is."

I take my glass and cautiously sniff it, wrinkling my nose. I can smell the sugary sweetness of it. It's a very dark red color, almost black.

Eve stares at her glass. "When our parents set us up here, they must have forgotten about the wine. The church had a whole storeroom of the stuff. For communion, I guess. But really, it's pretty good. More like grape juice than anything else. Drink."

I take a sip. Hmm. She's right; it's not bad. But for someone used to drinking almost nothing but water for the last few years, it's so different I can't tell if I like it or not yet. It's warm as it slides down my throat, which is a pretty interesting sensation.

Eve smiles, but she has to work hard at it. Her lips are going through the motions, but the rest of her face shows as much life as a creepy American Girl doll. The white streak in her hair has grown to three or four inches wide already. If it weren't so terrifying, it might actually be pretty, like some Hollywood fashion statement. She holds her glass out to me. Her hand is shaking a little, but not enough to spill any of the wine.

"Cheers," she says, and clinks her glass into mine. She doesn't wait, but tosses down the entire thing in one huge gulp. She shivers a little bit. "Your turn. Drink up."

I take another sip, a little bigger one this time, but nothing close to what she did. The liquid slides down my throat, warming it all the way. Okay, I'm coming around. It's pretty tasty.

Eve fills hers up, and tops mine off. She clinks her glass into mine once more, and we both drink. After the warmth passes, I point out at the gym.

"What's going on? Why are we up here?"

"It's a going-away party. For both of us."

I shake my head at her, trying to keep my cool, even though I'm on the edge of losing it. It's all I can do not to jump up and scream at all of them. Instead, I turn to her. "That's pretty damn ironic, isn't it? I want us to go away, to get out of here, but you won't let me. But we're having a 'going-away' party? What the hell, Eve?"

She stares out at the room. "Yeah, I never really thought of it that way, I guess. But the party is not for us, Scout, it's for everyone else. It's closure, you know? We'll go down to the furnace room when this is over, and most of these people will never see us again. At least not the way we are now."

I lean toward her. "But that's insane! We need to go, to get off this island. I've told you before that something is going on here, that my change is different. And my brother. His change isn't like anything we've seen before, either. Look at me!" I grab a fistful of my hair. "Does this look the same to you?"

She reaches out and touches my cheek. The birthmark on her face has darkened a little, either from the wine or because of the change. "Scout, sweet Scout. I'm sorry, but this is the way it's done."

I lean back and cross my arms. "No, I won't accept that. And even if you won't do this for you or me, then what about the others? What about all the little kids here in this room? What about Carly? And Tiny? If we do nothing, we're condemning all of them to the same early death! That's completely against what you stand for!"

She doesn't say anything, at least not right away. She holds her glass up and stares at the dark liquid again, gently swirling it around. The gymnasium is almost full of people now, and everyone starts to find a place to sit. Some of the younger ones jostle with others to get a prime spot.

"Scout," she finally says, as the room starts to quiet down, "do you really think there's anything we can do? When the greatest minds on the planet couldn't stop people from changing? What hope do we have? Think about it. This is the way it is."

"What if I refuse? What then? What if I just get up and leave right now?"

She sighs and points around the room with her glass, and this time she does slosh a little. Droplets hit the table and stain the surface black. I follow where she's pointing, and with a grunt I see some of Jacob's guards scattered around the room, bows in hand. There are at least four of them that I can spot, and maybe others that I can't. I don't have to think too hard to figure out why they're there.

"They'll stop you. We're united in this, Scout. No one who's changing ever leaves." She touches my cheek again, her fingers lingering there. "I'm sorry."

I roughly brush her hand aside. I'm feeling trapped and anxious, close to bursting. "Yeah, I'm sorry, too."

Before I can do or say anything else, she stands and raises her arm. The sound in the gym drops to nothing in seconds and all heads swivel our way. The faces I see staring at us range in age from as young as Carly to nearly as old as me and Eve. Singer and the others are all at one table nearby, but I don't see Hunter. For a second I wonder where the hell he is, but I don't have the time or desire to consider it for long. He's probably on guard duty in the sanctuary or something. I find that I really don't give a damn.

"Thank you all for coming today," she begins, her voice clear and strong. The acoustics in here are terrible, but her words and her presence completely fill the space. The windows up high don't let in much light, but even in the dim glow her green robe and gold belt seem to radiate with an inner power all their own.

Everyone starts to clap, slowly at first, then louder, until the gym walls almost vibrate with the sound. Eve lets it go on for a few minutes, then holds her arm up again. The clapping stops as quickly as if they lived on electricity and the power had been cut.

"Tonight is the last time I will be with you. No, it's the last time both Scout and I will be with you," she amends, looking down at me with a grim smile. There are moans from the crowd, and I can hear a few soft cries. I see Carly, her face buried in Annie's shoulder. The expression on Singer's dark face is unreadable. "But this is not a time for tears. It's a time to celebrate! Our lives may be short, but here at Home we're safe, we're well-fed, and we're together. The world outside may be terrible, but we've been spared all that. Here, we are more than friends. We are family."

There's another round of applause, but it's more subdued this time around, more formal. A few people stand in her honor. She raises her arm a third time.

"Before we begin the celebration, you should know that I've already chosen my successor. Jacob?"

Jacob is leaning against the far wall. Upon hearing his name called, he stands up a little straighter. He doesn't seem at all surprised that he's been chosen, and maybe he knew beforehand. I've never figured out what sort of governing system is in place here, but whatever it is and however it works, Jacob is the new leader of Home. People applaud again. He holds up a hand and smiles.

"Jacob may be young, but he's wise and kind. He will serve you all well after I'm gone. Listen to him. Obey him." More clapping, along with heads nodding in approval. He seems to be a popular choice. I take another drink of my wine. A bigger one this time. It's really quite good.

"And now, let's celebrate. To Jacob!"

The back door to the kitchen bangs open and Harold and a few of his assistants enter, two huge sheet cakes held between them. One is dripping with vanilla frosting, the other with chocolate. They set them with a flourish on our table, a look of satisfaction suffusing their sweaty faces. The warm, sweet smell hits me in the face. Everyone jumps to their collective feet and rush toward us, eventually lining up in something bordering on orderly. I see my glass has been filled again. That was thoughtful.

Harold cuts the cake into squares and hands out pieces to each person, not bothering with plates or utensils. It's crumbly and messy, but no one cares. They laugh and gobble their allotment down, licking and sucking the frosting off their sticky fingers. In minutes it's all gone except for two small squares, one for me and one for Eve. Harold steps up and hands each of us a piece with a flourish.

"Here you go," he says solemnly, his voice so low I can barely make it out in the din of the gym. "I hope you like chocolate. It's all that's left."

"Where on earth did you get this?" I ask in open wonder. I feel a little silly that this small square of pastry has suddenly consumed my attention, but I can't help it.

He shrugs. "It's a mix from a box. Well, a dozen boxes, actually. Just add water and a few other odds and ends. We've got a very limited supply for special occasions like this. Trying to cook one over an open fire is a bitch, but we've learned a thing or two. These actually turned out pretty good. Enjoy."

I gratefully accept the small piece and take a bite. Oh. My. God. It's still warm, and the sugary chocolate frosting is gooey and gets all over my hands. I don't care. There's only enough for four bites, but it's without a doubt the most awesome thing I've ever put in my mouth. I may have moaned out loud. Next to me, Eve laughs at my overblown reaction. She holds my wine glass out to me.

"Drink up," she commands.

We both toss back our glasses, and while I'm greedily sucking my fingers clean she tops my glass off again. Then she opens another bottle and fills hers. She splashes some on the table but something this trivial doesn't bother her any longer. We both notice that we've got frosting smeared on our faces, and we begin to giggle at each other, that infectious laughter that feeds off of itself and doesn't let you stop.

"Damn, that was good," I whisper.

"The wine or the cake?"

"Yes," I answer, deadpan, and we start to laugh again.

I swear, I don't know how she does it, but each time my glass is even a little bit empty, it's magically full again. She's some kind of wine wizard, like Gandalf the Grape or something. My head starts buzzing in the weirdest way, and I keep laughing at the dumbest things, including a vision of Gandalf with purple robes and a bright purple beard. And all the while people keep coming up to us and saying nice things, giving us hugs, and before I know it I'm hugging everyone back, whether I know them or not. My mood must be infectious, because now even Carly is laughing and smiling with me. The only person in the entire room not joining in is Singer. He's staring at me with his huge brown eyes, concern etched into his dark skin, his forehead pulled low.

I throw back another glass. "Singer! Play some music for us!"

But he won't, and I can't help but feel my good mood has been dented. I cajole and wheedle, but he won't break out his harmonica. I make a clumsy grab at his back pocket, and grab his ass instead as he spins away.

"Woo-hoo, nice butt, Singer!" I shout happily,

giving him an overblown wink, which I find extremely humorous. He looks down, and pushes through the crowd and disappears, which I also find way too funny. "Don't go away mad, Singer!"

"Yeah, just go away!" Eve shouts at his receding form, squealing with laughter.

We fall into each other, and once again I find my wine glass is full. Hey, how did that happen? But now I view a full glass as a challenge, and chug it, slopping a good third of it down my front where it stains my shirt.

I'm not sure how much time passes after that. At one point I'm spinning around and laughing with Carly while Annie watches from a short distance away, ever vigilant. Then I'm dancing with Eve, who is so close to me I can't move without bumping into her. She doesn't seem to mind, so neither do I. It's all so much fun, even though I'm having a harder and harder time staying upright and my vision is going wonky. Then I trip and fall over in a messy heap. With some effort and grunting, Jacob and Eve help me up, but my two legs have become as limp as well-cooked noodles and I can't stand under my own power. I slump down in a chair, where I slouch so low I'm mildly concerned that I might slip right onto the floor in a tangle of arms and legs. I take another sip of wine, and close my eyes, and that's the last thing I remember of the day.

CHAPTER
TWENTY-TWO

How many times do you have to have a dream before it's considered "recurring?" I used to have this one way back when I was in school, usually before a big test. I'm in my classroom, parked in my seat right behind my friend Teddy. The bell rings and everyone gets up and files out. I follow them into the hall, then remember the upcoming test. I turn to head back into the room, but the door is gone, and no matter how hard I search I can't find it. In fact, I can't remember even studying for the test. I start panicking, because I already have a C minus (more like a C minus minus, if I'm being honest), and if I bomb it I'm going to fail the class. In the dream, I'm furious with myself for paying so little attention that I can't even dredge up a single formula. Each time when I finally woke up and realized it was just my subconscious screwing with me, the relief was almost overwhelming.

So now I'm in the same basic dream, and everything is nearly identical, except this time we're all older. Okay, so it's not exactly the same, because Singer is sitting where Teddy was. But I'm so worried about the test (what test?) that I'm not talking to anyone. I'm fidgeting with my backpack, shooting worried looks at the clock, tapping my fingers on the desk. When the bell rings I jump in my seat, startled, before we dutifully march out of the classroom. Kids are bumping into me in the crowded hall and their mass is carrying me along. I have no idea where I'm supposed to go, or what I'm supposed to do. I'm getting more confused and concerned by the second, when a hand settles on my shoulder. I turn, and see Lord standing there. He hasn't gone Gray at all. I'm so happy I could reach up and hug him, but his stern, cool expression glues my arms to my sides.

I try to speak, but nothing comes out. That's weird. Why can't I talk?

Lord doesn't say anything either. I don't know if he can't, or he won't. But he points over my shoulder. I look behind me and see a red door at the far end of the hallway that wasn't there before. I turn back to him, but he's gone, and the hallway is empty. I'm alone. I spin around, terrified for some reason. I drop my backpack and books fall out of it. Dozens of them, then thousands, fanning out on the floor like decks of cards. The floor is suddenly tilted, but all the lockers around me are still straight up and down. The red door is beckoning me toward it, and I walk to it, slipping and sliding over the thousands of books. Just as I touch the old doorknob, I wake up.

I'm lying in the dark. No, it's not completely dark, but that early morning grayish dawn we've all come to know. There's an arm draped over my back, and someone's head is nuzzled in the crook of my elbow. Singer? It's very comfortable, or would be if my head would stop throbbing and my tongue wasn't as dry as an Arizona sidewalk. Ugh. This must be what a hangover feels like. I try to generate some moisture in my mouth, and wonder why, if this is how you feel after drinking, why anyone in their right mind would do it over and over?

I force myself into a sitting position, and quickly determine that I'm not in my bed. I'm on a mat, and this room smells of fuel oil and grease. I bolt upright.

Oh, no! I'm in the damn furnace room! I twist around, and hear a muffled thud. Whoever was snuggling with me just hit their head on the floor when I pulled away.

"Ow!" Eve exclaims, rubbing her ear.

So it wasn't Singer at all. Eve's hair is in her face and even in this low light she looks like hell. Her skin is pale, and she's steadying herself like she's about to throw up. The white streak is no longer a streak, but has taken over nearly half the hair on her head. With a shaky hand she pushes it back and stares at me with narrowed eyes.

"That hurt. Why'd you do that?"

But I'm not concerned about Eve right now. I

try to stand and feel a weight around my waist, holding me back. Looking down, I see that a thick chain is locked around my midsection, tightly secured there with a heavy padlock. The chain is about ten feet long and affixed to one of the steel anchors that I noticed during my first visit there. Barely holding back a deep, feral panic, I tug and pull at the chain. It's secured to the foundation of the church, and isn't going anywhere. I spin to Eve.

"What the hell is going on here?" I scream, my voice bouncing around the unyielding surfaces of the room. I'm breathing hard and the pounding in my head is enough to turn my stomach.

Eve calmly sits against the wall and leans her head back. She starts to talk, then her eyes fly open and her gaze darts this way and that. She spies a bucket a few feet away, grabs it, and vomits noisily into it, her own chain rattling as she shudders. In any kind of normal circumstances, I would do the honorable thing and hold her hair back. These are not normal circumstances.

After the retching has stopped and her gut is empty, she sits back down hard and wipes spittle from her mouth. Now the room reeks of hot vomit and sweat, which is not an improvement. Dim light from the thin band of windows up high slants in at crazy angles against the far wall. I'm not claustrophobic, but it feels like the walls and ceiling are bulging in towards me.

"Sorry," she mutters, wrinkling her nose and pushing the bucket away. "Not sure how much wine I had, but it was a lot."

"Screw the wine!" I tug at the chain again. "What the hell is going on?"

She shakes her head, eyes still closed and a hand up near her mouth. I can tell she's trying not to puke again. "Dear, dear Scout. This is where we end up. I told you that. When we start to change we're locked down here until...well, until the end. The chains are so that we can have some freedom of movement, but not threaten anyone that enters the room. We still need to be fed and cared for, you know. We're not animals. We'll be treated with kindness and respect until the end."

My hands fly to the side of my head. "How can you be so calm about this?" I scream. "They're leaving us down here to die. Don't you get that?"

"I know. Believe me, I know. But when the end comes we'll be so far gone that we won't even notice. It's better this way."

Something inside of me snaps. I don't know what it is, but all my anger and frustration just starts spewing out of me. I take three purposeful steps and grab a handful of her green robe in each hand, and lift, picking her up off the ground. Her feet dangle and kick at empty air. I shake her and slam her into the wall.

"I am not dying down here!"

Eve grabs and slaps at my arms. "See what's happening?" she manages to force out, her voice pinched. My hands are up and shoved into her neck, and she's having trouble breathing. "Just look at you. Look how strong you are! You're already changing! You're going Gray!"

I hold her effortlessly above me as her words slowly chisel through the wall of my rage. She's right. I am changing. I've known it for a while now, I guess, ever since I smashed in the trunk of that car at Dog's funeral. Or when I rowed so long, so effortlessly, without getting tired. Or how fast I healed from Lord's bite. Or when I slammed that warehouse door shut. Or that my hangover seems to have vanished already. Now I'm holding Eve in the air as easily as I would pick up Carly. This sort of thing is not normal. Normal people can't do this.

I abruptly let go of her, and she tumbles to the floor, gasping for air.

"Don't you think I know that?" I shout at her. "Don't you think I haven't figured this out already? Yes, I'm changing. But it's different. Deep inside I'm still me. By now anyone else would have no more intelligence than a damn border collie, you know? That's what I've been telling you. And that's why I need to get out of here, so I can figure out what's happening and maybe do something about it! For me. For you. For everyone!"

Eve sighs. She reaches up for my hand but I smack it away. My rebuke doesn't faze her.

"I'm sorry, Scout. That doesn't change anything. You're down here now, and there's nothing we can do. Jacob and the others will never let either of us go. It's our way. You need to accept that."

Just then the door handle turns, the chains rattle, and Jacob and two of his fellow guards enter. One of them has a five-foot long wooden rod with a gold cross on the end, just like the one our minister used to carry down the aisle at church on Sundays. They've got bowls in their hands. Jacob is armed with his bow, but it's slung over his shoulder. They take a few steps in and stop. He looks at Eve, his head tilted. His eyes brim with sadness.

"Good morning. How are you doing?" he says slowly and carefully.

Eve smiles at him. "Good morning, Jacob. I'm fine, thank you. I'm still 'me', too, in case you were wondering."

He perks up a little. "Oh, good. Would you like something to eat? To drink?"

Eve starts to say something, but I move quickly toward him. When I'm a few feet away I'm stopped short, the chain jerking me back at the waist.

"What I would like is to get the hell out of here!"

This is not their first rodeo, and they know exactly how far away they need to stay in order to keep out of reach. I'm surprised they don't have a painted demarcation line on the floor or something. Even so, he takes an involuntary step back, bumping into one of his men.

"Yeah, that's not going to happen. Sorry." He turns back to Eve. "I've brought both of you something to eat and drink. I'll leave it here." He sets the bowls down, and the one with the stick pushes them toward us. Two of the bowls are filled with oatmeal, and the other two contain water.

"Can I get you anything else?" he asks kindly.

"Keep your eye on Singer. I wouldn't put it past him to try something. Like break her out."

"One step ahead of you," he tells her proudly. "We've each got two men watching him at all times. He won't be interfering."

"Good. And bring Hunter here, too."

He nods. "Hunter? No problem. He's out patrolling the perimeter so it could be a little while. Anything I need to know?"

"Just get him. I'll explain then."

When I hear Hunter's name, my ears prick up. "What do you want with him?"

Eve ignores me, and the two of them talk for a few more minutes, the guards hanging back. I'm too pissed to listen, so I growl and turn away. Eventually the three of them leave. At the last moment I turn and look, and I see another guy positioned outside. He and Jacob are talking, then the door clanks shut and both of them are lost to view. My heart sinks; the room is guarded, and so is Singer. Even if he is planning on trying something, there's no way he'd be able to overcome so many of them. I'm trapped and anxious and I don't know what to do.

I hear a rustling sound. Eve has gotten Harry Potter and the Sorcerer's Stone out and is holding it in my direction.

"Can you please read this to me? I'd really like to find out what happens, before...you know..."

I cross my arms and stare down at her. My immediate reaction is to say no, to punish her like she's punishing me. "Really? I'm not in the mood, as you can imagine. Read it yourself."

The book doesn't drop. "Please, Scout."

I feel my face go all hard and bitchy. "I said no. Read the damn thing yourself if you want to figure out what happens. That ending's a hell of a lot better than this one."

Now she lets the book fall, along with her eyes. Her hair tumbles across her face, the bright white a sharp contrast against her cheek. In the low light her robe has been washed of color and appears almost black. She nervously traces her finger along the words on the cover. When she finally speaks, her voice is low, low enough that I have to turn an ear toward her to catch what she's saying.

"I can't read. I was never able to. The words... the words always looked smashed together, with no spaces. The doctors called it attentional dyslexia. I can read single words by themselves, but I can't figure them out if they're in a sentence." She hides most of the writing on the cover with her hands, except a single word. "Harry," she says slowly. Then she covers up the rest, exposing another. "Potter. See? I can read them one at a time, but not all together. Please, Scout," she implores. "Read it to me? I want to find out what happens, while it still makes sense to me."

Seeing her there like that, this proud young woman, this leader, begging me to help her, is more than I can take. I've said and thought so many times about how nasty and evil the world has become. I've railed and complained about it since the Storm began, and now I've got a chance to do something positive, and I won't take it? My hypocrisy slaps me hard, and I feel most of the bitchiness slide off my face. I shake my head and exhale noisily. Home's rules may be her doing, but what's happening in the rest of this lousy world isn't. I have an opportunity to do the right thing, and I realize that I can't screw that up. I kick my chain out of the way and plop down next to her. I hold out my hand, and she gives me the book with a bashful grin.

"Thanks," she says.

Despite myself, I smile at her, warmed by her honest expression. "You're welcome. Now, where were we?"

She points to the bookmarked page, and that's

where I pick up. While I read, Eve sits back and closes her eyes. To me she looks infinitely tired, as if we're pulling an all-nighter and it's four in the morning. Several times she lifts the bowl to drink some water, but she ignores the now-cool oatmeal. I urge her to eat, but she gently refuses, insisting that she's not hungry. Each time I look up from the book, I can see that the white has consumed more of her brown hair. The speed is glacial, the movement of a clock's minute hand, but it's there, and my heart continues to fall. Seeing someone you care about slide away like this in just a matter of a few days is the part that kills me. It's all so horribly unfair.

When I finish the last sentence several hours later, she opens her eyes, blinking a few times. I'm not sure she was even awake for the last chapter or two.

"Oh, yes, I heard everything," she claims when I ask. "I was just resting. I'm so tired for some reason. Thanks for finishing it for me. It was such a good story. Those poor kids went through so much, you know?"

We talk about the book a little more, until I notice she's dropped off to sleep. She's curled up on her mat like a kindergartener at naptime. I don't know what time it is, but I guess that it's early afternoon. The light coming in through the grimy windows is faint, but it's moved a good halfway across the room since this morning. I drink some water, then dip a finger into the oatmeal and take a taste. The cold paste sticks to my mouth, but I manage to gag some down. I lean back against the wall, and think. It's the first time I've effectively been alone for days, and I welcome the solitude.

Eve is going Gray fast, that's clear. But what about me? Mentally I feel the same as I always have. Although, ironically, I suppose someone who's losing their mental faculties may not recognize that at all simply because they're losing them. But I'm not having any trouble thinking, or remembering, or imagining what could be, so I'd have to say I'm okay. My physical attributes, however, are another matter.

I've got the whole slow motion thing going on, whatever the hell that is. And when I'm in that slo-mo zone, I can think and move faster than any human has a right to. Talk about an advantage in a fight. I wouldn't be able to dodge a bullet or anything, but I bet I can dance clear of an arrow. You know, like a… like a fast Gray.

Oh, shit. Yeah, like a fast Gray. And I'm way stronger than I should be. And I haven't even considered how fast I heal now. Yeah, again, like a fast Gray. Shit.

But what does this all mean? What am I, some sort of hybrid? Do I have a weird partial immunity? I've concluded that Lord's bite passed something on to me, but if that's the case then why is his change so different than mine? I wish I knew. But looking at Eve and how quickly she's going downhill, I feel both relieved and horribly ashamed that it's her and not me.

I don't know what I'd do if I were fading as fast as she is. It terrifies me.

Sometime later, Eve is still asleep and I'm still considering my current and future state, when I hear some muffled sounds outside the furnace room. I sit up straighter as the door clanks open and Hunter walks in, trailed by Jacob and his pair of guards from earlier. Hunter looks down at me and I swear the son of a bitch smirks when he has a second to take everything in: the chain around my waist, the puke bucket, and the cold, gray walls of the furnace room. Jacob steps forward and sees that Eve's asleep. He shuffles his feet a few times, then clears his throat softly at first, then coughs. Eve stirs and opens her eyes. She's got that bleary, deep-sleep look about her.

"Um, yes?"

"You wanted to see Hunter," Jacob tells her.

She sits up and rubs her eyes. At first I think she's going to drift off again, but she shakes herself and sits up straighter. She brushes the white hair from her face and tucks it behind her ear.

"Of course. Thanks, Jacob." She nods to the guards and they push Hunter forward a few steps. He's confused and a little pissed off at being manhandled, his eyes flashing, but for once he doesn't say anything. Being bossed around by a woman really eats at him. For the life of me, I can't figure out what she's up to.

"I know I passed my authority away yesterday," she begins, "but with Jacob's permission I'd like to issue one final order. Jacob?"

Jacob tilts his head, then looks at the two guards and shrugs. "Sure. Go ahead."

"Thank you." She turns to Hunter. "Hunter, I'm officially banning you from Home, effective immediately. Jacob, give him supplies for a few days, a boat, and his gun. If he ever sets foot on the island again, he's to be shot on sight. And not just in the shoulder. Am I clear?"

The order may have caught the two guards by surprise, but they quickly grab Hunter's arms before he can make a move. It takes Jacob a few heartbeats, but he nods at Eve to acknowledge her orders. I look back and forth between Eve and Hunter, shocked as hell. What is going on here?

The realization of his fate quickly sinks in to Hunter. His face darkens and he takes a menacing step toward Eve, but the guards are ready for that and plant their feet, holding him back. Jacob has his hands up, ready to jump in and help if needed.

"You bitch!" Hunter screams at her. "You can't do this to me!"

Eve doesn't bother answering him, but motions them all away with a simple flip of her hand. The guards tug and move toward the heavy door, Hunter still struggling between them. It's all they can do to hold him back. High-octane anger fuels his strength.

"Eve?" I start, but she holds up a hand and cuts me off. Her eyes drift shut and she leans back against the wall, exhausted. Even this short interchange has worn her out.

"Scout, help me!" Hunter yells, his hands reaching for me. There's no smirk on his face now. "Don't let them do this. I'll die out there by myself!"

"Eve, I don't understand. Why are you doing this?" I despise him, I really do. But the asshole is part of our group, and despite what he did to me I'm having a hell of a time letting them just toss him out into the wild. Hell, Lord thought enough of him to put in charge. That should count for something, shouldn't it? Of course, Lord didn't know what he was really like, and what he might do. To me. And maybe to others.

She doesn't open her eyes. "No, Scout. Don't defend him."

The door is open and they're dragging him away. He's grabbed onto the doorframe and is holding on like he'll tumble a thousand feet to his death if he lets go. The third guard in the hallway has jumped into the fray and has Hunter in a headlock. He's swearing up a storm and is swinging and kicking, trying to make contact with whomever he can. I don't make a move toward him.

"Help me, Scout, dammit!" he's screaming from the hallway.

Eve stirs again. "He knows what he did. Have you noticed that he hasn't even asked why I'm kicking his ass out?"

They've dragged him out of the furnace room.

He's still struggling like mad, cursing and shouting. Just before the door closes, he makes eye contact with me one final time, only now the bravado and anger are vanished and replaced by what can only be terror. He sags in their arms and I'm pretty sure he's starting to cry. He's suddenly a little boy, vulnerable and terrified. I can't help it, I still despise him.

"Help me!" he pleads. "Don't let them do this!"

Eve pats my leg tenderly. "By the way, dear Scout, did you know you're chatty when you're drunk?"

I feel the color drain from my face. What did I tell her?

"You and I had a nice little talk last night when we got down here," she continues. "I know all about what he did to you before you got here. Trust me, he'll never hurt you again. And he sure as hell won't hurt anyone here."

My gaze whips back to Hunter. Eve has spoken, and there's nothing I can do for him now, not that I want to. He senses this and something snaps inside him. His back arches and it's everything the three guards can do to hold him. They're all screaming and yelling at each other, but Hunter's belligerent roar cuts through their shouts with knife-edged clarity.

"You're dead, both of you. I'll get you, bitches, I swear! You're all dead!"

Then mercifully the heavy door slams shut,

and his furious rant is chopped off in mid-curse. I can hear some indistinct shouts for a little longer, until the only sound left in the room is my rapid breathing.

TWENTY-THREE

Eve is asleep. I'm on the floor next to her with her head in my lap. I'm stroking her white hair. Hunter's been gone awhile now, long enough that the light through the window is nearly gone. It must be late afternoon at least. Maybe later.

I'm thinking about Hunter, even though I don't want to. I can't get that final little boy image out of my mind. As talented as he is, I don't think he'll be able to survive for long by himself. He's too rash and brash, and without others to temper him I'm sure he'll do something stupid and get himself killed. I should be worrying about myself, I know, but I'm having a hard time doing that right now. I've thought horrible thoughts about him since that day, but I'm having a hard time coming to grips with his sentence.

I'm still stroking Eve's hair when I hear some noise from outside. The door opens and in come two other guards, with Singer tucked between them. The two are some of the older and bigger guys who report to Jacob, and are at least as tall and a lot bigger than

Singer. The larger of the two is named Dustin, I think. He's not very bright as I recall. For a kid his age he's got really broad shoulders and a thick neck. His little piggy eyes set deep into his face don't blink much as he stares at me. I don't recognize the other one, but he's almost as large as Dustin. Jacob is taking no chances with Singer, that's clear.

"Hey there, Scout. You okay?" he says softly. He's carrying a tray of food.

"Oh, Singer, I'm so happy to see you," I tell him, doing my best to stay strong and not break down. On the tray is a bowl of steaming au gratin potatoes and sliced peaches. The heavenly aroma gratefully masks the foul stink in the room.

"Damn, it's good to see you, too."

"How is everyone? How are the kids?" I ask, feeling my stomach rumble. I realize then just how famished I am. In fact, I'm so hungry I'm almost shaking.

He takes a step forward, but Dustin grabs him with a big meaty hand.

"That's close enough," he says. "Just put it down there and step back."

Singer tenses for a second, then shrugs and follows orders. "Sure thing, Dusty."

Dustin's little eyes squint almost to the point of closing. "Not 'Dusty,'" he corrects him. "My name is Dustin. Dusty is a kid's name. Get it right."

Singer shrugs again. "Sure thing, Dusty."

I laugh, not able to help myself. Singer ignores Dustin's growl and sets the tray on the floor. Dustin uses the pole with the cross on it to roughly push the tray toward me, but the peaches slop around and some of their juice splashes in my potatoes. He chuckles, and now I'm not laughing anymore. Jerk.

I dig into the food like it's my full-time job. Of course there aren't any utensils so I have to use my hands, but it's not the first time. Singer and his guards watch in silence as I stuff my face. I scoop up every last bit, and even drink the remaining peach juice. When there's not a crumb left I stare with longing at the empty bowls and wish there were more. I can't understand why I'm so famished.

"How's everyone else doing?" I repeat, wiping my hands on my clothes. I take a big drink of water and then use what's left to clean myself up. I've gotten used to being clean and tidy these last few weeks, and I like it more than I care to admit. It's amazing what becomes normal after such a short time.

Singer motions behind him with his head. "Annie is with the little kids and Tiny, and Carly's running around playing. They'll be down later, when Annie's got a break." His face clouds. "What the hell happened to Hunter? Do you know? No one is saying anything. They took him outside and put him in a boat and kept guns on him until he rowed out of sight. He's gone."

I turn away, unable to look directly at him. I

want to tell him, I really do, but for some reason I'm still embarrassed at what he did to me. Plus, Dustin's staring at me like a piece of meat, and sharing this in front of him is the last thing I want to do.

"Um, yeah, but can we talk about it later?"

Singer kindly doesn't bring up the fact that "later" may never happen. He sees me glance at Dustin and I can see he understands that for some reason I'm reluctant to talk in front of anyone else. "Sure. No problem. Whatever you want."

"Thanks."

He nods at Eve. "How's she doing?"

I shake my head and touch her hair. "I don't know. She's so tired she can't stay awake. She's been asleep for a long time now." My voice drops. "She's changing really fast."

"And you?"

I don't stop running my fingers through her hair. "I'm okay, I guess. I mean, I feel pretty much the same as before."

"Hmm. You know, we never had a chance to talk about what happened down here before. Remember? We were supposed to talk about that."

That's right. Singer saw me in slo-mo when we were down here yesterday, but we haven't been alone since then. The problem is, we're not alone now either. My gaze drifts towards the two guards again.

"Can we table that, too? I'm not sure I can explain it anyway."

He understands again, although from the look on his face he really wants to know what's going on with me. I don't blame him; I want to know what's going on with me, too.

"Sure. No problem." He points to the ground next to me. "Hey, is that Harry Potter? Can I see it?"

I'm not sure why he's suddenly interested in my book, but I slide the hardback over to him with my toe. He picks it up and starts thumbing through the pages, leafing backwards and forwards through the story, not reading any of it. He hefts it in his hands.

"Damn thing's pretty heavy," he says to himself. Then he proceeds to fill me up with random small talk, which I don't get at all. He starts with the weather (it's cloudy and raining, what a shocker), what they had for breakfast (oatmeal and pancakes), followed by how they're planning another raid into town in a few weeks (he's already volunteered). Singer's never been the chatty type, but this is getting ridiculous. I want to ask him what's going on, but each time I try to slide in a word he launches into another topic and shuts me down. Behind him, Dustin and the other two guards have decided we're way too boring, and are leaning against the door, mumbling to each other. Singer's still holding onto my book.

I look sideways up at him to give him a "what the hell are you doing?" expression, and our eyes meet. His face goes flat and cold, and I find myself sitting up straight, the hair on the back of my neck going porcupine stiff. Think of a sprinter's expression as he waits for the starter's gun, or the face of a gymnast as she's about to begin her floor routine. I've never seen this expression on him before. I notice that his knuckles are white as he grips the book tightly. In contrast to that, when he speaks again his voice is still casual and light.

"Hey, remember when we were in the boats, after the Motel 6, and the can of bullets was there? You were afraid your little fire would set them off. Remember?"

Yes, I do. Singer was watching when Lord told me not to worry, that it would take a lot more heat than that to light them up. I don't say anything, but I nod slowly, trying not to look as confused as I feel and follow along.

"Yep, it was rough out there," he says, his voice conversational and sincere. "Sometimes I wish we were still there, though, you know? At least we knew where we stood. Sometimes it's better just to keep running."

Given my current predicament, I'm inclined to agree with him, when there are two loud explosions close by, not far from the furnace room. Boom! Boom! They're loud enough to make me jerk and jump to my feet.

Dustin isn't bored any longer. "That's gunfire!" he yells. He stabs a finger at my original guard. "Matt, stay here and watch these two. Sam and I will check it out."

The two of them swing open the heavy door, and I see more people running toward the kitchen as they take off. Before the door can close, there are several more huge booms. There's more shouting and confused yells, and I catch the faint, acrid odor of gunpowder. My original guard, Matt, is suddenly very nervous, glancing this way and that, dancing on the balls of his feet. It hits me then that he's just a kid, younger than me by many dozens of months. There's not a hint of a beard or whisker on his round face.

Then there's another boom, and Matt jerks toward the door. At the same moment, Singer sets his feet and swings the book with both hands, a big, arcing swing that he puts his back and shoulders into, like a hammer thrower. The heavy book smashes into the side of Matt's head with a deep thud. I wince as he leaves his feet and his head crashes into the wall. He slides down, toppling onto his side when he's halfway to the floor. There's a red mark on his forehead where Singer smacked him, and a nasty gash where he hit the wall.

In less than a second, Singer's straddling him with the book held high, ready in case the guy comes to and is ready to fight, but the kid is out cold. Singer flips the book to me and starts searching through the guard's pockets.

"My God, Singer, what the hell's going on!"

He's too busy searching the guard to answer.

After he's gone through all of his pockets twice, he stands up. His hands are shaking.

"Where are the keys?" he says, his gaze shooting to all corners of the room.

"Keys? What keys?"

"To your belt lock thing. The keys! We don't have much time before the others are back. Where are they?"

"Hell, I don't know!" I tug at the chain. "I woke up and it was already on me. I never saw who did it."

Singer redoubles his search efforts, but I'm not hopeful, not if he hasn't found them already. I mean, the unconscious guard doesn't have that many pockets. There are two more booms, loud and close enough to make me flinch again. While Singer's search escalates to the next panicked level, I grasp the chain in both hands, and eyeball it down to where it's joined to the steel bracket. The bracket is a steel plate mounted to the wall with four large bolts, very strong and imposing. The chain itself is beefy enough to lift a truck. A really big truck.

But I block out Singer's increasingly frantic searching and all the muted noises coming from beyond the heavy door, and I think back. I remember punching the trunk of that car and the massive dent I put in it. I remember seeing that Gray rip the door right off the SUV. I remember picking Eve up like a doll. I remember, and I wonder.

I wrap the links around my hands and I tug, long and hard. The chain goes as taut as a guitar string, so tight I feel it humming and singing in my grip. I strain for a good ten seconds with no result. Then I place my foot against the wall, take a deep breath, and pull again, straining and groaning. The chain is biting into my hands, each link digging deep into my flesh. I'm pulling so hard I'm afraid something in my own body will snap. Bones in my hands. Tendons or muscles in my arms. My back. And still I pull. I am not going to die down here!

But. Nothing. Is. Happening!

And then I'm flying backwards. I land hard on my ass and do a backwards roll, ending up in a tangled mess near the door. I stare in shocked amazement at the chain in my hands. It's still in one piece and locked around my waist, but I yanked the bracket right out of the wall. Chunks of rock and gravel are strewn on the floor. There's a softball-sized piece of concrete still clinging to the bracket. Singer is staring at me in stunned silence.

"Okay, I guess that'll work," he finally says, brushing some dust and grit from his face.

"Yeah, I guess," I reply, panting a little. "No questions now, okay? Let's just get out of here and I'll explain later."

"Later, along with everything else, right?" he replies, looking sideways at me, eyebrows raised. As we turn towards the door, I hear a noise.

"No! You can't leave me!" Eve screams, launching herself at Singer. Damn, I forgot about her. I start to warn him, to shout something, but before I can do anything I feel it coming, I recognize the sensation now. It's a gentle tingle in the back of my head, no more than a feather brushing against my neck, and I go into slo-mo again.

Eve is caught in a freeze-frame. Her mangled expression is not like anything I've ever seen on a human face before, at least not one that hasn't already gone Gray. Her inherent and exterior beauty are gone, peeled back and replaced by something twisted and dark, something horrible. Her once-dark hair is almost completely white now, and it's fanned out around her head in stunning, perfect symmetry. She is no longer the Eve that I've come to know and like, the girl willing to take in a group of strangers, to take us in and care for us. The thing that is Eve is in mid-leap, going after Singer with fingers like talons, and if I don't do something she'll shred him.

So I move. It's so damn hard, but I move. I'm pushing through Jell-O with fifty-pound weights strapped to each arm and leg. Every movement I make is torture. I strain to turn my body, and I take a labored step toward her. In the time I've moved a few feet she's only crept forward an inch, maybe less. Out of the corner of my eye I spot Singer, but it's all happening fast and he's still oblivious to the danger. He doesn't have time to react, but I do.

I take a slow, ponderous, second step forward, and I'm almost to her. With nearly as much effort as it took to rip the chain from the wall, I raise my hand and plant my open palm into her chest and gently push. And then, just like that, time snaps back. Eve soars backwards like she's been hit by a bus, and crashes into the back wall, the chain around her waist flying backwards and landing in her lap. She slumps to the ground and lies still.

"Oh no!" I yell, and rush to her side. I kneel down next to her and take her slack face in my shaking hands. "Eve! My god, Eve! I'm so sorry!"

She moans softly, and raises a limp hand to her chest, rubbing it and wincing. Behind me, Singer grabs my shoulder and spins me around. The surprised look on his face is so extreme it borders on comical, although there's nothing funny going on.

"What the hell was that?" he shouts. "What did you just do? How'd you do that?"

I take his hand. "I don't know! And I don't know how to control it, either." I turn back to Eve. "I'm so sorry! I just couldn't let you get him."

He pulls at my shoulders. "Scout, I think she's okay. But we're not going to be unless we get the hell out of here!"

She's far from okay, but I stand there, torn between Eve and escape, unsure of my next move. Then he takes my shoulders and turns me around, making the decision for me.

"It's time to go," he insists, enunciating each word individually. His hands move to my cheeks, and he makes me look him in the eye. "There's a boat waiting outside for us. We've got to go!"

"What? Just the two of us? But what about Annie and Carly? And Tiny?"

He shakes his head. "We kept Annie out of this on purpose. She's got no idea what's going on. She'll be fine, trust me. And Carly and Tiny will be, too. They're staying. It's safer for them here. But you're already changing, and I can't be far behind. None of us want to get locked down in this crappy furnace room and left to die, you know?"

I look back over my shoulder, down at Eve. Her eyes are fluttering as she begins to regain consciousness. She moans softly. If I had any doubt that she was going Gray, those doubts have been vanquished: no normal person could have survived what I just did to her.

I finally nod, and with some difficulty I gather up the chain and hold it close to my chest. It's heavier and more awkward than I thought it would be. I pray that I don't have to run too far or too fast, because even with my new strength I doubt I'll be able to. Singer cautiously pulls the door open a crack, and after a moment motions me out with a flick of his head. Closing it quietly is impossible, but we do our best. The hallway is dark. We can hear commotion everywhere, especially near the kitchen.

"Who was shooting?" I whisper as we edge our way toward the steps. We hear pounding footsteps coming, and we quickly duck into one of the storage rooms. Two of Jacob's guards run past us, little more than dark blurs. They're yelling something.

"Carly did it. She's the only one not being guarded."

"Carly? You gave her a gun? Are you crazy?"

"No, of course not," he says. "I gave her a bunch of shotgun shells from the tin. She tossed them into the kitchen fire and then ran like hell. We needed a distraction, and she wanted to help."

Brave Carly. She will never stop surprising me.

It's pitch black in the storage room. We inch out and make it to the foot of the steps, pressing ourselves against the wall. The chain keeps doing its best greasy snake imitation by trying to slither out of my hands onto the ground. Singer leans close to my ear, and I smell mint and realize he must have brushed his teeth.

"Okay, here comes the tricky part," he whispers.

"Wait. You mean the furnace room wasn't the tricky part?"

"Ah, no. Now we go up the steps, then straight out the red door, and go right. Run and don't look back. I'll be right behind you. I've got a boat waiting there."

"When did you get that ready? I thought you were being watched?"

There's more noise coming our way, and we merge into the shadows. He leans close again. "Last night. During the going-away party. After I left. Now let's check out of this damn Hotel California, okay?"

Hotel California? I don't know what he's talking about, but I take a deep breath and we fly up the steps, taking them two at a time. We're up the stairway and into the church sanctuary in seconds, and the big red door is right in front of us. We don't hesitate or look around, but hit the heavy door at a sprint. It crashes open and we almost tumble down the steps. I drop most of the chain and have to slow down to gather it back up. The wooded area is to our left, not very far away. The water's edge is only twenty or thirty yards to the right, and one of our row boats is there.

"There it is. That's the one!"

Just then one of Jacob's guards bursts through the red door behind us, a bow in his hands. Singer spots him and without hesitation turns and runs right at him.

"Go for the boat!"

"Singer, no!"

The guard is young, just a kid, and so nervous and shaky he can't even notch an arrow. He finally fits it in place, but by then Singer's on him. He tackles him and lays him out. The weapon goes flying. The two of them tumble around in the mud, but the guard is no match for Singer's wiry strength and determination.

"Go!" he screams. "I'll be right there."

I hesitate for a second, then turn and continue slogging through the mud. The chain slithers out of my hands again, and I fumble with it, trying desperately not to trip over the damn thing. Behind me I see movement, and here comes Singer. He's covered in mud from head to toe.

"Come on!" I yell, completely unnecessarily.

He's pounding through the slop like there's a thousand Grays in hot pursuit, slipping and sliding as he goes. He's quickly narrowing the gap just as two more guards rush out of the red door. They spot him, pointing and shouting. Seconds later I'm at the boat, and in no time Singer slides up to me. There's so much mud caked on him he's almost unrecognizable.

"Let's go!" he yells, gasping for breath and wiping some of the brown goop from his eyes and mouth.

I chance a look over his shoulder. The two guards are coming our way, slowly. They've got bows up and aimed in our direction but they haven't shot at us yet. I jump in and nearly trip over something. I take a split second to see that it's Hamlet, the big edition with the English translation. It's wrapped up and sealed in a Ziplock bag. Singer, still standing outside the boat, grins at me as he picks up my valuable cargo.

"We couldn't very well leave that behind, could we?"

He's holding it in front of him, smiling and proud, when I hear a crack! Singer jerks and spins around, then staggers forward and stumbles, twisting as he falls into the boat. The back of his head smacks on a metal cleat so hard the boat vibrates, and he goes completely limp. My hands fly to my mouth when I see a bloody smear growing on his chest, near where a shirt pocket would be.

"No!" I scream in horror, gathering him up. My hand behind his head is wet and warm with blood. His hair is soaked. The full length of my chain falls overboard and splashes into the brown sludge as I fumble with him. The book slips from his hands but stays in the boat. My vision suddenly blurry with tears, I wipe my eyes and look up. The guy that Singer tackled is on his feet now, and all three guards are looking away from us, staring and gesturing into the wooded area behind them. I peer over their shoulders, and I see him standing back there, by the trees, with his gun still leveled in our direction.

Hunter.

I don't know how long I stare at him, shocked to my core. That son of a bitch shot Singer! More guards pile out of the church and fan out, no longer interested in the two of us. They want Hunter, the more obvious threat. They've taken cover behind trees, the church itself, and whatever else they can find. After they banished him, he must have snuck back. It's always so dark and gloomy. If he was careful and quiet, he could have crept back and stayed hidden all day long. He's a hunter. He's used to sitting still for hours on end, waiting on his quarry. It wouldn't have been hard for him at all. I don't know if he knew about Singer's escape plan or was just biding his time, but it doesn't matter now.

Cursing and crying, I reel in the chain. The wet chunk of concrete on the end hits the bottom of the boat with a crunching thud. I grab a paddle and begin rowing as hard as I can. My strokes are strong but uncoordinated, and I'm doing little more than weaving around like a drunk. But just like back at the railroad tracks, I force myself to calm down and concentrate on taking even, measured strokes. Once I get things under control and I'm pulling away from shore, I shoot a glance back at the church. The guards are trying to surround Hunter, but instead of staying put and doing more damage, he turns and sprints off. I wish in my heart of hearts that someone would kill that son of a bitch!

Jacob has arrived and is standing at the water's edge with several of his men, with more coming. One lifts a bow in our direction, but Jacob's hand goes out and the guard lowers his weapon. I keep paddling, each stroke putting more distance between us, until the dozen or so people on shore are no more than tiny, indistinct figures against the brick backdrop of the church. The red doors are astonishingly bright in the dim light.

TWENTY-FOUR

I paddle farther out, well into the channel separating Home from Cedar Ridge. My eyes are still cloudy with tears, and I'm sweating from rowing like a crazy person. This is one of the few times that the light mist feels good on my skin. I stop only when I'm far enough away that Jacob and his gang can't easily follow me. I toss the paddle aside and spin around to Singer, careful not to move too fast. The last thing I need now is to capsize this thing.

He's still unconscious. I grab the first aid kit from under the seat, and toss open the lid. On top of the gauze and bandages sits my knife Chuck, complete with its leather sheath. He must have smuggled it onboard when this escape was being planned. I set it aside for later, but I'm happy it's here.

Singer coughs and moans, but doesn't wake up. The front of his shirt is drenched in blood, and I don't think it's stopping or even slowing. I stare down at him and a sensation of total and complete helplessness overcomes me. I have no idea what to do for him. I'm no doctor. I grab the sides of my head and bite back a scream. What do I do? I don't know how to save him! My hands are shaking, and I feel my eyes filling up with tears again. The last scraps of my self-control are being blown away by the winds of my futility.

I barely manage to tamp down the scream that's clawing to escape, a scream that, once it starts, I'm afraid will never stop. I can't lose control. Not now. I have to keep my head, or he'll certainly die.

Oh my god. Singer might die.

The shakes hit me again, and this time my entire body starts shivering. My heart aches. I can't let Singer die, I can't! I start rummaging through the first aid kit. When Hunter was hit they pulled the arrow out, but that wound wasn't nearly as severe as this one. Plus, Singer hit his head so hard when he fell into the boat that it knocked him out, so he's probably suffered a concussion or something, too. I am so out of my element here.

Shit. Someone tell me what to do! Now I wish I had found and read more reference books, not just my escapism fiction. Why am I such an idiot?

But I can't just sit and do nothing. Using Chuck, I take a deep breath and carefully cut away his shirt from around the wound. I try to act all clinical and detached like Annie, but when I see the huge furrow of ripped open flesh across his chest, I can't. He's bleeding badly, blood puddling below him. My level of freaking out jumps all the way up to eleven. Using what little gauze and tape I can find, I wrap him up, running the tape around his chest and up and over his shoulder, but it's not nearly enough. Singer groans a few times, and through my tears I whisper soft words of encouragement to him. I hope he can hear me.

I tear my eyes away and look back the way I came. The outline of the church is barely visible through the haze and drizzle, a dark square like a tombstone on a hill. In the other direction sprawls Cedar Ridge, its buildings and streets dead and desolate. I'm close enough that I can make out the tumbled-down white and brick houses with caved in roofs, the movie theater, and the vacant streets lined with shattered store-fronts. There's no help in that dead place, I'm sure of it. In order to help Singer, I know what I have to do.

I strap Chuck onto my thigh, and I start paddling.

In no time the prow of the boat scrapes bottom, and I step back into the flooded parking lot. I wrap the chain around me and tie it into a huge clumsy knot around my waist, then lean over and pick up Singer, being careful not to jostle him. I stumble a little in the muck, and he moans and his eyes flutter open, but they're sightless and roll back until only the whites are showing. His head falls against my chest, his long black hair draped over my arm. With my newfound strength, carrying him is no more difficult than lugging a bag of groceries into the house from the car.

Under my breath, my voice breaking, I apologize and kiss his cool cheek. I trudge out of the shallow water with him limp in my arms. When I reach my destination, I bang on the familiar red door.

"Jacob!" I yell. "Jacob, I need your help."

Long moments pass, and then the doors creak open. Jacob, Dustin, and a few others are standing there. I expected him to be furious, was sure he'd immediately order his gang to jump me. But he's calm and, strangely enough, he actually appears relieved to see us. His maturity continues to surprise me. Lord would have liked him.

"Scout. Are you okay?"

Dustin doesn't wait for an answer, but growls and shoulders past him, coming at me. His little eyes are filled with fury, likely directed at our whole group but localized here with me. I mean, I present a pretty meek and easy target for an overblown thug like him. His beefy hand is almost to me when I feel it coming, that now-familiar tingle, and I go into slo-mo. I can't say I'm used to it or that I ever will be, but at least I'm ready for it this time. Straining, I force my hand up and grab hold of his upraised arm. I close my fingers on his wrist and give a gentle yank. Time resumes normal operation, and Dustin goes soaring over my head. He flies ten feet and lands face first in the mud, sliding like he's stealing second base, and plowing up a Dustin-sized trench along the way. When he finally comes to a stop, his screaming starts. He's clutching his arm and wailing. I'm sure I dislocated something, or maybe multiple somethings, which gives me a little more satisfaction than it probably should.

Jacob's head ping-pongs comically between Dustin and me. His eyes are big and round, his white eyebrows arched, and he may have gone a shade paler than usual, if that's even possible. He finally settles on staring at me, and try as I might I'm not sure if it's in awe or fear, but I'm leaning toward fear. The other two guards are just as shocked at my parlor trick with Dustin, but after seeing what I can do, they're understandably hesitant to come at me. They've just learned a valuable lesson; big surprises can come in small packages. And that's good, because I'm not going to take any shit from them.

Regardless, they huff and puff and take a few steps my way, but Jacob throws out his arms and orders them to stand down. They grumble and glare cold death at me, but I can tell they're secretly relieved they've been told to back off.

"Singer needs help," I tell him, although it's obvious to see. My eyes start misting up again, and my voice cracks. It jumps up that annoying octave as I struggle to keep calm. "I...I can't do anything for him. He needs Martin and Annie right away. Maybe they can do something. If he stays with me he'll die for sure. Please help him."

Jacob stares at me, unblinking. He's had a moment to gather his wits, and his shocked expression has gone flat, a study in neutrality. "Tell me, Scout. Why? Why would we do that? Look at the trouble you've caused, and he was a big part of it. I'd be completely within my rights to slam the door on both of you right now."

I look at each of them in turn, thinking madly. How can I convince them to save Singer? As strong as I am, as tough as I've become, I can't just force them to do it. They have to want to. What can I say?

"Jacob. Please. Help him. He had no intention of hurting anyone. He just wanted to get me out. He didn't want me to die down there. Please, take him to Martin."

He crosses his arms. The two guys behind him glare daggers at me. I'm not winning any arguments here. Begging won't do it. I think of Eve, and Lord, and what's happening to them.

"Okay, let me ask you something," I say to him, changing strategies. "How old are you? One hundred and forty months? One hundred and fifty?"

He blinks once or twice before answering. "One hundred and fifty. Why?"

"So you've got some time left, good for you. Probably eighty months, more or less. Not much time in the grand scheme of things, is it? What about Dustin over there? He looks a lot older. In fact, I bet he's pushing two hundred and forty right now. Am I right?" I point to the other two behind Jacob. "And you two. What about you? You can't be too far from going Gray either. Am I close?"

No one answers, but the anger in their faces has diminished, their brows no longer furrowed at me. In fact, both of them behind Jacob look increasingly uneasy at my blunt observations. Good.

"You know as well as I do," I continue matter-of-factly, "that my change is different. If any of you have a prayer of not dying in the basement of this place, then you'd better hope I can figure out what's happening to me. Because I am going Gray, but not in the same way everyone else does, the way you guys will. If I can determine why, I promise I will come back here and share that with you. You don't have to go Gray and die."

Jacob shifts on his feet. His arms uncross a little. He looks over his shoulder at the pair of guards behind him.

"You would do that?" he asks.

I nod. "Yes, I will. But only if you take care of Singer. I will find out how to stop this, and I'll come back and share it with you. But," and I point my finger and poke him in the chest. "But when I come back, if Singer isn't alive, then I'm leaving. If I come back and Singer is dead, then you can all go Gray, and to hell with you."

Several seconds that feel like minutes tick by. Finally, he nods his head. "Okay, yeah. Bring him in."

I shake my head. "No, I'm not going to do that. If I come back inside, you know I'll end up in the furnace room again. I won't do that. I won't go back down there to die. There's too much to do." Plus, I don't want to see Eve now, not the way she's become. I want to remember her as she was before.

Jacob opens his mouth to disagree, but sees the determined set of my jaw, and stops. He purses his lips together for a moment, thinking, then nods. He motions to the remaining guards.

"Carry Singer downstairs. Carefully. Then get Martin and Annie." He looks over my shoulder and shakes his head in disgust. "Jesus, Dustin, will you please quit whining? Pick yourself up and head downstairs so Martin can check out that arm."

The two guards take Singer from my reluctant hands. To their credit, they handle him gently and with greater care than I would've given them credit for. Before they go, I grasp Singer's arm, lean over, and give him one more kiss, this time on the lips. I linger, willing the warmth of my body into his. His eyes flutter open and for a second I swear he's looking not just at me, but into me. As they carry him away, I see him voicelessly mouth my name. Not my longstanding nickname, but my real name. Jean Louise. I wrap my arms tightly around myself, and it's all I can do to not grasp the door for support as they vanish into the darkness. I flash back to the last time we were together, at the going-away party, and I cringe inside at how Eve and I treated him. Don't go away, Singer! Just go away! My hand drifts to my forehead and I close my eyes. I'll never forgive myself for that. I wonder why that one bad moment is front and center in my mind instead of the good ones we shared together?

Still cradling his arm, Dustin clumps up the steps and warily detours around me, like I'm an unstable explosive or something. Mud sloughs off of him and splatters on the floor as he ducks inside. Jacob watches them all go, then turns his blue eyes to me.

We stare at each other wordlessly while the mist falls all around us, dampening our clothes and hair. Tiny water droplets cling to his fair eyebrows, highlighting them and making them more visible than usual. He's looking older already, more seasoned, and he's only been in charge a few days. Poor guy. I feel for him.

"So what's next?" he asks me. "Where are you going to start?"

I glance out over the channel, toward Cedar Ridge. "I'll head there first," I tell him, with a nod toward the town. "I think I need to stay on land from here on out, so I can find my brother. Maybe together we can figure out what's different about us. Like I said, we're not going Gray the same way everyone else is. If we can learn why, or how this happened, then maybe we can find out how to stop it completely. The town itself is dead, but who knows what's beyond it. I gotta start somewhere. I'm going to start by finding Lord."

He follows my gaze across the still channel. "Okay. Good luck. And I mean that."

I tilt my head at him. "I believe you. And please, tell Eve goodbye for me. I...I never got a chance to do it myself."

"I will." He doesn't volunteer any updates on her condition. He doesn't have to. I'm sure she's pretty far gone by now.

I start down the steps, then stop and stare at him over my shoulder. "So what's going to happen to Hunter? And everyone else in my group? What's going to happen to them?"

He lifts his blond eyebrows. "Hunter somehow managed to get away. He took off in his boat and headed away from the town and us. He's not our problem anymore, unless he tries to come back." He pauses for a moment. "He must really hate you, you know? I heard what he said he'd do to you and Eve, down in the furnace room. And that obviously went for Singer, too. I'd watch out for that one while you're out there, away from Home."

I don't know what to say, so I say nothing. The truth hangs there between us.

"As for Annie and the little ones," he continues, "if they want to stay, they can stay. If they want to leave, we won't stand in their way. We only stop Grays from leaving. Everyone else can come and go as they please. And speaking of leaving..."

He fishes in his pocket and pulls out a small brass key. He joins me on my step and unlocks the chain from my waist, then watches as I wriggle free. It feels so good to have that weight off of me. I kick the heavy links away and they tumble down the steps and into the mud.

"There. Remember the warehouse?" he asks with a small smile. "Now we're even."

I do remember. I nod at him in thanks.

He pockets the key and stares at me, not un-sympathetically. "We were sure you were changing. But now? Now I don't know. And Eve was the one who ordered you down to the furnace room with her. Since there's been, shall we say, a change in adminis-tration, I'm free to make my own decisions. Honestly, I don't think hers was the right move."

"Well if that's the case, why were you chasing us? I don't get it."

"Scout, I never ordered anyone to shoot at you or hurt you. My orders were to stop you if possible, but no one was supposed to get hurt. Gunshots were going off in the kitchen. Hunter attacked us. If my guys went a little crazy, can you blame them?"

I step off the stairs into the slop. Without the chain dragging me down I feel like I can float across the surface of the mud if I want to. This sensation of freedom is intoxicating. I keep walking away from the church, while the entire time I sense eyes on me from the stained-glass windows high above the sanctuary. I ignore them.

"Take care of my friends," I call back to him. "And do not let Singer die." There's a satisfying hard edge to my voice that I never thought I had in me, not even a few weeks ago. I hear a bit of Lord there, and it makes me happy.

"We'll do our best," he calls at my receding back. "Don't worry."

I draw Chuck from his sheath and point it at him. I wonder what distorted image of myself I'd see in its blade now. I'm not the same person I was. Jacob and I lock eyes.

"I don't want to find out otherwise. Trust me, you won't like it if I do. I'll be back when I have answers."

I climb into the boat, grab an oar, and start paddling toward Cedar Ridge. I'm not at all sure I like being alone out here, but I'm much more confident than I used to be. In the past I've always had someone watching out for me: my mom and dad, my brother, Singer. I can't remember a time when I've been totally on my own. Hell, I never even walked to school by myself when I was a kid. But if I'm being honest, whatever change is happening to me has proven pretty damn helpful so far, too, so that blunts the edge of my anxiety.

Now if I could just figure out how to control it. Yeah, that would be great.

But I can't worry about that now. I know now that my overriding concern is to locate Lord, and hopefully the two of us can find a cure, or an antidote, or at least figure out what's different about the two of us. And this isn't just for us. I'm thinking of all the people in the world that haven't gone Gray yet, including my friends at Home, and good people like Jacob. Hell, there could even be other weird changes like me and Lord out there. If everything stays the same, their time on this Earth will be short, probably violent, and will almost certainly end horribly. Even if it's too late for the older ones and me, the thought of Carly going Gray is almost more than I can stand.

I can't go through the motions and be a by-stander any longer.

I continue to paddle, and my strokes are even, strong, and determined. Cedar Ridge, dead and emp-ty, looms directly in front of me, and I aim for the familiar road that dips into the toxic water. I'm sure there aren't any revelations in this once sleepy little country town, but after so many months of sticking to water, it's time I travel on foot. It's sure to be more interesting in oh so many ways.

The hull scrapes bottom on the muddy con-crete. I step out of the boat and easily pull it ashore, happy to leave it behind. I grab Hamlet and check to make sure Chuck is secure in its sheath on my thigh. I head up the muddy road, detouring around the dead, discolored husks of cars and SUVs, wary of Grays. Several turkey vultures wheel effortlessly overhead, loving this new world. The smell of rot and death here is a physical presence that threatens to overwhelm my senses. I keep walking. Lord is out there somewhere, and hopefully answers are out here, too.

I'm the Firebrand, and I'm going to find them.